Local Girls

Local Girls

CAROLINE ZANCAN

RIVERHEAD BOOKS
New York
2015

RIVERHEAD BOOKS
An imprint of Penguin Random House LLC
375 Hudson Street
New York, New York 10014

Copyright © 2015 by Caroline Zancan
Penguin supports copyright. Copyright fuels creativity, encourages diverse voices,
promotes free speech, and creates a vibrant culture. Thank you for buying an
authorized edition of this book and for complying with copyright laws
by not reproducing, scanning, or distributing any part of it in any form
without permission. You are supporting writers and allowing Penguin
to continue to publish books for every reader.

Library of Congress Cataloging-in-Publication Data

Zancan, Caroline.
Local girls : a novel / Caroline Zancan.
p.   cm.
ISBN 978-1-59463-364-5
1. Young women—Fiction.   2. Friendship—Fiction.   3. Coming of
age—Fiction.   I. Title.
PS3626.A6293L63   2015   2014042225
813'.6—dc23

Printed in the United States of America
1   3   5   7   9   10   8   6   4   2

BOOK DESIGN BY AMANDA DEWEY

For Mom, Dad, Sara, Wally, Emma, and Ben.
When I count my blessings, I always count you twice.

Let us all be from somewhere.

Let us tell each other everything we can.

—Bob Hicok, "A Primer"

All of them had restlessness in common.

—John Steinbeck, *East of Eden*

The last summer we were teenagers was as hot as every other summer in Florida, but we spent it in the Shamrock, probably the only bar in the state without air-conditioning. It was the summer Nina got a ticket for public urination and Lindsey lost her virginity, although she wouldn't admit it until later. She had always told us that she lost it at seventeen to someone named Chad—no last name—a friend of one of her brothers, which should have tipped us off. Her brothers would have murdered anyone who came near her, never mind that there was no one any of us knew that the other two didn't. I got my own apartment that summer—the first one of us to do it—but when we weren't drinking or working, we hung out at Nina's mom's house like always.

"Blistering Love" was the number-one song on iTunes, and the only song we all liked. We sang it in Nina's car at the top of our lungs like maniacs—windows down, driving too fast, the city neon before us. Nina told us to put the third line of the first verse on her tombstone.

Despite all the singing, and the trips to the city, and the

small freedom my apartment afforded us the few times we were all there, we were miserable that entire summer, and furious at one another, though we didn't know it at the time. If someone had pointed it out to us, we wouldn't have been able to say why.

That summer was the summer we met Sam Decker on the last night of his life, a fact so strange we barely believe it ourselves, so we don't expect anyone else to, either.

There's a picture proving that we met him, though. It's still hanging in the Shamrock, or was the last time any of us checked—we haven't been back much, which is another thing we wouldn't have believed, had you told us back then. Sam Decker surrounded by three girls with faces still baby-fat round, smiles bigger than our disbelief at what was happening in that moment, skin shiny from humidity, the oppressive magnitude of which you could imagine only if you've been to Florida between the months of May and September. There is no sign indicating the date, so there would be no way for you to calculate what happened a few hours later. And you probably wouldn't be likely to guess, because in the picture, Sam Decker looks happy.

But then, so do we.

One

These are the things we knew about Sam Decker: Tacos were his favorite food. He had a collie-poodle mix named Rickie. He was a Sagittarius, and the first thing he noticed about a woman was her laugh. We knew that *Flight Opus* was his best movie but that *Sender Unknown* was the one he looked most handsome in, and that he fell in love with Abby Madison when they were filming *Dancing on Thursdays*. We knew he was the co-owner of cocktail bars in Manhattan and London, which made it even more surprising that he would come to a dive like the Shamrock, or even that he would be in Orlando at all. Lindsey was the first one to spot him across the room, and though none of us had any idea what he might be doing there, we intended to find out.

We took copies of the magazines that had taught us these things everywhere we went that summer. We read them at one another's houses, on car rides to and from the city, at swimming pools and beaches and barbecues. We exchanged facts we had uncovered about perfect strangers the way most people exchanged pleasantries. We delivered them as greetings, mid-sentence, and halfway through conversations about totally unrelated subjects, as one of us sat idly flipping through a worn, dog-eared copy of *Blush* or *Kiss*, half listening to the others. We managed never to pay for them, taking them instead from doctors' offices and the gym where Nina worked. We picked up the copies tourists left on the beach like they were seashells.

While the tourists would've had to turn these magazines aside halfway through them to close their eyes from the Florida light our own eyes had grown used to long ago, we could continue to worry and wonder and bask in the things we most wanted to know, even as the sun did its work: the cut and color of the dress Joni Parsons wore for her dinner out with which Hollywood director, and the name of Corey Jones's fourth-grade teacher, who he had recently thanked in an acceptance speech for an award that no one had heard of but that everyone got dressed up for—the pictures flew around the Internet, and bloomed from the pages of both *Rumor* and *Kiss*, even though they tried never to cover the same events. We cared less about how we would fill the empty nights that followed vast but indistinct days at the beach than we did the brand of toilet paper February Mathis was seen carrying out of the Whole Foods in Beverly Hills.

Until the night we met Sam Decker, it had been too hot for even the beach, even for us, because it was August in central Florida. August came to Florida every year, but it felt like the end of the world every time if only because of how empty the streets and sidewalks became—everyone stayed inside. It got so bad that you started to blame the heat on other things—the palm trees and the beach and the sunsets and the sand—

because heat that unpleasant had to be blamed on something. It surely wasn't benign. And for all its unpleasantness, it went unseen, measured instead by the size of people's pit stains and just how far out of their mouths the tongues of panting dogs hung.

There was always a day, usually during the second or third week of the month, when the heat broke. It was an unofficial holiday in the state. On the morning of the night we met Sam Decker no one would have braved the sand too hot to stand on without flip-flops, or the lukewarm water that offered no relief from the invisible palm the air held over your nose and mouth. But it dropped five degrees between noon and three, and we followed the temperature like it was the Super Bowl score in the fourth quarter. By the time we hit the outskirts of Orlando that night, it felt like something had been released, like someone had changed the radio from a somber symphony to a rock song, and change of any sort felt promising to us back then, because we were young, and lived almost a full hour from even Orlando.

That we could enjoy the coral-orange colors of the sunset without indicting them for their association with the sun was the first sign that it was going to be a good night. The second was that, after parking our car in the overnight garage and walking up and down the same drag we walked up and down every Saturday night, we had seen Lindsey's secret boyfriend's actual girlfriend, Carine, walk into the Shamrock. If she had been a color she would definitely have been a pastel, which was only the first of several reasons we hated her. Her equally horrible friends—reasons two and three—were with her. We had promised we were going to try a new bar that night, but it was late August, which meant Carine and Paisley and Polka Dot, whose real names we could not be bothered to learn, would be returning to out-of-state colleges in only a few weeks, and tormenting them was pretty much our favorite thing to do that summer. So we went to the Shamrock as always.

Carine and the patterns were Golden Creek girls, but wouldn't be for long. The whole point of attending the sort of colleges they were on summer vacation from was to move away from home for one sort of important career or another—in fields so competitive that you had to go wherever the work took you, which usually happened to be somewhere you wouldn't mind moving. Though we knew the distinction of having been from Golden Creek would never fully leave them—it would keep their postures straight, and it would always be one of the first things they told people upon meeting them. We knew they'd be precise—it would always be *Golden Creek*, never just *Florida* or *outside Orlando*.

Golden Creek was the home of the largest collection of salt-water pearls anywhere in the country, and a liberal-arts college that was just as expensive as the ones they had left home to attend. It was a land of golf courses and manicured greenery. It had Florida's vacation climate, but the houses there would've been extraordinary anywhere, with touches of character—a widow's walk on one, a two-story bay window in another—that seemed missing from the identical units in the condo parks and gated vacation-home communities Florida is known for. These houses weren't designed to look like tropical get-aways, they were sturdy, stately, and dignified structures that sat among majestic courthouses and schools instead of seafood restaurants and T-shirt shops. Golden Creek had cobblestone streets and more nonfunctioning lighthouses and designer stores than any other stretch in Florida. It was the kind of place presidents came to visit. Four American presidents had been to Golden Creek and publicly fawned over its beauty, including Obama.

I suppose they had their own reasons for hating us. Golden Creek was closer to Orlando than our neighborhood and a series of nameless towns just like it, and people like us regularly passed through Golden Creek to get to the city. It was more scenic than the highway, and faster. We weren't always sober and we didn't always follow the speed limit, and the people of Golden Creek were the sort who had the time and money to do something about this. In the last two years, extra speed patrols had been added at the Golden Creek community's urging, resulting in a speeding ticket apiece for me and Lindsey, and a whopping three for Nina.

That night, our plan of attack on Carine and the patterns quickly turned into a plan of descent on Decker when Lindsey, literally stunned into openmouthed silence, gestured at him with her giant head.

The Shamrock smelled like the inside of a beer bottle, or like a beer had spilled just a second ago, an illusion the always-sticky tables complemented. It smelled like hops and yeast and, because we were in Florida, salty, water-heavy air. It was that smell more than anything that made me doubt, before he turned to face us head-on, that it was really him. That made me think it was a trick of the light, or even wishful thinking.

That the resemblance was uncanny, but not exact, and that standing twenty feet away was only a handsome but otherwise average man, a banker or even a bartender, who had been pulling girls out of his league for years. They couldn't put their finger on it, but something about him just made them feel like they already knew him. The real Sam Decker couldn't possibly be in a bar the smell of which promised such a cheap, soggy Saturday night.

"Holy. Shit," Nina said, apparently not sharing any of my doubts. "We're definitely getting shitty with him tonight."

He turned then, and looked at us for just an instant, an empty, dazed half-smile on his face that we basked in until he turned back to the bar a quarter of a millisecond later.

There was no mistaking that smile, even at half-mast.

"Holy shit," I said, not able to think of anything to say other than what Nina already had. "It's really him."

Nina turned to look at me with her *Um, YEAH, if we're gonna pull this off you're gonna need to get your shit together* look.

"I'm just going to be a human and tell him that I like his movies," I said, edging one butt length closer to the end of the booth. I was bluffing, mostly on account of the look she had given me. I had no intention of being the first one to talk to him.

"Don't be an idiot, Maggie," said Nina. "Once you establish yourself as a fan you've declared yourself on a different level. Like, a level *below* him. He'll ask you if you want an autograph and move on to people who drool with their mouths closed."

"Okay," said Lindsey. "So why don't you practice whatever opening line you're going to stun him with on us."

Lindsey was constantly backing me up against Nina. Not because she liked me more, but because Nina never needed any help.

"That's just it," Nina said. "I'm not going to use a *line*. I'm going to ask him what he's drinking."

"What, like you don't know who he is and he just happens to be somebody standing there when you want a drink recommendation?" I asked.

"Exactly."

"Um, because you want him to think you're from Mars? Or, like, *homeschooled*?" Lindsey asked. "Everybody knows who he is."

Ironically, Carine was the one to save Nina, by picking that moment to walk across the bar to our table—Paisley and Polka Dot behind her—saving us the trouble of having to do something like send her a glass of milk with our compliments later.

"This is strange," Carine said. "Fred said he was going to be in Sanibel this weekend. I assumed he was with you."

She had the pouty, unhappy droop of the blonde girls in tampon commercials before they discover Tampax's otherworldly leak protection. Period Barbie, we called them.

"Whoah, Whoah, Whoah," said Nina merrily. "Carine, are you wearing a *romper*? Is that one *giant* piece of neon-green fun? Is there even a *pee hole* in that thing? And do you think you should be drinking in an outfit that's gonna make it *that* hard to break the seal? You gotta get outta here, man. It's just not safe in that outfit."

"I know, Nina, it's crazy, isn't it, that they sell pieces of clothing for more than twenty dollars?"

"What's crazy, *Courtney*," said Nina, emphasis on the far-less-exotic name Carine had been born with, a fact Nina had done considerable sleuthing to uncover, "is that you date a man under the age of forty named Fred."

"You know," Carine said, turning back to Lindsey. "You'd probably be less inclined to do trashy things like sleep with other people's boyfriends if you didn't hang out with such trashy people."

She tilted her high side ponytail in Nina's direction.

"Oh, wow," Nina said, showing no signs of ruffle, her voice all innocence and light. "I didn't realize the Brownies had started giving out patches for being a total cunt to strangers in bars. You'll be good at that one."

"Stay out of it, Scarfio," said Paisley, or maybe Polka Dot—we could never remember who was which.

"I'd love to," Nina said, nodding at her like she was a small child. "But your camel toe is precluding my enjoyment of this adult beverage."

Carine tried to knock Nina's drink off the table and into her lap, but she was not a girl versed in bar fights, and was too slow. Nina caught the glass mid-tilt with a lone extended index finger. She let it balance there for a minute, maintaining eye contact with Carine the whole time, before she picked it up and finished the drink without taking a breath.

"Anything else?"

They blew back over to their table in one triangle of evil, and before we even had time to do a *Fuck-you* shot, Sam Decker was at our table.

"Dude, what the fuck?" he said. "That was some ice-queen

shit. I didn't know people actually behaved like that outside of, I don't know, *Carrie*."

"I just happen to not believe in wasting alcohol," said Nina coolly. "Is that from *War Addict?*" she asked, nodding at his bomber jacket.

He looked down to check what he was wearing, a move none of his characters ever would've pulled. They had an answer ready for everything.

"Oh. No. It was my grandfather's."

It hadn't occurred to us until then that Sam Decker had a grandfather.

"But who cares about that? Seriously, what just happened? Did you guys even know each other? Is that, like, normal for this part of town?"

"Sit down," Nina said.

None of us so much as shifted the angle at which our legs hung from the booth during the one second he hesitated, looking at the door and then back at us.

"Why not?" he finally said. "I love a good story."

We were burnouts in a burnout town. It took half the length of a Sam Decker movie to get to Orlando from where we lived, and even the city was a four-year-old's dream, not a nineteen-year-old's. The high school that we had gone to was not the type whose graduates went on to Ivy Leagues, or first- or second- or even third-tier liberal-arts colleges. There was a community college in town where some of our classmates floundered and delayed having to look for jobs that paid by the hour, and the valedictorians usually made it to Florida State or the University of, but that was about it. By not bothering with these consolation prizes, we felt like we were making a point, though I'm not sure we could've told you what it was.

At first this rushed adulthood was all we had hoped it would be. Lindsey and I worked at the mall—her in customer service, me in the coffee shop, where I spent most of my time making new creations that the three of us rated using a complicated system of factors, like the aftertaste and the effect on the stomach, and never paid for. Nina started out cleaning machines at the nearest gym but had recently begun teaching an aerobics class, a concept we found funnier than YouTube clips of people falling, even when we saw for ourselves that she wasn't horrible at it. "Besides," she had said, a cigarette between her teeth, "I'm not exactly fit, but anyone not pushing two hundred pounds counts as trim in this state." Though we were often bored, our jobs were rarely humiliating or uncomfortable or hard, and there was still the novelty of having any job at all.

Life was quieter, maybe, without our classmates, but they had generally been white noise, noteworthy mostly for the extent to which they weren't us. We were well liked enough, but I doubt anyone who didn't live in a five-block radius ever wondered what had become of us. And the ones who did we still saw—they drove to their classes in hand-me-down cars instead of living in dorms.

At night we had money to burn. We had decent enough fake IDs to get into most bars in town even though everybody knew who we were—they were simply good enough to cover the bars' asses should the sheriff come in for a drink while we were there partaking underage—and we were attractive enough to get into the more upscale bars when we ventured into the city. Though by that night we had grown tired of the wardrobes those bars required, and had pled monogamy to the Shamrock.

We were still pretty in a high-school-girl kind of way, but we wouldn't be for long, and neither of those facts was lost on us the night Sam Decker walked into the Shamrock and renewed our dwindling confidence that we were living the right kind of life—the kind where anything could happen. We adored him ironically—we made fun of his movies but always went to see them opening weekend—but it was with pure earnestness that we watched him slide into our booth and ask us what our names were.

It was dusk, and I knew it would be dark by the next round. I loved the Shamrock as much as the other girls, but it was two different bars by night and day. During the day it was a distinctly Florida bar. Even though it was tucked into the last lot of the street it was on, dwarfed by the other, looming buildings that you had to pass to get to it, and surrounded on one side by dense Florida foliage that came closer to swallowing the entire building every day, the sun still found you there, like it did everywhere else in the state. The light was a tangible thing, another regular.

By night, though, Sal, the bar's owner, didn't do much to light the place. It felt like the inside of a ship. It was entirely dark wood—the tables, the floors, the walls—that dimmed even the brightest bulbs and made you feel small. Starting to drink in the Shamrock in the middle of the day and going straight through to the night was a little like going down for a nap when it's light out and waking up when it's dark. You always wake up a little panicky, like you gave up more time than you intended to, even if you closed your eyes for only the exact twenty minutes it takes the sun to drop out of the sky.

"Okay, I have to ask," Lindsey said just after the first bar light came on. "What are you *doing* here?"

All traces of whatever distress Carine had caused—which Nina and I both knew she had, even though Lindsey tried to downplay the fact that she, our most good-natured third, was the one to have found a nemesis—had dripped off Lindsey's posture and sat sweetly in a puddle at Sam Decker's feet.

"I'm here for some Disney Channel reunion," he said, clearly grumpy about it.

We remembered, then, that he had gotten famous because of *The New Mickey Mouse Club*, which seemed strange to us, even though we had grown up watching it, because we couldn't remember a time when he didn't have stubble. We liked to joke that there was a clause in all of his contracts that demanded he be allowed to keep it, no matter the role—he was the grungy heart surgeon and the baker who couldn't be bothered to wear deodorant.

"No offense," I said, "but aren't you a little too famous for that?"

"Are you *ever* too famous for Mickey Mouse? He's like the animated Harvey Weinstein. You don't say no to him."

We looked at him blankly. His eyes went wide at the fact

that we didn't know what he was talking about, but he deflated into the booth instead of explaining it to us.

"I'm kidding. My agent made me go."

"Does that mean Clive Bennett's gonna be here?" Nina asked, as if the reunion were going to be held there in the Shamrock.

Clive Bennett was another *Mickey Mouse Club* alum. He was currently on the show *Buckle Up*, about traffic cops and the crazy, heavy shit they got into that nobody would ever suspect them of because they were traffic cops. It was a good show—we all watched it—but we knew that even good television shows ranked far below movies.

"No, and that's the problem." Decker took a swig of bourbon that he put his whole body into, nearly finishing it. "But that guy's a dick anyway."

"Um, he goes to Rwanda like once a year," I said, putting on my snottiest voice and hoping he realized I was kidding.

"Ha. That guy couldn't show you Rwanda on a map if it bit him on the dick."

"Ouch," Lindsey said. "I had no idea that was a problem you people faced."

He had just taken another sip of bourbon and he almost didn't get it down. And we knew it was a real laugh because we knew his acting laugh intimately, and this wasn't it.

"Ha. That's really funny." He turned to me and Nina. "She's really funny."

"So if he doesn't have to be here, why do you?" Nina asked.

Lindsey gave her the *Seriously?* eyes, probably pissed that Nina hadn't confirmed how funny she was.

"My agent thought it would help me reconnect with my

original fan base. The box-office returns haven't exactly been what they once were."

It never occurred to us that Sam Decker checked his box-office returns, given how busy he was escorting Abby Madison in and out of expensive cars and five-star restaurants and parties full of people even more important than he was. We had noticed that one of his movies had gone right to pay-per-view, bypassing theaters entirely, but that happened even to people like Jennifer Lawrence and Christian Bale sometimes.

"He always has these big plans but never has the time to see them through."

He shook his head and reconvened with his bourbon, looking into the glass he tilted toward himself as if he expected a prize like the kind you find at the bottom of a cereal box to float up.

"So does that mean the reunion's off?" I asked.

"No, it just means he was supposed to come with me and canceled at the last minute," he said, looking back up at me with a face that was still jarringly beautiful even after twenty minutes spent looking right at it. "And now I have no one to drink with."

"Well," Nina said, "thank God you found us."

Though she had a rule against makeup and kept to a uniform of hooded sweatshirts and running shoes, Lindsey was the prettiest. She had deviant curly hair that couldn't decide if it was dirty blond or auburn, but didn't waste much time thinking about it. Like most things in her and everybody else's life, she tried to control this force of nature by pulling it into giant knots on the top of her head and into nautical French braids, but it usually got the better of her. The stray curls that escaped even her most intricately conceived hair plots were always leaping from behind her ears, where she tucked them. She had been awkwardly tall for as long as we'd known her, but somewhere in between sophomore and junior year even the latest-blooming boys had caught up with her, and she complained about it less. The hard, lean figure she'd always had from years of sports made her seem older than she was, chiseled and able, like a woman who knew how to garden and sail, but the freckles that covered her body kept her young-looking. Nina liked to say she had *an ass that wouldn't quit*, mainly to make her uncomfortable—she had skin that showcased every blush, so she could never hide when she was flustered, delighting Nina—but it was also true. She bought her jeans two sizes too big, but there was no pair of pants she didn't fill the seat of.

Her mother had died when she was four, but Lindsey still told stories that featured her regularly. They always sounded nice, but we assumed they were made up because we couldn't remember anything before six. We knew there was a chance that one of her four older brothers had passed them down to her, but because we had never heard more than three consecutive words out of any of them, we doubted it. They were sluggish, not terribly clever boys who Lindsey had a bond with that Nina and I could never understand, maybe because we were both only children.

Maybe it was because she played so many sports, and the

coaches at our high school loved to use battlefield metaphors, but Lindsey had no trouble doing what needed to be done, stoically, without asking any questions. If you needed someone to pull the plug on a beloved vegetative family member, Lindsey would have been your girl. Not because she didn't care, but because she understood that someone had to do it. She was our puller of splinters and killer of exotic Florida bugs. Maybe it was because nothing would ever be as bad as her mom dying and maybe it was because of her four older brothers, but she could do things like watch tigers disembowel antelopes while they were still alive on the nature channel without turning away or even starting to while everyone else squealed and demanded the channel be changed. The thing that made her a magical creature instead of just creepy was that she didn't sacrifice an ounce of cheerfulness or optimism to this acceptance of life's unpleasantries. She was as likely to be found baking cookies as she was looking for worms after a rainstorm. She drew hearts over her *i*'s and loved maudlin, sappy endings more than anyone I knew.

Though we counted Carine an unreliable source on all things, she wasn't incorrect about the fact that Lindsey was sleeping with her boyfriend, Fred. We didn't object to the affair on principle, but we were confused as to why she would ever want to see him naked. He was hot in a lacrosse-player kind of way, but his face was the human-face equivalent of vanilla ice cream. He had no distinguishing features whatsoever—not even the accidental cookie-dough chunk or Reese's Pieces that had snuck in. If Nina was the one dating him we would've asked her flat out what the appeal was, but we knew that Lindsey had said yes to him mainly because he was the first person who had ever asked.

I had spoken to Fred only twice—once when Lindsey invited him over to her father's backyard to drink with us without any warning, and once when he came to visit her at the mall—and I still couldn't pick him out of a five-man lineup. If I hadn't held him in such low regard I would have been worried that I was going to snub him one day through my sheer inability to recognize and respond to such a stock, cardboard-cutout face. Though we would miss Carine's horror at her inability to prevent Lindsey from having something she didn't want her to have, Nina and I were both looking forward to Fred's return to school in New Hampshire in September.

The one mark in his favor was that he bought Lindsey expensive gifts, mostly jewelry and flowy silk clothing in prints that girls who wear Laura Ashley when they're young wear when they grow up, and at first we were surprised at how pleased she seemed to receive them, given that she would rather shave her eyebrows than wear either. But then we remembered that, because she worked in customer service at the mall, she had no trouble returning them for cash. We knew exactly what they cost because she pointed the items out to us in catalogs and online. So while we appreciated the times she picked up the tab and insisted on one more round, promising to cover it, we also knew that this generosity wasn't putting a very big dent in her savings, wherever she was keeping them. Nina and I occupied the nights Lindsey was with Fred trying to guess what she would eventually spend it on, no easy game, given that she wore the same Fruit of the Loom uniform everywhere she went and had no aspirations to move out of her father's house. All of her brothers still lived there.

When I think of Lindsey now, I think of the time, right after graduation, when we were done with school but didn't yet have jobs, when we went to the beach every day. Outside of that one stretch we didn't really go as often as you would think we would, living so close, but we thought of the beach as some sort of kid brother—loud and attention-hogging—and all the tourists that it drew were the kid brother's loud, annoying friends who laughed too hard at his fart jokes. But for, like, six weeks we went every day, to the same spot. And this one day, halfway through that stretch, we saw this three-legged cat. It was big and muscular enough that it might have been a bobcat. Though this guy had certainly won his fair share of fights, in addition to missing the leg, he had about half the whiskers he was born with and generally looked like the first cat God ever made, but he was hopping around like it was no big deal. Like cats made do with three feet all the time. But there were no other animals on the beach when we saw him. Most stretches of beach, private and public alike, had about four different kinds of wildlife for every person. We knew that cats were territorial creatures, and that maybe this relative wasteland was only the result of him successfully claiming this piece of land for himself, but it felt more like the rest of the animal kingdom had smelled his three-legged fate and wanted to be as far away from it as possible. And it made the ocean look even bigger and more indifferent than usual.

We named him Ralph.

Nina and I were pretty impressed by how well he was doing

on three feet—he really was hopping every which way, getting his half-whiskered face into every potentially fish-bearing
mound of sand in sight—and we were pretty optimistic, really,
about his long-term chances of success. But Lindsey insisted he
wasn't long for this world. And she wasn't sentimental enough
to try to save him and make a pet out of him; this was a woman
raised by men. Instead, confident that Ralph was on his last legs
in more than just the literal sense, she insisted that we give him
half of our picnic food, because he should have one last nice
thing in his life before whatever savage end nature had in mind
for him. Ralph happily took our sandwich meat and buns, and
even the cupcakes we had brought for dessert. And he must
have been restored by these reserves, because for the next few
weeks, he was there every day, waiting to see what we had for
him, until finally he wasn't. All Lindsey would say about him
not being there was "fucking cat," as if, suddenly, she had forgotten the name we had been calling him even when we
weren't with him, finding it hilarious to wonder what Ralph
would do in various social settings if he was there. But when
Nina gave a blow job to one of the lifeguards who worked that
stretch of the beach, he told her Lindsey showed up every
morning at dawn—before even the old people who walked the
sand and waded for exercise—with miniature feasts under her
arms. And even though she never talked about Ralph ever again,
we knew that she was always looking for him when we went,
and that when we stopped going to the beach every day, it
wasn't because it had gotten too hot, it was because she had
given up on him.

The only story you really need to know about Nina to

understand *her* is that she didn't know the name of that life-guard she gave the blowie to. But that she cried over what he told her about Lindsey. Later, when she was alone.

She had one of those mothers who wanted to be "friends" with her daughter, which really meant not bothering with any parenting. The effects were more pronounced in Nina because her father wasn't around, either. She never even met him. As we got older, we came to appreciate Elaine more, because she actually gave good "friend" advice, especially where dating and love were concerned, and I think her intentions were always good, despite their results. But I think Nina would've gotten fewer detentions and drawn less ire from the teachers and maybe made it to a few more classes if her mother hadn't spent so much time during the early years out in the trenches, gathering the hard way the advice she would later gift us.

I, meanwhile, always felt a step behind—not just of them, but of the entire world—which led to destructive, nonsensical decisions that confused even me. Like moving out of my parents' house that summer with no money saved, into an even dumpier part of town and pretty much the one apartment in Florida I could afford on a mall-coffee-shop salary. I think my parents assumed I was moving in with my boyfriend, Jay, and their feelings were hurt all over again when they found out I was living alone. I would've complained to Lindsey and Nina about how measured my parents' voices had become in the weeks before my move, even more polite and distant than usual, but I don't think either of them understood why I, the only one with two parents, wouldn't keep living the dream for as long as I could.

We sound ordinary, I know, like a million girls everywhere. But we weren't. Lindsey had taught herself to play the piano without a single lesson; even though her father couldn't afford a piano, she just kept getting better. We used to stay after school with her so she could play the piano in the band room that Nina figured out how to pick the lock of when we were sophomores. Nina and I would share Ho Hos and read *Kiss* and *Blush*, pointing out particularly beautiful or awkward or compelling pictures to each other, or just listen to her play. Lindsey could play just about anything without the music for it—theme songs to our favorite after-school sitcoms, commercial jingles, the latest radio hits. We used to try to stump her, demanding she play this or that, but she got it right every time. She never joined the school band, maybe because it would have been a bore to someone like her, but it's equally likely that it was in service to spending more time with us.

We were the only ones who ever heard her play.

Nina's imagination was a beast the likes of which only she could've created, even if she just showed you the tip of it. She told stories better than anyone else I knew. And not just recaps of the absurd things she actually did. She used to make up wild stories to captivate the school psychologist when our high school principal threatened to expel her if she didn't go, after she was caught miming fellatio to the baseball team with the erasers she was supposed to be cleaning as punishment for talking back to the school's least popular teacher. Mrs. Horvath had stopped her in the hall and asked to see her hall pass and when Nina said she forgot where she put it, Mrs. Horvath asked her where in the world it could've gone during the short walk from Nina's seventh-period math class to the stretch of hallway Mrs. Horvath's classroom was on. Nina told her it might very well be caught somewhere between Mrs. Horvath's second and third chins. She never had any trouble coming up with a line like that, when the rest of us would've just surrendered with an apology. And while the totally over-the-top sagas she created for her therapy sessions were amusing to her and to us, on whom she tested each story she had planned for the next appointment, she claimed she was doing it for the school psychologist—an eager, unimaginative woman just out of grad school who had moved away from her family and friends in order to fix our problems, whose eyes just went so deep when Nina painted her mountains of pain. She gave that psychologist a purpose, and made sure she never knew that Nina had been making the focuses of their sessions up, even when Nina stopped having to go see her. She wasn't making a fool of her, Nina swore, but fulfilling all the expectations that had drawn her to the job. People who felt fulfilled by their jobs were probably better at them, she said, which meant she was doing it for all the screwed-up kids who came after her, who would probably need a good therapist. One who had heard it all.

Someone might have noticed this cleverness, and the ease with which she told complicated, gripping stories, and helped her do something with it other than make us laugh, if Nina ever bothered to attend an English class. But she skipped as many of those as she did all of her other classes.

I was their audience, a generous one, the witness to their lives. Whenever one of them came alive with fury at the mistreatment they perceived from one party or another, I showed them a kinder, more generous version of what might have happened. I reinterpreted their lives in a way they could stand. I was patient with them when they lost patience with each other, and tried to distract them from the flaws they couldn't change. They said that I was gifted at doing this because I had come from a stable home where the curtains matched the rugs and I wasn't allowed to eat Fruit Roll-Ups for dinner, but I think I did it because one of us had to.

We loved one another purely, without the complications teenage girls so often bring to everything. But I wouldn't be telling it right if I didn't also tell you that it felt, by that night, that a sense of uneasy anticipation filled any room the three of us were in. It felt like someone had just farted in a very formal setting, and there was no pretending that it hadn't happened, but nobody wanted to be the one to acknowledge it and move things along. Nina hadn't even taken that much pleasure out of calling Carine a cunt, which normally would've had the power to turn a Wednesday afternoon into a Saturday night. It felt like we were running out of things to say, and in the silences we let settle, resentment had time to mount. At the fact that we had all reconfirmed for each other that our collective aimlessness was a good idea. That none of us would have been bold enough to forgo any investment in our future without the other two, and that we wouldn't be sitting where we were, in seats becoming worse by the minute—obstructed view, with no padding, and at the back of the house—if it weren't for the others. We were starting to panic, and when we looked around for something to pin our regret on, all we found was one another. Sam Decker being at the Shamrock was a miracle, our miracle, and my first thought when I saw him was that he might be miracle enough to give us back to each other.

S o, man, this is like a *real* bar, huh?" Decker said.
He tapped his fingers on the table as he looked around. We would measure the number of drinks he had across the night by the pace of those manic taps. Like the rest of him, they mellowed with every round. They had no rhythm or beat, which made their sound feel frantic, more caged animal than I *have this tune in my head.* He looked expectant, like he was waiting for someone who was supposed to meet him there, even though he had already told us he was alone.

"As opposed to what?" Nina asked.

"I mean, these are people who come in here just to drink."

"Um, yeah, it's a *bar*," Lindsey said. "Were you hoping to have your taxes done or something? There's an accountant's office next door, but they don't sell booze. They probably wouldn't mind if you brought your own, though."

"Didn't that guy go to jail for fraud?" Nina asked.

"Probably," Lindsey said. "I guess you'll have to stay here," she said to Decker.

"That's not what I meant," said Decker. "I just meant it's not somewhere you come to see or be seen or meet up with people. Like those old guys over there." He nodded at Bob and Jax, two of the most dependable regulars. "They look like they've been here awhile."

"Yeah, probably," I said. "I've never been here when they weren't."

"And they'd keep on drinking even if they were the only ones here," he said.

"I'm pretty sure they think they are," I said.

"And this *music*," Decker said.

Frankie Avalon's "Venus" was playing. The oldies were pretty much the elevator music of Florida, not least because the stereotypes about the number of old people here are true. While Nina, Lindsey, and I normally preferred the Katy Perry/ Lady Gaga fare that most girls our age did, we had grown used to the oldies that Sal made his patrons listen to, and maybe even liked them a little by the night we met Sam Decker. Sal told us it was good for us to get to know these older musicians—they told whole stories in three minutes, while our generation tried only to shock, he said. But we knew that at least part of the reason for the limited selection was that he didn't have the time or desire to listen to any of the new music he claimed to hate so much, and would never let any foreign influences find their way into the Shamrock.

"You could live a 1950s *childhood* in this bar. It's like a time capsule."

"I mean, if that's your thing . . ." said Lindsey.

"That's awesome. I love that. It reminds me of this bar I used to go to in Anchorage," he said. "The décor was pretty much the same, too."

None of us made any indication that we had known he was from Anchorage, even though this, too, was in our catalog of facts. We couldn't figure out what he meant by *décor*—the kitsch and posters and random collection of garage-sale rubbage that covered the walls of so many bars like this one had been outlawed along with pop music. There was wood, and there were beer taps, bottles of liquor, and glasses to put them in, and that was pretty much it. In that way, Decker was right. It really was just a bar.

"There just seem to be so many fewer assholes here than in your average bar," he said.

"Eh, I think you'd be surprised," said Lindsey. "Assholes look different in different places."

"Yeah, and what constitutes an asshole?" I asked.

"People who see bad movies."

"I'm so sorry not all movies are as good as yours," said Nina, warming up for her A-grade flirting.

"Oh, no, I was counting my movies in that category. Well, most of them."

We had not seen this coming. Self-deprecation was not a trait we associated with Sam Decker. He was one of the few actors of his generation whose career wasn't built at least partly on irony.

"I bet half the people in here have never heard of me," he said. "And I love them for it."

Our favorite section of our favorite celebrity magazine that year was "10 Things You Don't Know About Me." It was exactly what it sounds like: Each week a different celebrity listed ten facts about him- or herself, ranging in gravity from their favorite TV show or their favorite nail-polish color to their ethnicity, or the person they were named after, or how old their Sicilian grandmother lived to be. You might read that someone's splurge food was truffled macaroni and cheese right after you discovered that they raised money for and participated in the AIDS Walk every year because they had an Uncle Tony who died from the disease. We loved the pictures of stars in action, going about their daily lives, unaware of the trailing camera, that ran before and after these lists, but it was the lists that gave the photos their power. As intimate as those pictures were, there was a distance to them, too. The subjects rarely looked right at the camera, and there was a danger of feeling like you were spying on them, no matter how little you pretended to care. But with these lists, our most beloved stars—the ones most worth watching even when they didn't know we were—were inviting us in. You could argue that Chelsea Pauly might not have worn so short a skirt if she had known there were going to be photographers outside her brunch, or that Bobby Lobo might've held the door for the old woman walking into Barneys after him—that they never meant to subject us to such bad behavior—but with the lists there was a sort of willing participation that gave credibility to everything around them. It felt as close as we would ever get to these people we loved.

We spent a fair amount of the time we spent drinking in the Shamrock lauding what some celebrities chose to divulge about themselves in this section of the magazine, and lambasting others. What people chose to reveal about themselves changed how much we liked them, and the degree to which a celebrity came off as profound and thoughtful or shallow and douchy didn't necessarily correspond with the impressiveness of his or her career. It was a risk, we learned over weeks of reading the column, to show your hand like that. It was like going on a first date with all of America at once, only you got to the restaurant first, so they had a chance to study you from afar before approaching the table, and even bail if they needed to.

Sometimes there was a particularly disastrous week of "10 Things," or one that inspired us to give a flailing career a second chance, or to try at least one episode of a show that had never captured our imagination because the second lead proved he was quirkier and less predictable than we ever would've guessed. Then it became clear to us again how important it was to be able to present yourself neatly and colorfully to the world. To spin the facts of your life. Those weeks, we debated the ten most noteworthy or surprising things about each of us, and how we'd word them in the magazine. We never discussed how or why we might become famous—why anyone might care that Lindsey had broken seven bones or that Nina had pet hermit crabs as a kid—but we took discussions of the list as seriously as if we had an actual plan, or at least a talent, to reach a point in our non-careers at which people would demand access to this trivia. The night Sam Decker walked into the Shamrock, my list might have gone something like this:

- I was eight weeks pregnant by Jay, my boyfriend of four years, who I loved, but was no longer in love with.
- My favorite drink was called a fire engine, which was just a Shirley Temple with vodka in it. It never occurred to me that the fact that I still liked grenadine might be an indication that I was too young to be drinking.

- I had assumed since junior year, when I tried to break up with Jay and he started crying and then said "no" just once, that I would have his babies, but now, not even showing yet, this baby felt like an actual person, and it felt far crueler to let another person waste away in a town with one bar for every ten churches than it ever would have been to tell Jay that I was sorry but he would find somebody better if he would stop crying long enough to try.
- My rent was due in nine days, and I had less than half the amount I needed, and my next paycheck was eleven days away.
- I knew that Jay would be a good father—he was a good, kind person who was both reliable and hard-working, and was unbothered by the limits to his charisma and intelligence. I knew he would do all the right things, like whisper to my stomach—I couldn't stand to call it a belly even then, which is maybe the first sign I wasn't ready for motherhood—and hold my hair back when my morning sickness got a jump start in the middle of the night. But also that all those things and others would be wasted on me, and that our child would grow up having no conception of love except for one she formed from movies like those Sam Decker was in.
- I had never seen snow, and when asked to think about my ideal vacation spot—a popular topic for the "10 Things You Don't Know About Me" column—names

of places never came to mind, but I always pictured a big open field covered in an untouched layer of snow.

- I had started looking online to see if at that point in a pregnancy a baby had fingers and toes yet, and when it would start to grow eyelashes or be able to feel pain. If it was the size of a walnut or a fist or a piece of fruit, and I had Planned Parenthood's price list memorized, but also the numbers in my bank account.
- I used to live two blocks away from a girl named Becca Voigt, who I played with when I was in a fight with Nina or Lindsey, or when they were grounded or on vacation. When we were in the tenth grade she got knocked up, and a few days after the news broke, she was sent to live with her grandma in Idaho before she had a chance to say good-bye to any of us. Her grandma had come to visit once when we were nine, and we had spent a full week after she left talking about how bad she smelled. Becca told me that one time, when her grandmother was napping on the couch—she was always napping on the couch—she was so still that Becca thought she was dead, and it was only when she started sucking on her dentures that Becca realized this wasn't the case. She imitated what that sounded like and, accurate or not, thinking about it still makes me shiver and then brush my teeth. Even all these years later, her having to go and live with a person who had horrified her to such a degree still felt like punishment for going past third base. Even if it was meant to protect her.

- Lindsey and Nina had proven to be my most reliable and creative allies in outsmarting the conundrums I'd found my way into since the second grade, when the peanut butter I had put on the earpiece of our telephone after watching the movie *Little Monsters* broke my own grandmother's hearing aid, but I hadn't even tried to tell them yet.
- I had not stopped drinking—had, in fact, started drinking more—in the weeks after marking my menstrual cycle on a calendar with cats posing in different Halloween costumes each month, confirming for certain that I was either going through menopause at the age of nineteen or pregnant. I knew from those late-night online searches how bad that was for whatever project my body had started against my will, and also that this decision seemed to imply that another one had been made.

Two

We were finally starting to feel comfortable with Sam Decker—our hearts had returned to a semi-normal, sustainable pace, and we stopped having to sit on our hands to keep them from shaking, and we had a millisecond or two to think about the things we were saying instead of just blurting them out, relieved every time that what we said sounded casual and conversational even to us—when Lila Tucker walked into the bar and we all froze. Lindsey and I immediately looked over at Nina, causing Sam to do the same. When Nina didn't say anything, he looked back at the table where Lila had joined Carine and Paisley and Polka Dot and greeted them with a round of kisses, and then back at us with a smirk. We had enough reasons to hate Lila without this reminder that Carine and the patterns never would've been on our radar if it wasn't for her. They would have blended in with all the other little blonde girls Golden Creek was known for growing, the way the rest of Florida was known for growing oranges. They hadn't come after us until Lindsey and Fred met at the dance club in the stretch of Orlando where all the under-21s hung out at the start of the summer, but we had been wary of them since Lila had taken up with them years ago.

"Oh, yeah. That's right," Decker said, turning back to the table. "I believe I was promised a story."

"Well, that's simple," said Nina. "Lindsey over here is fucking the frigid one with the lazy eye's boyfriend, and in the long tradition of shitty things that happen to women, Lindsey's the one taking the shit for it even though *she's* not the one who made any promises to that lizard."

"I mean, she *is* fucking her boyfriend," Decker said, like it was the funniest thing he had ever heard. Nina laughed.

"True," she said.

"Jesus," I said, trying to motion with my eyes at Lindsey.

"I mean, *obviously* I'm not saying Lindsey's the one to blame. There's no dealing rationally with a woman who dry-cleans her jeans," said Nina.

We all looked into our drinks. Apparently even Decker didn't know how to hijack a conversation back from Nina once she had taken it to weird or awkward places.

"She *does!* I've seen her at Ace dry cleaners."

"But who's the other one?" he asked, studying Nina. "The one who just walked in."

Lindsey and I opened our mouths to speak at the same time.

"No one," Nina said, cutting us both off.

"That's one way to put it," said Lindsey.

"Lila Tucker's worse than the rest of them," I said. "But she knows better than to come over here."

"Man, you girls are *intense.*"

None of us said anything.

"I mean, no, I love it, but you realize this isn't normal, right?"

"Please," Lindsey said. "You live in L.A. Aren't people just as brutal to each other out there?"

"I don't know," said Decker. "I guess they're just a little more . . . How do I put this . . . *discreet* about it."

"Maybe you're all just really good actors. So you fake it really well. Not hating each other, I mean."

"Yeah, right," Decker said. "You've clearly never seen most of the people in L.A. act."

"I Get Around" by the Beach Boys came on, and Decker looked like someone who had just spotted himself on the Jumbotron at a sporting event—he popped up involuntarily from an affectless slouch, eyes cartoonishly wide. He would have similar reactions to the songs that came on throughout the night, and every time he did, it reminded us how much older than us he actually was. From his outfit—an expensive-looking but rugged chambray shirt with a soft-looking cotton waffle weave under a low button job, and brown motorcycle boots that matched his bomber jacket—and his meticulously groomed-to-look-effortless hair, he looked too hip, too timelessly cool, to be old. But at thirty-four, he was closer to our parents' age than our own, and while he wasn't old enough to have grown up listening to these songs, his parents surely had, and hummed them over his shoulder while they helped him with his homework, or while making dinner or taking out the trash, the way ours did Bruce Springsteen and Billy Joel.

"Maybe your old uncle Sam should gather you silly girls around and we can sort this out so that you can all drink together." He raised his eyebrows, clearly satisfied with his deviance.

"It's early yet," Nina said with unreadable eyes, their vacancy more unsettling because of how big they were, making it impossible not to go right to her eyes when trying to decode her mood. "Too early to tell how this night is gonna go. But I can promise you that's one thing that's not gonna happen."

We didn't always hate Lila Tucker, and in fact, as far as we knew, Nina still didn't. She rhapsodized about the empty black hearts and the lonely dismal futures of Carine and the patterns with all the creativity and malice she showed to their faces, but Lila was the one subject that ever drew silence from her. This befuddled Lindsey and me into hours of circular conversation, because Nina had more reason than either of us to hate her.

Years ago, they lived on the same block, and we had all gone to school with Lila. The concept of a parent who stayed home full-time to take care of the kids was totally unheard-of where we lived—a home with two parents was rare enough—so our parents relied on us as childcare for each other. It was understood that while some dark, unthinkable deed committed by or upon any one of us might go unreported by any other one of us, if a large group of kids witnessed something worth talking about, eventually one of them was going to talk, and the truth was going to leak up to the older, disciplinary generation.

So while our parents could not afford the Disney World

camp that we begged them to send us to every summer, they did encourage us to get together with all the other kids in the neighborhood to engage in the same activities we would have if they did have the money to send us. "Who needs to spend five hundred dollars so your kid can play capture the flag?" and "My kid's got a good enough imagination to entertain himself" and "Only boring people get bored" were the mantras overheard in our neighborhood when our overworked parents gathered in fraying lawn chairs in the middle of the streets after double and triple shifts, cheap beer finally in hand, content at the energy we seemed to have collected across the day that was at the point of bursting as we rode our bikes in loops around where they sat, whooping and shouting the happy, nonsensical calls of summer.

These mantras and the cheap beer were flimsy covers for the sense of dread that pervaded Florida in the summer of 2009, the summer before our freshman year of high school, and the last year we were all friends. The biggest industry in the area before September 2008 was real estate. Second homes. Vacation homes. It was the land of getaways and escape. By living there year-round, we were the minorities. Our parents worked as secretaries or handymen in real estate offices, construction workers on the new condo developments going up every month, or as waitresses in theme restaurants that catered to sunburnt men in Hawaiian shirts who had chosen to spend their two weeks of vacation with their families in a brutal, blistering climate that none of them were conditioned for. After the crash, the second-home class of people could barely afford their first homes, and foreclosure rates in the area rose to an all-time high. Everywhere you looked, half-built housing developments loomed, like skeletons whose flesh had been picked off. The sounds of bulldozers and drills and concrete mixers was the symphony of our home, and the silence that replaced it in the fall of 2008 burned our eardrums and put everyone on edge. Our neighborhood had always been working class, but when their old jobs ceased to exist, our parents had to settle for even less reliable, less rewarding work with longer hours and lower pay. We had thought that after a few months or a year these developments would be back on track, that it was only a matter of time before their completions gave way to new blueprints and plans and buildings in progress that would call for even more manpower than before, but by that summer it was clear that the silence was there to stay.

The result was a pessimism that colored every interaction, and every decision, and went deeper than our smooth brown skin. There was not much good luck anywhere you looked, and as a result, our parents were prepared, at all times, for the worst: for the gator that always gets too close to finally strike; for soft, weak plots of land to finally give way to the sinkhole beneath; or for the rebellious teenager who always has something to say to just not come home one night. The only guard against these ever-lurking dangers, it was understood, was to combat them together—to pool safety in numbers. This meant that Nina's mom was allowed to yell at me, and my own mother never felt bad about asking any of the neighbors to watch me without any warning. Everyone's house was open to everyone else's kids, and which kid was struggling in algebra and which kid had just landed the lead role in the school play were common knowledge. Good luck had abandoned all of us at once, and we would make do together.

This meant we walked one another to and from school every morning and home again every afternoon five days a week from September through June, and gathered in the hallways according to the neighborhoods we lived in, with the people we both commuted with and played with after school. We spent nearly every waking minute of the summer with each other. And when I say we were like family, I don't mean that as a cozy, sentimental concept, but a practical one. We spent more time together than most siblings do. The only time I used to spend away from Nina and Lindsey and Lila were the eight hours I spent sleeping every night.

We had been friends our entire lives—the shit economy can't be credited for that. I can no more remember meeting Lila or Nina than I can my own parents, and there are pictures of all of us in plastic wading pools in each other's patchy front yards, and flying around so joyfully, so urgently, in nothing but diapers that it looks like our happiness is about to sprout wings. But while there is no hard beginning any of us can point to, that summer does mark the start of the stretch of years I think of when I think of them now.

Even in the hard times our state had fallen on, it wasn't entirely unpleasant to be young when and where we were, and not only because we knew one another. When we were kids, our neighborhood was in the middle of nowhere, a strip of empty land between swamps. But we had charted the spread of upscale vacation developments and the bougie shops and restaurants to accommodate them optimistically—in the years just before the crash, we were surrounded. The gated communities-in-progress we lived in the shadows of were designed so that each cul-de-sac within each community had a different aesthetic—missionary, ranch, whitewashed with red roses climbing up the sides—and was named accordingly. The Sierra. The Rose Bed. And all the identical units of each street were clustered around a pool. While each cul-de-sac was halted midway through its completion after the crash, there were always one or two occupied houses on every street. Which meant they had to keep the pools open and operating, since it was one of the amenities that had been promised in the brochure.

All of these cleverly named, meticulously styled and crafted lanes of identical homes were lumped and gated into larger planned communities with equally charming names—Alligator's Walk, Sunset Point. The guard towers you had to pass to get into these communities—"welcome points," they were called—ran along Route 49, across which sat the ungated, unplanned streets that our less colorful, unnamed homes lined. The men who manned these welcome points really were fairly welcoming. Most of the guards were retirees who lived in the gated communities, pleasant and probably a little bored old men who were happy to show you pictures of their grandkids if you had the time. They wore matching polo shirts and had perfected the art of the friendly nod. In general, we didn't mind the people of these communities the way we did the Golden Creekers. They were vacationers and retirees—we had no idea what kind of lives they led in the real world, and this made any interactions we had with them impersonal, and very low-stakes. They were individual entities, all of them, whose polite waves at each other when they passed made it clear they didn't know each other. They had not gathered into a force that was threatening to us. That they had gone so far out of their way to spend time in our home seemed promising.

One of the guards, a widower, had a brief fling with Elaine, which is how we all had stickers on our bikes signifying the right to come and go from Panther Crossing whenever we pleased, giving us access to twenty-seven different half-finished cul-de-sacs, and the swimming pools that sat unused within them. That these pools were maintained for no one further drained the already dwindling funds of these communities, but was great for us.

Elaine had eventually tired of Henry's early bedtime and his lack of interesting stories after long days spent nodding at the cars that had windshield stickers proving they lived in Panther Crossing, and punching the button to raise the bar to grant them entrance. But he still nodded at us every time we went cruising down the bike lane that ran past his guard tower.

These bike rides and pool crashings were, like everything else, a four-person event. I can't remember a single ride or swim that summer that one of us missed. Nina and Lila never excluded me or Lindsey—it was understood that any gathering that any combination of the four of us held was open to every member of the group—but there was a physical component to the bond between Lila and Nina. I don't mean they were lesbians, as the older boys who lived in the neighborhood always screamed at them when we rode our bikes through their street hockey games, just that they were constantly drawing each other in some magnetic, physical way. Their bodies were always turned toward each other in a way that didn't seem entirely voluntary. Even by that night in the bar, the one thing that made me even a little insecure in my friendship with Nina was having seen her with Lila. I knew friendship could become even *more* intimate, more intense, for her, and that our friendship, as important as it was to me, and as influential as it was on every other aspect of my life, had not yet reached the level of friendship Nina was capable of. But I don't think I would have believed that if I hadn't seen it for myself.

It wasn't so much that they borrowed each other's clothes as that they shared a wardrobe. They combined their allowances to buy the pieces of clothing that always hung exactly the same on both of them and never looked quite right on me and Lindsey even though we were invited to their trips to the mall to purchase them. Whenever the four of us agreed to meet somewhere at a given time, they always showed up together, even though we had seen them part ways when we all said good night after we made the plan. And we knew they hadn't called each other in between to work out an earlier meeting time, because Lila's family was so poor then that their phone service was cut off half the time. It wasn't so much that they finished each other's sentences as that when either of them was speaking it was understood that she was speaking for both of them. The other nodded along, smiling neutrally, confirming that she had signed off on the statement being made. People who lived in our neighborhood and had known them for years sometimes mixed their names up, and not just because they had the same four-letter structure.

They even *looked* alike. Or complementary, really, given that they were either identical or opposite on any given physical front. Their bodies took up the same amount of space volume-wise, I guess you could say—they were both small, compact girls who managed to afford Abercrombie clothing by virtue of being able to fit into the children's line, which had most of the same styles as the adult store but cost less. But while Nina was all nobs and hard angles, boyish in hip and bosom, Lila was lithe. She seemed almost stretchy on account of how smoothly each part of her body flowed into the other. My mother called her Gumby. They both had thin, silky hair that they wore in face-framing bobs that curtained classic features. Nina, who loved to be surprising, suffered from the fact that her features and mannerisms were as Italian as the name Nina Scarfio promised they would be. She had the skin tone of a character in a Fellini movie and could never help gesturing with her hands as she spoke. Lila looked rich even before she was. She was the picture of an East Coast blonde rather than a California one, with delicate, straw-looking hair and china-doll skin that was never meant to spend as much time in the sun as it did. She was the kind of girl you knew would look great in a turtleneck, even though the weather kept her from ever confirming this. She had blue eyes the color of the swimming pools we were constantly trespassing in.

Where Lindsey had the consolation of knowing that her mother *would* have been around if she could, and Nina had never met her father—did not, in fact, know his name—so didn't have anyone to miss, Lila's story was a little less tidy. Her mother had lived with her and her father until Lila was ten. She didn't disappear completely, but went to work on one of the cruise ships based in Miami. Whenever she docked, Lila went to Miami to stay with her for a night. We would have been jealous, but Lila never came back from these trips with any good stories, or souvenirs, and only offered bland, one-word answers when we pressed her, until finally we stopped. I never saw Lila shed a single tear over her mother, or voice a single complaint, but after she left, Lila laughed less, and you could sometimes tell she was tuned out from the conversation we were having around her. She had always been the least silly of us—the one with the most proper grammar and the cleanest nails—but after her mother left she seemed adult in a serious, reserved sort of way.

Lila's father, Mike, was what was known as a dreamer in our neighborhood, which was certainly a notch, on the philosophical hierarchy, below a stern, nose-to-the-grindstone hard worker. But it was also understood that dreamers were broken by The Man, and The Man was the enemy. Which meant that while men sometimes shook their heads when they saw him sitting on his porch drinking a forty as they came crawling home after fourteen-hour shifts, they shared cans of beer from their own six-packs when his malt liquor ran out. He pitched new gadgets and schemes to the clusters of lawn chairs that gathered each night—an automatic baby bottle, a talking ball that would train your dog, a bookmark that was also a flashlight—and over time he became our parents' very own court jester. At the very least, sentiment went, he made people laugh.

The other reason people gave Mike a break was because of Marie, Lila's younger sister. She was four years younger than us, and the only person Lila might've conceivably loved as much as Nina. She was rabid about her, often insisting that Marie come along on outings she probably shouldn't have been part of. All of us knew better than to argue.

Marie was a strange, haunting child who rarely said more than a handful of words that anyone could remember. She was gracious to adults and did well in school, but she was a chalky white color that unsettled her golden peers and made more noticeable the dark circles under her eyes. Her and Lila's mother was generally blamed for this, along with just about everything else that went wrong in those first few years after she left. And every small, kind gesture directed at Mike was understood to be compensation for his wife's unthinkably self-ish exit.

Occasionally when a new product hit shelves with an uproar, Mike claimed he had been only a step or two behind arriving at that very same one. He had seen the hole in the market for it, he said, but the product that hole called for hadn't taken a concrete form in his mind yet. The consistency of his confidence didn't keep anyone from being shocked when one of his ideas finally did pay off. It was so simple, we couldn't believe we hadn't thought of it ourselves, and it was only later that our parents realized they were having a taste, finally, of what Mike had been going through for years. Sick of having to buy new crayons for Marie when she broke them, he patented a small piece of rubber that would fit perfectly around the two halves of a snapped crayon, making it whole again. It was rumored that Crayola had bought the patent for more than three million dollars.

The deal had gone through in the summer of 2008, and

though no one thought his sessions of make-believe would finally come to something, no one was surprised that he waited until everyone else was particularly poor before landing his fortune. He had never managed to get in line with what everyone else was doing. At the same time, no one was surprised that once he had money to spare, he didn't change much, or pick up and leave altogether. He was a simple man who showed no frustration or regret at the simple life he led. He made a change here and there, but so gradually that we didn't notice at first—a nicer backpack for Lila right in the middle of the school year when her old one was perfectly fine, top-of-the-line tires on his crumbling car. I don't think now that he put off the new house in the nicer neighborhood and the private school for as long as he did only because the dual concepts of money and having any were so foreign to him that he had not had time to figure out what he would do with it.

I think that, for all his trouble with social graces and reading people, he understood that his small family relied on our neighborhood for things he could not give them.

So what about the rest of you?" Decker asked. "Are you all spoken for? I mean, if that's what you want to call it," he said, looking at Lindsey. "At what age do people sign their lives away around here?"

"That's romantic," Nina said.

"You know what I mean."

"Yeah. I guess I'm kind of seeing someone," I said.

"Ha! You've been wearing his promise ring since sophomore year," said Nina. "*Kind of seeing someone.* I would love to see Jay's face if he heard you say that." She turned to Decker. "They finish each other's sentences more than twins and old married couples combined. It's actually kind of sweet, if that's your thing."

"I don't think I've ever finished one of Jay's sentences," I said.

"Does Jay even *speak* in sentences?" Lindsey asked. "I mean, no offense. You know I love the guy like a brother, but he's more of a word-here-or-there kind of guy."

"Yeah, like you need any more brothers," said Nina.

"That's cool," said Decker. "So where is he tonight? Do couples not, like, go on dates around here?"

"We do. I mean, sometimes we do. He just started working as a salesman for his uncle's company. They're on some sort of corporate bonding retreat."

That was a lie, kind of. He sold refrigerators from his uncle's store, which was in a strip mall. They were stainless steel, state-of-the-art, but still, they were refrigerators. The corporate retreat was him drinking in his uncle's basement with two of his cousins. He wanted to meet up later in the night, but this was becoming increasingly unlikely.

"Got it. So what's his deal? Other than the sales thing?"

"I don't know," I said. "He's just a guy who lives in Florida."

"Okay, I know I made fun of him before," said Lindsey. "But c'mon. Jay's the *best*. You know that better than anyone."

She turned to Decker.

"He once drove an Egg McMuffin sixty miles to her apartment from his grandmother's house on a Sunday morning because she complained she never got up in time for McDonald's breakfast, which everyone knows is the best."

"I feel you on that," said Decker.

"Yeah," said Nina. "And his dick would, like, knock you over if it hit you in the face. He's a bull."

I wasn't sure if she said it for the shock effect or to return the focus to the table's sexuality, but Decker was the only one flustered by the nature of this statement.

"Uh, that's cool," said Decker. "But how have you seen her boyfriend's dick? Is that, like, a Florida thing?"

Nina hesitated for exactly zero seconds.

"Oh. He's my brother."

He looked genuinely horrified.

"She's kidding!" said Lindsey.

He exhaled loudly the breath he'd been holding, and laughed wearily, without his heart in it. We were relieved that he was beginning to understand how inappropriate Nina could get, and that while she may have been joking, she was also measuring what, exactly, it would take to get a new person to squirm. Having hung out with Nina in mixed company dozens of times, Lindsey and I knew intimately how awkward it usually was before this moment was reached.

"Good," he said. "That's good."

"Oh, c'mon, it's Florida," said Nina, "not a cult in, like, Nevada or something. All the appropriate sex taboos are upheld. I did date her brother once, though, which was actually pretty incestuous."

She nodded at Lindsey when she said this, whose rare

agitation was already showing itself in red splotches on her neck and cheeks. Nina had dated her youngest brother, John, for two weeks in response to Lindsey's insistence that none of her brothers were sexually attracted to Nina. It had ended badly. Not because of bad behavior from either half of the couple, but because Lindsey totally lost her shit.

Nina's favorite game to play that year was a hypothetical scenario in which nuclear apocalypse wiped out everyone on the planet except for the people living on five specific blocks, and to preserve the species we had to do it with someone who lived on them. It was a different five blocks every time we played. This was her way, of course, of getting us to admit feelings for people we saw every day and whose presence we could be made uncomfortable by, but she could never do something as simple and orthodox as just asking us. Lindsey and I found all kinds of ways to get out of this trap, and I suspect that Lindsey's insistence that Nina's own answer that day—John— would only result in the end of humankind since John would never do it with her, was only a way of distracting us from her impending turn, but Nina pounced on it. I don't think Lindsey would have cared so much if her father, not realizing that the relationship was anything but sincere, hadn't been so excited about it. All of the men in her family generally avoided us when we congregated at Lindsey's house, heard, in basements and garages and everywhere else that had troubled engines and pipes that needed tightening, but not seen. But once John gravitated into our circle by pairing up with Nina, Lindsey's dad took it as a sign that we were all one big happy group. He started inviting us to dinner, or to watch TV after, which only reminded all of us how lonely he probably was.

Nina must have been pretty desperate to get the controversial nature of her love life across if she was willing to bring it up. She and Lindsey stared at each other without saying anything, and Decker kept looking from one to the other.

"Okay, fine," he said. "But what about now? Can anybody around here keep up with you?"

"Yeah, right," said Lindsey, who was still the color of a jellyfish bite.

Decker didn't say anything to this, but kept his eyes on Nina, waiting for her answer. She was suddenly captivated by the beads of condensation gathering on her glass. She kept sliding them together with all the concentration she might've applied if she was in a class perfecting that very skill.

"If it requires this much thought, I feel bad for whomever you're seeing," he said. "You're either taken or you're free."

She looked up all *Who, me?* as if she hadn't realized that it was her dating status he was after. It was too convincing to be entirely coy. Lindsey and I were the only two people on the planet who could see through her every time.

"Free as a bird," she finally said.

I guess you could trace the start of the trouble to the ninth grade, when Lila transferred to the Orlando Country Day School in Golden Creek. Not because she ditched us when she made new friends, but because that's where she met Max.

We had been worried when Lila finally confessed that she

wouldn't be moving with us from the junior high in the middle of our neighborhood to Culver High School, which was a full ten-minute bike ride away. We thought that we had finally lost her. She only told us because we were discussing first-day-of-school outfits, and what the seniors would be wearing, forcing her to mumble something about the uniform she'd be confined to. We'd thought people wore uniforms only in movies. The fact that she had waited until the days had already started growing noticeably shorter, cutting down the hours we spent at the pools we had come to think of as ours, didn't exactly make us confident that she would be keeping the lines of communication open. Nina, of course, already knew. Lindsey was halfway through her description of the fluorescent green shorts with stars on them that she was trying to find the right shirt for when Nina turned to Lila, who had been suspiciously interested in the surface of the diving board we were sitting on, and said, "Just tell them." When Lila did, Nina looked like a disappointed parent who was listening to her child confess a crime that she was already privy to, to the other parent. Stoic, resigned to it, but still not unaffected.

The day school started a full week earlier than Culver did, so Nina, Lindsey, and I were free to go over to her house that first morning and vote on how she should wear her hair, and if she should use both straps of her backpack, or let it hang off one shoulder casually. We laughed along with Lila when she made fun of how fascist her blazer was, but later we all agreed that it reminded us of Sarah Jessica's blazer in *Girls Just Want to Have Fun*, and we got depressed about Lila being gone all over again. We cheered ourselves up with how funny it would be to be sitting on her porch when she got back from her first day, as if we had never left the spots from which we had seen her off, even though we'd each had a Slurpee and a half and two corn dogs from the 7-Eleven, and had rescued two baby frogs from the pool by the time she was due back. It was a flimsy conceit because we knew she'd be able to measure our day from our skin—skin just abandoned by the sun looks different than a tan even a day old. We're girls from Florida, we know.

She got to be the one to surprise us, though, because she didn't come back alone. She walked ahead of him, either to lead the way or because her backpack, which was slung over his left shoulder, was slowing him down. She was a girl by then used to turns of good fortune and generosity, and had probably accepted the offer easily, gracefully. Without having to think about it. We assumed she would have lost the blazer by then—it was over a hundred degrees—but she still had it on. The only difference was that she had rolled her plaid skirt so that it fell an inch higher on her late-August thighs. Her porch was western-facing and the sun had already started its descent, so as she approached us her backlighting was about as flattering as a person can hope for. It was stunning, supernatural light that almost made the heat that held us all hostage worth it. It obscured her features, but we wouldn't have recognized her anyway.

We had all prepared ourselves for some distance to open up between us and her—silently, to ourselves—but even in our worst prognosticating, we hadn't foreseen a take-home friend on the first day. It was like learning that someone you loved with a slow-moving but terminal cancer had been hit by a bus.

We braced ourselves for her to wonder out loud what we were doing there, or to make some thin excuse about how she and Max had to study. But instead she threw her head back in relief and said, "Oh, yay, you're *here*. I thought I was going to have to round you up. Max is dying to meet you."

"I've heard so much about all of you," he said, as if they had been on a long trip somewhere together.

So we gained a fifth instead of losing our fourth. We never figured out when she had time to catch him up on our shared history, but he knew all our inside jokes, and all the million ways in which we were connected, or liked to think that we were. When they weren't with us they were in school, and he was two years older, so it's not like they were passing notes in class. He insisted on coming to pick her up every morning even though she was forty minutes out of his way, round-trip, which we thought might have explained it, but she once confessed to us that she usually spent the ride cramming for the tests teachers were regularly springing at the day school or, in a confession that horrified us, given her inability to breathe through her nose and her habit of drooling, sleeping.

It's not what you're thinking. It didn't escalate into a competition for his affection. He always loved Nina the most. From that first afternoon, when she was the only one to stand up to shake his hand, you could see how much of a kick he got out of her. He was careful never to take his eyes off her, and not only in admiration or attraction, but because he knew if he did he'd miss something—he realized quickly that she was the one who made the plans, that she was always moving toward something that she just knew you'd like and wanted to share with you. He had a formality about him, an antiquated set of manners that made it feel like he was wearing a button-down, tucked in, even when he was wearing a T-shirt, which he almost never did. We couldn't picture him at any social gathering attended by anyone other than us, and he managed to put an end to all the fun we had with irony—he took everything at face value—but he was kind, and he was smart, and he was beautiful. For all the turns Sam Decker had made in high school movies at the beginning of his career, he could never have played Max Thompson, because Decker, with his scruff and his jawline and his build, which managed to be fantastically chiseled but lithe at once, was always a man, and Max Thompson was a boy, in the very best way possible—flushed and curious and eager. And Nina was the source toward which all of his energy flowed.

Max was never embarrassed when he didn't get the pop-culture references that cluttered our conversations, and when he stood up once after a big meal and farted audibly he didn't get flustered or start blushing, he just said "Excuse me" and kept talking about whatever he had been. Someone he loved once told him that you should never be embarrassed unless what you were doing was wrong or dishonest, and it had taken. Watching him with Nina, you could practically see his neural pathways grow, and his synapses fire at different angles and speeds—she was the only thing he was a quick study in. There was a blank look that his face fell into right before whatever fact or phenomenon Nina was trying to explain to him took root.

For all the time he spent with Lila, there was a sibling quality to their relationship that was surprising mainly because Lila
was so clearly a girl without a brother. She was always the
most surprised and horrified at the penis myths that girls
begin to circulate sometime in the sixth or seventh grade, and
was more polite and careful than the rest of us in our interactions with the boys in our neighborhood. She was generally
averse to plots that might end in grass stains or muddy shoes.
She was at ease with Max in a way she didn't seem to be with
even her own father, and because we were fourteen-year-old
girls acquainted with how you acted, sometimes against your
will, when you were "into a guy," we understood without ever
talking about it that there was no sexual or even playful, mischievous element to her relationship with Max. We never
teased her about the amount of time she spent with him.

There was such little natural energy between Lila and Max
that it occurs to me to wonder how they became friends in the
first place. I can't help but suspect that in Lila, Max saw an
opportunity. A person who didn't yet know where in the hierarchy Max fell, which I can't imagine was terribly high—he
was a sixteen-year-old who wore cuff links and knew the middle names and birth and death dates of all the presidents. He
might've worried about impressing her, or fooling her—afraid
of her discovering how benignly but completely alienated
from the rest of his classmates he was—but there was no need
to. She had no more interest, when they met, in making new
friends than we had in her making them. In Max she found
someone to walk the halls with and sit with at lunch who was

totally free and willing to spend every minute outside of class with someone else's friends. Someone without any friends of his own.

I'm sure all of this was terribly obvious even then, but we were so worried about Max liking us enough so that Lila wouldn't have to choose between old and new, we didn't stop to think that there might've been something in it for him, too. The thing that makes me wince now, looking back, is that I don't think he wanted friends in order to feel better about his social standing, or to have a less embarrassing amount of free time. I mean it when I say he was benignly set apart from his classmates—he was too beautiful a physical specimen to be teased on that front, and too busy studying to draw any other sort of attention. Plus the day school was a place where it wasn't a crime to be smart.

I think he was lonely. I think he was an outcast by virtue of being overlooked, not realizing until it was too late that you had to scramble to make friends. I think he wanted someone to talk to. And there we were.

The first year we knew Max was the last year that we used our neighborhood as one giant playground. We still played games like capture the flag and flashlight tag and, in the unlikely event that there was a ball around inflated enough to play with, kickball. Max seemed happy enough to join us, but there was a stiffness to even the way he played that we laughed about when he wasn't around. He played games of chase with us the way a butler would have when the nanny was out sick—enthusiastically, but like he was playing in a foreign country where there was a barrier in even the body language. One night, when we had known

Max just long enough to know the name of every pet he'd ever had, we were playing a game of hide-and-seek. Max, as usual, was it. He didn't understand that it was a role you were supposed to try to get out of.

I had found a spot I was pretty confident in underneath the tarp Mr. Miller kept over his grill, but a mosquito bite I had been clawing at all day finally broke, and I started bleeding all over my new white shorts. I could see it even in the dark, which meant it would be disastrous by day. So I started walking toward Lila's house, the giant tree in front of which we always used as base, in an unannounced time-out. As I approached, I saw that Nina was hiding in the hole in Lila's father's bushes on the side of the house—a spot we were all very well acquainted with, but that Max still hadn't caught on to. I was about to call out and blow her cover when I saw him coming from the other side of the house. Instead of tagging her, he crawled into the hole with her. He sat with his knees tucked under his chin and his arms wrapped around them. As soon as he was settled, it looked like he'd been there all day, watching television or lounging in a circle of friends. She didn't show any signs of surprise at his arrival. She just turned and looked at him without saying anything. They both seemed utterly relaxed and at ease, though I couldn't see their faces. After a few moments, he handed her a note. She accepted it, slipped it into her pocket, and dashed out of the hole and toward the tree. She screamed in delighted panic as he followed right behind, just grazing the back of her T-shirt, a handful of which would have made her "it." I never heard them talk about whatever half-event I'd witnessed, that night or anytime after, and they were never alone, so I don't know when else they would have. I can only imagine now that he handed it to her when the risk was the lowest. Even if she welcomed whatever he said in the note, she would have had to run away from him immediately after he handed it to her.

The rest of the night was uneventful. Max failed to tag anybody and kept asking questions about the origin of the game and why certain rules that felt counterintuitive to him existed, as if he were a Ph.D. student in hide-and-seek. Lindsey quit out of hunger and Lila found a half-bag of cashews, two pudding snacks, and a can of peaches, which we passed around on her front steps while we each tried to be the first one to shout when a lightning bug flashed, each winner getting one of the final spoonfuls of the pudding. And Max asked why we used the male pronoun for lightning bug, out of curiosity more than any sort of political agenda, and we all agreed that we associated different animals with different genders and that because we awarded the same number of animals to each gender, it was okay, but we couldn't decide on the distinctions we used to determine which animal was lumped where. I had almost forgotten about what I had seen until Max pulled away after making a plan with Lila for when he would pick her up the next morning.

"What do you guys talk about?" Nina asked. Quickly, like she was ripping off a Band-Aid and trying to make it as painless as possible. "All those hours you spend together."

"Don't be an idiot," said Lila, in the first time I can think of that she ever talked down to Nina, or even disagreed with her. "You. We talk about you."

. . .

We were about to ask Decker about his own love life, even though everyone who spoke English and a few million people who didn't knew that he and Abby Madison, *Maxim's* third hottest woman in the world, had been dating for about two years, when his phone, which was laid out on the table next to his drink, started vibrating, and her picture, a selfie, flashed across his screen. If someone had run into the bar totally naked, or a man with a gun had demanded that everybody freeze, our eyes could not have been more perfect circles of surprise and alarm, even though it made sense that a twenty-four-year-old woman would want to talk to her boyfriend on a Saturday night. Especially a woman as happy and in love as everyone knew Abby Madison was with Sam Decker. The thing we had no way of expecting was when he touched the button on the side of his phone that sent the call directly to voice mail. Even after he put the phone in the inside front pocket of his jacket we kept staring at the spot on the table where the phone had been.

"Has the iPhone 5 not made its way to Florida yet?"

"Dude, why didn't you get it?" Lindsey asked.

"Yeah, we don't mind if you have to take that," I said. "We can wait."

Now it was Nina's turn to make the *Seriously?* eyes.

"She's on a press junket for *Existential Madame.* She's in Spain right now. Or maybe France? I don't know. They were gonna hit them both at some point. She probably just got up."

He had become animated in his playful ribbing about Lila

and our love lives, but with Abby's cellular presence hovering over our table, he fell into a slouchy, defensive posture, as if he were answering complaints from his male friends about how much time he was spending with his new girlfriend.

"Isn't it, like, three in the morning over there right now?"

"Oh, you're right. She's probably on her way to the gym, then."

"At *three* in the morning?" Nina asked.

He shrugged. "Workout time isn't built into these tour schedules. But she would probably rather have her eyelids removed than skip the gym."

"Do you need to call her back?" asked Lindsey. "Seriously, we don't mind."

"I don't know." His face made it clear that he was less uncertain than he'd said. "What could she possibly have to tell me about a European press tour that I don't already know? Second-tier, middle-aged journalists with bad breath and paunch that you get to watch grow with every movie."

"Maybe she wants your help fielding a tough question they might ask her," I said. "You know, since you have so much more experience with this kind of thing?"

He laughed unkindly, but not at me. It was an internal laugh, at some private joke we hadn't been granted access to.

"No. Abby's a pro. She knows exactly what she's doing. Plus, the press loves her. She's fine."

He said most of this into his bourbon, and a lock of his hair, which had been expertly groomed and combed back so that it looked styled and natural at once, fell into his face. I wouldn't have thought it possible for the Sam Decker we had met an hour ago to get any more attractive, but this lock of hair proved me wrong. It made him look more vulnerable in the way we want all of our heroes to look, making their ultimate victory that much more triumphant.

"Maybe she just wants to hear your voice?" said Lindsey. "You know, homesick and all that."

"I guess I'm just not a phone person," he said. "It always makes me feel like I have nothing but pointless, banal things to say, and I end up asking about the weather where the other person is. Even if it's someone I really like."

"So I guess that's why you guys never go more than two weeks without seeing each other, huh?" Nina asked, finally conceding that Abby Madison existed, and that we weren't going to stop talking about her anytime soon.

He started laughing, loudly and for a beat too long, making sure his point registered.

"What in the world makes you think that?"

"I read it in *Blush*," she said, more sheepish than I'd ever seen her. She looked like a dog waiting to be struck for eating the Thanksgiving turkey.

"Don't read that shit. I mean, unless you like fiction. But even then, I'm sure you could do better. The writing's pretty bad."

"What, so they make stuff up?"

"Sometimes. Sometimes we make stuff up. Why do you think we hire publicists?"

"No way," I said. "The stuff they report always *eventually* ends up proving true. Like, they report that there's trouble between certain couples, and then a few weeks later the couple admits they've broken up."

"I don't know. The publicist probably starts leaking that there's trouble when his client finds a younger, prettier girl-friend, so that when he has to actually announce that it's over, people are primed for it. Minimal damage to the reputations involved."

Getting to exhibit expertise was having the effect on Decker that it had on most people. It was drawing him out. He was talking to us now, instead of to himself. Making eye contact and using his hands and body language to emphasize his points.

"That's crazy," Lindsey said.

"I'm telling you. That's how it works."

His jacket started vibrating.

"Dude, just pick up and tell her that it's raining here!" I said, half joking, suddenly panicked at the thought of Abby Madison alone in a dark hotel room in Europe, unable to speak the language of the excited bellboys and desk clerks who kept inventing excuses to talk to her, already exhausted with a long day ahead of her, her adorable little face scrunched up in frustration at not being able to talk to the one person who might be able to make it okay. There are some things in life you have to believe in, even if you have no evidence of them, and up until that moment, the fact that Sam Decker picked up Abby Madison's calls on the first ring was one of them.

"Seriously," said Lindsey. "Who doesn't pick up when Abby Madison calls them? She's the world's best human being. Even her *name* is perfect."

His *That's absurd* laugh got bigger every time.

"That's not her real name. Of course it's not. That's nobody human's real name."

We all spoke at once.

"What?"

"So what's her real name?"

"I'm confused."

"Stacy Berliner, of the Tennessee Berliners."

"Wow," I said. "That's not a *bad* name, but I guess it doesn't have the same ring. I mean, are there *any* famous Stacys?"

"No, because all the Stacys and the Nancys and the Joans change their name before they even get their union cards. You actually all have first names that might work," he said. "Except for maybe you," he said to Lindsey. "No offense."

She put her hands up to ensure none was taken.

"But you'd probably have to come up with new last ones."

"Wait!" Nina said. "What about Lindsay Lohan? Lindsey's a totally vanilla name." She looked briefly at Lindsey to reiterate the benevolent spirit in which her name was being taken down. "And Lohan is her mom and her siblings' name!"

She looked like a *Jeopardy!* contestant who had just gotten the Daily Double right, an achievement that happened surprisingly often when she watched the show at home, given that she had graduated high school with a 2.3 GPA. Decker shook his head.

"Child actors," he said. "Parents feel bad about subjecting their kids to such a crazy life so early. They go to absurd lengths to keep things 'normal' even as their kids start making ten times what they made last year in a single week of work. Changing their names would be out of the question."

We nodded like good students, confirming the logic of this explanation. This was the Decker we knew. The one who had an answer for everything. His stepping into his role made us all more confident and easy. It was like we all suddenly remembered our lines.

"I just missed the era when parents and managers started worrying about these things. When I started, the kids were paid talent just like everybody else. I don't know if that makes me lucky or un."

"I just can't believe we didn't know this," said Lindsey. "Like, that Rumor and Kiss haven't uncovered it yet."

"They don't report it because it's not a big deal. It's a well-known fact that everybody does it."

"Wait a minute!" said Nina. "Does that mean—"

"Matt Brandon," he said, offering up his bourbon, ready to receive our glasses. "Nice to meet you."

My own parents, meanwhile, didn't have even the consolation of the lawn chairs in the street. They would have been welcome—it was never a terribly exclusive gathering, though you were generally expected to bring beer, which they didn't drink—but they made less noise than any two people I've ever met, even now, and I get panicky just thinking of them in such a rowdy, expressive circle.

My parents decided early on, it's apparent to me, to be good parents. And they succeeded. They reprimanded me when I broke curfew and monitored the length of my skirts in a place where hems moved upward with age until you became a parent yourself, and they always insisted that the three of us sit down to meals that didn't come out of a box. Maybe the problem is that they were too good at it, and by that I mean that I have trouble identifying for you much about them outside of that role, and not only out of some selfish, ego-driven insistence that the world see them as I do.

I never heard either of them raise their voices in the eighteen years I lived with them, and their laughter, also scarce, was almost always something elicited by one of the detective novels they read with a fervor they applied to little else, or the one hour of old sitcom reruns they allowed themselves a night, rather than something one of them said. Their idea of spending time together was being in the same room reading books that they would both read at some point, though I'm not sure they even discussed them. They had one glass of wine a night at dinner, always the same bargain brand, two on Saturdays, and I never saw any indication that they were ever tempted to have more. There were never lulls in the conversation, but we always talked about the same things—events we had coming up, things we had read about in the news, a new dish my mother was thinking about making, though I can't think of any time now that she actually did. I couldn't have told you what they worried about, or what they had wanted to be when they were young. The only time I ever saw my mother cry was when I spilled a tall glass of Coke on a couch she and my father were still paying off, even though the three of us were the only people who ever saw it. She started covering it in plastic that smelled like the rubber sheets I had to use when I wet the bed as a child and made awkward squeaking noises that sounded like flatulence, and even then she stared at it like it might run off.

Even if it was just one of the girls who was over—Nina or Lindsey—they were considered company. My mother never called them this, but she came just short of bowing to them in all her nervous fussiness over whether everyone had enough to eat and drink and whether the room was just the right temperature. Elaine dropped the f-bomb every other sentence and was constantly enlisting our help—be it manpower in moving their ratty couch when the concept of feng shui reached her, or matters that were literally trivial, as when she couldn't place the name of an actor or a movie. We rolled our eyes every time she burst into Nina's room—every query or request was urgent—but there was an easiness, a lack of formality, that made us gravitate toward Nina's house without saying anything about it.

To be fair, there was no question I ever asked my parents that they didn't answer or scolded me for having asked, but I learned long before I left their house that they would not have been much help on the emotional festers that sometimes made their way into my life. If I had talked to them, for instance, about Lila transferring schools, my mother simply would have said, "Oh, how nice for Lila. I'm sure there'll be a lot of opportunity in going to a school like that," and my father would've said, "I hate to think what that's costing Mike." And it would never have occurred to me to tell them how seeing her in that blazer was like the moment the person you're waving off at the airport finally disappears from sight on the way to their gate. There was such a tediousness to the number of times they turned around to wave at you where you were standing, just before the security checkpoint, feeling a little sheepish that the security agents could see how many times you were waving, that it never occurred to you that the waving would eventually have to stop. Or that when it did you'd have lost something. If I had told them, my mother might have said something about how dramatic girls can be, shaking her head at the silliness of it all, before pointing out that Lila still lived less than a tenth of a mile away from me. But I also think a comment like that would stir up in her a panic, a discomfort, not unlike the one being in the middle of all those lawn chairs would have.

I had thought this is just who they were—the settings they were born on—until my mom's ne'er-do-well younger sister, Donna, spun in and out of town on a doomed fund-raiser for OxyContin my sophomore year. I came home from school to find her rifling through my mother's jewelry box in an empty house, muttering to herself. Or maybe to my mother. She was smaller and wirier than my mother—she had Madonna arms that you could actually see distinct muscles in, which Nina was always talking about and was determined to have, though I never once saw her lift a weight. Donna had dirty-brown hair and mosquito-bite scars up and down her legs that somehow smacked of debauchery even though everyone in Florida was covered in bug bites. I had seen pictures of her and though they were faithful to the woman in front of me—she had not gained or lost any weight and her hair was the same color and about the same length—when she turned around from the jewelry box to face me in the open doorway I didn't recognize her. I realized after she left that it was because in every picture I had seen of her she was smiling, and everything about this woman, from her posture to her facial expression to the stains on her white T-shirt to the shake of her hands to her eyes, made it clear that smiling was no longer something she did a whole lot of.

She gave no indication that she was embarrassed at having been caught.

"What are you looking at?" she asked, holding up a handful of my mother's jewelry, a cigarette in the other hand. "Don't worry, I'm not gonna take it. There's nothing but shit here. She has a two-bedroom house and nothing but fakes. I should've known."

I remained frozen in the doorway, petrified both that she wouldn't leave and that she would, and I'd have to decide whether or not to tell my mother that she'd been here.

"What has she told you about me?" she asked.

"Not much," I said, telling the truth, which must have pissed her off more than any insult I could've invented.

"Yeah, well, you tell her at least I didn't have a baby I couldn't afford."

She looked me up and down, as if she were trying to decide how much she could get for me at the pawnshop around the corner.

"And a bastard at that," she said, pretty pleased about the whole thing.

I didn't mind the label. Most of the kids I grew up with already wore it. If not with pride, then without shame, either. It isn't a slur where I'm from. But I had never stopped to think that my parents, in other circumstances, might not have chosen each other. It had been clear to me for some time that they didn't suit each other—they never rushed home to share the particulars of their days, and I rarely saw them touch, outside of items passed across the dinner table. But I had had no way of knowing until then that the monotone setting on which they lived their lives might not have been hardwired into them.

I became obsessed with other lives they might have had. Not grander, more ambitious lives, just different ones. My father, in reality a casual, mediocre golfer and the only pasty man in Florida, as a caddy at one of the Disney resort courses, lean and brown from his work. My mother a flight attendant who ushered the tourists back to where they came from, smiling, as she fetched pillows and directed people to turn off their phones, far more than she ever did at home.

Jay called me every night at the same time to say good night, even if he was out with his friends, who ruthlessly made fun of the ritual and asked to be tucked in as they threw bar nuts at him. He let me pick the restaurant on the rare occasions we could afford a dinner out. He held open doors and ordered dessert when I was in the bathroom—knowing that I wanted it but didn't want to spend the money—and though he no more wanted a child than any other nineteen-year-old boy did, I knew he would pick up double shifts or get a second job to afford one.

I just couldn't let go of the other lives.

You know your friend over there," Decker said, nodding at Lila. "Her name might actually work. Lila Tucker could be a screen name."

"She isn't our friend," said Lindsey.

"Yeah," said Nina, ignoring her. "You might be right. She's got a good name."

I will save you the suspense—suspense not being our genre, simply because it was not Sam Decker's genre, and his were the only movies we would shell out ten dollars to go see. In his movies there was usually a girl in trouble—because she either had too much money or not enough, or either was too beloved by men who ended up getting her in trouble or couldn't get anyone to notice her. Something usually blew up, but you always saw it coming.

So I will tell you now that this is not the night when Sam Decker swept us away to Hollywood or even to a better bar. This is not the night he taught us some valuable lesson, or that we began long, meaningful friendships with him, because this is the night that Sam Decker died from a mix of alcohol, heroin, and prescription antidepressants in a hotel room in a city where he had nobody to drink with and had to settle for us.

We should have known from the red of his eyes. From the fact that a man who had the money for daily manicures, and lived in a place where he would have felt no shame in getting them, had nails bitten down to the quick, into jagged little promises of disaster. Of bad things to come. But we were too busy loving him, and not just because he was a movie star, and one we happened to like. We loved him because he was buying our drinks. We loved him because from the coy manner in which he set out making Abby Madison's life miserable, we saw in him every boy who had ever ignored a call or text, and this made him seem less alien to us. We understood what he was doing, at least as much as we had when it was done to us. We loved him because he didn't recognize all the things that distinguished us from Carine and Lila and the patterns. To him we were all just young, prettyish girls in a bar in Florida, which, had it been true, would have solved all of our problems. We loved him because no matter how many times we laughed during parts of his movies not meant to be funny, we felt something in those darkened theaters that we sometimes called upon after we had left them, and because he didn't seem to approach our conversation as one big practical joke, the way we did, with knowing smiles and loaded eye contact. He talked to us like people. Like girls he met in a bar that reminded him of his hometown. I'm not sure what we were expecting—an entourage, maybe, a trail of screaming fans or a publicist monitoring every word he said—but not that.

Three

The Shamrock was owned by a man named Sal Pisatori. Yes, he was Italian. He weighed at least two-fifty, but he had a dainty, elegant mustache just starting to gray that called to mind men in top hats and made him seem much smaller, and though he spoke with the lilt of a Long Islander, he wasn't the bumbling, clueless wise guy you might be imagining. He was keenly aware of most of what happened in his bar, and able to participate competently in most of the conversations conducted there on an endless number of topics—bait options for deep-sea fishing, and which excuses wives generally swallowed and which ones they saw through—and he had interests that your stereotypes might not take into account: gardening and classical music. We knew without having to ask that he had less education than us, but he knew that Russia shared a border with Kazakhstan and Mongolia—countries most people we knew couldn't have given you a continent for, or had forgotten about altogether—and the exact date that the Second World War ended and which languages they spoke in which countries, even when it wasn't an easy match, like

Portuguese in Brazil, and other facts that you didn't used to have to go to school to know. He was always moving, confusing everyone as to how he stayed so fat, and whenever he stopped at our table while making his rounds he started with, "Did you girls know . . . ," trying to impress us with his most mind-blowing pieces of trivia: the length of the largest bird's wingspan, the country with the smallest population. He also knew we were not twenty-one, and gave us his *You're gonna get me in trouble* eyes every time we walked in, but the first round was always on the house. Sal was a man who respected loyalty more than he did the law.

We asked him, once, why he didn't open an Italian bar. Wine Time, maybe. Or Mozzarellas.

"Italians, we're known for our food," he told us. "I give it a name like Mozzarellas, people are gonna start expectin' to be fed. Mozzarella sticks, fried calamari. That kinda thing. What are you gonna eat at an Irish bar? Potatoes? Cabbage? If they come in thinkin' we're an Irish institution, they'll feel spoiled— taken *care* of, you know—by just the option of the burger. I put it in the name, so right away people know what they're gonna get. Simple. Everybody's happy."

We knew this was a dig at his Irish counterparts and their cuisine—he was, after all, an Italian, even if he did own a bar called the Shamrock—but he was right. No one ever asked for a menu at the Shamrock.

Sal came waddling over to our table just after we had finished processing how uneasy Sam Decker's real name sat on the tongue.

"Sal!" we cheered in unison, realizing, as we said it, how

cinematic his real name was, and then wondering if that's what we called him by. A shady past that needed erasing didn't feel like a stretch for a man like Sal.

"Let me ask you girls a question," he said.

"Sure, but whatever it was we didn't do it," said Lindsey, referring to his obvious agitation. He was normally much happier to see us.

"What do you girls know about a movie star being here in the bar?"

"Why, Sal?" Nina asked, not looking at Decker.

"Jax over there," he said, nodding at the bar where Bob and Jax sat not talking to each other, fisherman caps pulled low, "said he heard something about some big shot's here, havin' drinks."

We were impressed at the possibility that Jax—who we had never heard speak—might know who Sam Decker was at the same time we were embarrassed for Sal for not knowing.

"Well, what are you gonna do if you find him?" I asked.

"Take a picture!" he said with all the incredulity he would have if I'd asked him how many noses I had. "You know, for the wall."

The wall had exactly four photos—two soap-opera stars, a child actor a good twenty years after the only sitcom he was ever on ended, and the guy from a series of beer commercials who was famous for saying "It's Saturday night where I live" as he held up the beer he was advertising in the middle of settings that got increasingly more inappropriate as the commercial series went on: boardroom meetings, parent-teacher conferences, and finally the delivery room where his wife was giving birth. "I don't know about *movie star*," said Lindsey, "but this guy used to be on *The New Mickey Mouse Club*."

"*This* guy?" he said, nodding at Decker skeptically.

"That's the one," said Lindsey.

"How long ago?" he asked.

"I mean, it was a while ago," said Nina, "but he was a big enough deal on the show that they asked him back for the reunion."

"Yeah, and we all watched it all the time," I said.

"I'm on billboards for vodka in Asia," Decker offered.

"Well, we are a bar . . ." Sal said.

"Look, I'll take as many pictures as you want," said Decker, realizing that as funny as the gag was, whatever he posed for would be on the wall for years—the beer guy had allegedly been dead for a decade. "But I don't want to be in it alone. Get one of all four of us."

I could feel the others trying not to squirm at the thought of being in a publicly displayed picture of Sam Decker, one that people we actually knew would see, but the air at the table was suddenly full of manic, juvenile expectation, like that moment when the person you're all pranking walks into the room you've rigged, unaware of the trap waiting for him.

"The pictures are normally taken with me," Sal said.

"You seem like a nice guy," said Decker, "but c'mon, given the choice, who would you rather be photographed with—yourself, or these girls?"

"Well, I see what you mean, but—"

"C'mon, Sal, we're here every weekend. We count as bar representatives."

"And maybe if the other patrons see the wall celebrities mingling with the customers, they'll be even more inclined to come back. Like, they'll actually *see* the celebrities, they don't hole away in some VIP section."

The absurdity of a VIP section in the Shamrock should have tipped Sal off to the joke, but he caved.

"All right, all right," he said, pulling a silver camera smaller than his palm out of his shirt pocket. "Smile big."

So we did.

Though there were many bonuses to having a new member in the group, and a male one at that, it was clear pretty early on that the perk Nina took the most pleasure in was that it expanded the geography across which the prank war could be conducted. The prank war had started innocently enough the spring before we met Max, and grew from the same seed that I now know most bad ideas do: boredom. We were having a sleepover at Nina's, and she was the first one to fall asleep, which almost never happened. She had trouble sleeping, and normally went to great lengths to keep me and Lindsey up for some company, resorting to both flattery and a strange sort of bribery in which she started confessing things she swore she'd never told anyone before, in the hopes that curiosity would function as a substitute for caffeine. Lila always managed to fall asleep just minutes before Lindsey and I remembered that by going to sleep early we'd be exempting ourselves from late-night Nina duty later.

Lindsey and I were both so shocked when we heard Nina's

steady breathing join Lila's light, trademark snore in the middle of the first movie we put on that we tore our eyes away from the lead-up to the sex scene we'd been waiting for—both of us too shy to suggest we just fast-forward to it—and looked at each other at the same time, baffled. We both agreed that waking her up would be too mean, given how rarely she enjoyed the pleasure of sleep, but that we couldn't let this go unremarked upon. She could be ruthless in her campaigns to keep us up, outlining the many things one could miss out on with an early bedtime. So we spent an hour and a half swapping the entire contents of her sock and underwear drawers with the kitchen cabinets.

I'm pretty sure that I speak for both Lindsey and myself when I say that, had I known how far Nina was going to take what was meant to be a onetime amusement—a nod to our past, and the silly escapades of earlier sleepovers, rather than our future—we would have left the bras and the tomato soup where they were.

She loved it. The next morning, after the thirty seconds it took her to process what we had done when she opened the pantry where her mother normally kept the cereal, she laughed like Chris Rock was performing stand-up in her kitchen.

"Oh, my God," she said. "That's funny. I can't believe you guys came up with something like this without me. Whose idea was it, seriously? And, man, how long did it take you? I have a lot of underwear."

To be honest, by the time the red-and-white-checkered bikini briefs landed on Nina's bed head, Lindsey and I had forgotten all about it. We were anticipating the Lucky Charms on the other side of the fake wood door as hotly as Nina was. I'm pretty sure, looking back, that the only reason we spent all the time the move required was that neither of us knew how to conduct a sleepover not punctuated by Nina's insomniac rumblings.

The event had considerably more staying power with Nina. The next weekend, she convinced me to help steal all of Lindsey's jeans from her bedroom and replace them with jeans a size smaller. It wasn't difficult to do—like all her other clothes, Lindsey's jeans came from the Target by our house.

That she was not the mastermind behind the prank war's first move is probably hard to believe for anyone who has seen Nina's face bloom the moment a new idea for a prank occurs to her. But it would surprise exactly no one who has spent more than an hour with her that she was the one to raise its stakes. Her big jeans plan had a bite that was missing from the underwear swap Lindsey and I came up with.

Lindsey showered only when she broke a sweat, and brushed her hair before she went to bed but not when she got up, and wore her brothers' hand-me-downs because her beauty was totally unconnected to and independent from any effort she made. It was in the proportions of her figure and the glow of her freckly skin, and the beautiful chaos of the hair that really could've used a second brushing. And you could smell it on her in the exact moment the button on the too-skinny jeans popped—horror at the possibility that she might have to start trying. Not to mention what effect this new weight would have on the many athletic fields she dove and charged and dribbled across.

It was two weeks before she realized what we had done. Motivated to eat less during those fourteen days—during which she wore sweatpants, since she didn't have the money to buy new jeans—we got all the good snacks from her lunch. The pudding cups and the Oreos. Because she never gained back the five pounds she lost, you could say that she was the only winner in the prank war.

I didn't think to worry once—not while I was smashing the green ceramic alligator bank that I'd kept next to my bed for the last two years to help pay for the smaller jeans, or pricking my fingers trying to sew the old jeans' tags into them—that by helping Nina prank Lindsey a week after Lindsey and I had pranked Nina, I was declaring myself prey. But I saw it in Lindsey's eyes in the same moment that the truth behind the push of her waistband registered—I was next.

And I was. And in this plot, too, was a brand of humiliation tailored just for me—this time in the fact that the prank I was the victim of was the first one to be conducted publicly, where anyone other than the four of us could see it. Lindsey, Lila, and of course Nina had heard me stutter enough times when called upon without having raised my hand to know that I hated attention of any sort, never mind that they knew intimately the silences and wooden good behavior that my mother's household was run with.

They convinced me that I was being stalked by the register guy at the new McDonald's that opened down the street, proven by the free McFlurry he had waiting for me there every day—a ritual he engaged in only after they convinced him I was their "special" cousin, whose temper tantrums (which often entailed rogue bowel movements, they later confessed) were soothed only by ice cream. On the fifth day of the McFlurry stretch, when I screamed that I would *never* sleep with him, we were banned from the premises.

Though I hated that my pulse grew loud and violent enough that you could see it pumping through the skin on my wrist and my squealing laughter was less hearty than the other girls' as we plowed through the new glass doors still miraculously unfingerprinted by high school kids in search of sodium and sugar, I understood that I was always going to have to take a turn, and tried to convince myself to be grateful that it was over, for now.

That was the thing about the prank war—allegiances were fluid. They had to be. It prevented them from creating small cracks in the group that opened into abysses over time, dividing any portion of us against any other. It kept us from being just another group of catty girls who claimed to be friends but caused just as much anxiety and heartache in each other's lives as every other asshole they had to deal with. By constantly mixing up who was on the receiving end of the prank, and who had teamed up to deliver it, the pranks stayed random. Who was on what end and with whom didn't mean much, because everyone would be there at some point, and every possible two- and threesome would mastermind how they ended up there. It kept the prank war pure—a source of fun and creativity rather than malice and exclusion—but it was also the thing that totally baffled Max about it.

Max was a boy of logic, of military strategy and algebraic equations. He relied on and took comfort in the unchanging nature of the facts in the books he dipped into while the rest of us were sunning ourselves, or playing games, or conducting bike races. He was loyal to a fault. All of which countered the logic of the prank war, which was actually devoid of any sort of logic at all. He first encountered the prank war—it didn't really feel like something you could explain—when Lila had her meltdown at the frozen yogurt place they went to every day after school. When you bought nine frozen yogurts— measured with a tiny paper card and an adorable little frozen yogurt stamp—you got the tenth one free. Lila had been one punch away for the last three trips, because Nina kept replacing her card with nine stamps with cards that had eight stamps, which she purchased from the teenage acne victim who ran the store after school.

The point of this one was so clear it should have been apparent even to Max, who was still struggling with the prank war's tenets by then: Lila had enough money, now, that she had no business fussing over free cones.

On her third eight-stamp trip, Lila apparently lost it, though Max was the only one to see it. She told the guy behind the counter that if he didn't learn to count he was gonna be "left behind," and kept trying to explain why it was "literally impossible" for her not to have earned her free cone. She cited the fact that she and Max never came in without the other, and pointed out that he had scored his free cone two trips ago. When this didn't work she knocked the tip jar on the counter—whether this had been accidental or intentional was unclear.

It was the first prank we didn't all laugh about together, after. Lila had the good sense not to make it a thing, but she said she was too busy with her science fair project to make enchiladas at Elaine's house with the rest of us. It's not that we thought she was lying about the project. But she normally spread her science or English or history homework around her in a paper circle while the details of our day buzzed drolly past her.

Nina wasn't trying to be cruel. It was a control thing, to be sure—she knew all of us well enough to know the Achilles' heels to aim for with her pranks, and she wanted us to know that she recognized those weak spots. But Nina took the time to get to know people that well only when she really liked them. That much attention from Nina was a gift. And while some people might have found these jabs at our tenderest parts unforgivable, I think Nina saw them as well-timed jokes, and everyone knew that being able to laugh at something was the first step to moving on. If you could laugh at some silly little fault of yours, it was less likely to trip you up. And while I am maybe being overly generous to Nina in this assessment, I think these pranks were her way of saying that she loved us in spite of the weaknesses they exposed. That we were fine as we were. And that the things that worried us most were laughing matters.

Regardless of her motives, after the free-cone debacle, the prank war was the only subject Max didn't seem to have an opinion on. He fell silent every time it was mentioned, or said only "I've never seen her act that way," more to himself than to any of us, making me feel bad for both him and Lila, because if it was as bad as he made it sound, I wouldn't have wanted to see it, either. Because I had been on the receiving end of these things, I couldn't fault Lila entirely for her behavior, extreme as it sounded. I was familiar with how involuntarily your entire muscle system could clench when you encountered the evidence of things you *knew* couldn't be true, which was a big part of the sport. After marveling quietly about how unrecognizable the spirit of the game had made Lila, Max would stay silent while the rest of us continued planning or recapping the latest prank, as if it were a pretty girl he didn't know what to say around, which it kind of was, because at some point Nina and her prank war had become indecipherable from each other.

Unfortunately for Max, his discomfort was mounting at the exact wrong moment. We were not the only ones who had noticed the rising stakes of the prank war. So had our parents and teachers. Nina had been strenuously warned against "any further nonsense" by both our principal—who lost a teacher to the vodka Nina poured in his coffee, not realizing he was a recovering alcoholic, before stashing the bottle in my locker—and our parents, whose laundry loads had doubled over the past months on account of the pranks that left stains, the ones that relied on desk chairs coated in honey and milk cartons that had been filled with vinegar. In Max she saw fast-food joints and parents and teachers and school corridors that would never see her coming.

He had to be broken.

Nina decided that the best way to change his mind about the game was to involve him in one of the pranks. Not only that, but to make him central to the prank's going off smoothly. Until then he had seen only the effects of the pranks—the mess left to be cleaned up and the embarrassed, flush-faced girl who happened to be a friend of his who stood there trying to convince herself and everyone watching her that she was a good sport. That she thought it was funny that her pants had ripped, or that a small dog had just dry-humped her in front of a large group of people; the extent to which she actually wanted to lie down and cry evident in varying degrees, depending on the prank and the girl. If he experienced the triumph of having been the one to place the awkward, puberty-has-just-begun photo over the face of the mascot in the school lobby, or plant the pot seeds in the garden, Nina was convinced he would know what it was all about. He would be ready to play.

She drafted a plan that she needed his help with. That, while he wouldn't have to be the one to pull the trigger on, he would have to provide the bullets for. This, of course, meant a prank pulled on Lila in the school that only Max would be able to help her navigate. What she needed, in the end, was to know where to find Lila's locker.

The plan was simple. Nina would cut the lock on Lila's locker and replace it with a new lock with a different combination, one unknown to Lila. After several failed attempts to get into her locker, Lila, who was always the first of us to turn an unopenable jar over to a parent, or seek parental intercession into sibling battles that had gone physical, would go to the principal's office or a trusted teacher for help. Whenever she and her adult aide forced the locker open, they would find the pornography that Nina would have plastered all over the inside of the locker before securing the new lock. She had admitted *almost* all of this to Max, omitting only the exact nature of the "surprise" that would be waiting for Lila when she opened her locker.

This would have been a brutal prank on any one of us, but for Lila, who wasn't much more comfortable with those penis myths than she had been when they first started circulating, and unquestionably the most sexually prudish among us, it was unthinkable. She couldn't get through a PG-13 movie without making excuses to leave the room half a dozen times during sexually loaded scenes.

Nina was excited enough about this plan that she decided it was worth not only her but also Lindsey and me taking a sick day from school, so we could all take the bus—an indignity Nina normally avoided at all costs, bribing the older boys in the neighborhood to either escort her or lend her their car so she could drive herself illegally—to the day school.

The bus ride was uncomfortable, and not just because the bus was full of strange adults and we were all a little nervous about cutting class. It was a long drive. With every inch of scenery that glided across the windows we looked out of without talking, it registered a little more—how far Lila went from us every day, the exact distance between her old school and new.

We liked, back then, to measure the distance from one point to another by the number of McDonald's franchises between them. It was virtually impossible to find any franchise in our part of the state not in walking distance to the closest sister store, so it was a measuring system of fine gradations. To get to the day school, we had to be on the highway at one point, and I kept seeing whispers of the golden arches just far enough to the right and left of our course that I wasn't sure if they could be counted. I realized it was a distance that couldn't be measured in franchises—it wasn't a straight enough line—and it bothered me more than I would have guessed before we set out.

Lindsey and I kept turning to look at Nina every few minutes, searching her for signs that she, too, was picking up on how long we had been riding, but there were none. Nina, of course, had realized it long ago. It was a huge part of why we were there, making the trip in the first place.

Max was waiting for us at the front of the school when we walked up, as planned, and I realized only then that the plan required him to skip class in the middle of the day, and how much he must've hated that. As uncomfortable as he looked, and even though the tie he had normally shed by the time he got to us each day made his uniform look even more stuffy, he smiled when he saw Nina.

"Let me show you around," he said, eager both to be the one to get to show her things and to delay the inevitable. Even though Nina's eyes were greedy, blinking twice with disbelief at everything from the vending machines our school didn't have, where Lila and Max presumably met to get the name-brand candy we didn't have access to, to the buoyant, bright blue rubber track that sat just to the left of the school, where we had only a balding patch of grass that needed watering, she didn't want to linger.

"After," she said. "We've got to get going, or this is never going to happen." She was so sure that we all understood how tragic it would be if this didn't happen that she let it go unsaid.

I was feeling as uneasy about this as I ever had when I looked out at the field of wildflowers that separated the campus's main buildings—magnificently large and stately, all of them—from a thick, untouched tangle of foliage that I would later learn had running trails for the cross-country team and a zip line the day school kids used in their gym classes while the rest of us made our way through wilted, half-games of dodgeball and kickball.

Little Marie Tucker was there, sunning herself, her plaid skirt pulled up to give the most amount of skin possible to the sky, her face turned to the sun. She couldn't have been there more than twenty minutes, given that it was a school day, but the fact that there were flowers growing all around her, except for the exact patch she was sitting on, made it seem like she had been there forever. Like they had grown up around her. Though I spent more time with Marie than almost anyone else in my neighborhood, I had always secretly found her as strange as everybody else did, her silences as unsettling. And seeing her there like that was one of the first times I could remember when she looked perfectly at ease.

As if she could hear my thoughts, she looked down from the sky and opened her eyes. She looked right at me, even though I had to be at least two hundred yards away. She smiled and waved, a small, girlish wave I wouldn't have thought her capable of. Like my being there was the most normal thing in the world. And it felt, in that moment, seeing her there, like everything was going to be fine.

And it was. At least that day. It went off as planned. Lila smiled when she came out to greet us at Max's car, where Nina sat smoking and flipping music stations in the front seat. Lila didn't even get mad when she told us that it was the creepy *male* eighty-something-year-old janitor who ended up cracking her locker, and that he whistled when he saw the magazine cut-outs, instead of politely ignoring them. Nina almost peed her pants, and Lila only rolled her eyes, smirking vacantly.

Max took it less well. In a turn that surprised only Nina, his vital role in one of the most daring, humiliating pranks yet left him unconvinced of the game's merits.

"Listen, Nina," he said when he was driving us to the frozen yogurt place twenty minutes away from the school, since he and Lila were still banned from the one where she had made her scene about the free cone she could have afforded twenty times over. "This was fun. I mean, I see how much you like doing this. How much fun it is for you, and I'm glad you have that."

He didn't look at her while he was talking, and I might have assumed that it was because he was embarrassed about what he was trying to say, to ask of her, really, but based on the rigid ten-and-two position his hands made on the steering wheel, I suspect it was also partly because he was a cautious, serious driver.

"Yeah," she said, her brown, newly non-awkward legs hanging out the open window, as if to give the unrelenting sun a fresh target to hunt. She blew confident lines of smoke that traveled away from her mouth with a purpose, like they were chasing something. "I'm glad I have it, too. You'll be glad to have it once you start coming up with ideas. Once you put your mind on that setting, they come easier than you think."

"I don't think so," he said, his voice just shaky enough to be perceptible. "You're good with things like this. Things that draw attention. I'm not as good with surprises. I like to think about things for a while before I do them, or even react to them."

"It's just fun," she said in a voice that might have sounded, if I didn't know her any better, like she was pleading. "It's just for fun."

"I know in your own way it's announcing you like someone. I know you would never prank someone you don't like. And I guess in a weird way it's sort of like being in a club or something," he said, his remarkable talent for stating things the rest of us were happy to know without comment striking again, "but maybe there are other ways to show that, you know? Just where I'm concerned."

"Don't be silly. Where I live, it's the highest form of flattery," she said. "And I happen to like you a lot."

Just then, Veronica Beecher came walking into the bar, and we knew it must be ten after. Veronica's shift started at ten, and she had never once been on time. It was one of a million reasons we couldn't understand why Sal didn't fire her. Technically she was a waitress at the Shamrock, but we hadn't seen her lift more than a dozen glasses since we'd been going there, never mind filling them and bringing them out to people. The real reason she bothered to show up at all, we were pretty sure even Sal knew, was that she was determined to hook a man. What she expected to do with a man she hooked at the Shamrock was less certain. Her silicone valley, as we called the deep line of cleavage that she consistently showcased between the V-frame of her soft-looking, colorful T-shirts designed to draw even more attention, was wasted on the eyes of men like Bob and Jax, who had seen too much in this life to appreciate the simple goodness of a rack like Veronica's. To her credit, she made sure each seat in the house afforded patrons an equal view of the show, bending low even in front of the bar stools occupied by men too drunk to remember where they parked the car or too poor to have one. Her eight-year-old son, Bobby, came in ten steps behind her, as he always did. We were never sure if she orchestrated this delay so that potential suitors would have already fallen for her before they realized she came with offspring or because he was pouting about having to spend another summer night inside, among adults, and waited in the car to lodge another formal complaint against his mother's job before resigning himself to it and going in to find Sal.

Bobby was the reason we forgave Sal for Veronica's presence. He was a cool little kid, and we knew all the time he spent with Sal was going to make him cooler. Sal gave him jobs to keep him occupied, so we didn't get to spend as much time with him as we would've liked.

Sal turned from our table, photo safely captured, to direct Bobby to a stack of glasses that needed drying, which we were pretty sure he had rinsed for just that reason five minutes earlier.

"Roni must have gotten new shirts. That V is working even harder than normal," Nina said as soon as Bobby and Sal were out of earshot.

"Nah," said Lindsey. "It's the bra. They're riding high."

"Don't tell me," said Decker. "Another warring faction."

"No," I said. "We don't hate Roni."

"I mean, don't get me wrong," said Nina. "She's not in the Sisterhood of the Traveling Pants or anything, but we don't have any beef. It just feels like all the brain cells allotted for her personality somehow misfired to the chest."

It was true, we didn't hate her, but we unanimously agreed the Shamrock would be better without her. She was always thanking you with her smile and body language for compliments you hadn't given her yet. She was that sure they were coming. She would be horrified at the suggestion that she thought less than the world of anybody—she was the first preschool teacher with fake tits in that way—but she was one of those women who feed you that line about not really having any female friends. That she just didn't "trust" other women, a sure sign of untrustworthiness if there was one. It occurs to me now, though, that maybe Decker had a point. There weren't that many people outside the three of us we did like. I'm not saying we bullied Roni or that she was actually a really good person, just that the only other adult allowed at our table during the year we went to the Shamrock was a movie star.

"Yeah," said Lindsey. "She's the kind of waitress who, if she got my order wrong, I would never tell her because I know she'd spit in it before she brought it back. But she would, like, bring it with a smile."

"Exactly," I said. "She's just not that nice."

"Yes, but of course she's not," said Decker. "That's actually one of my two life mottos."

"What, slutty waitresses with too much cleavage aren't nice?" Nina asked.

"No," said Decker. "But, I mean, kind of. It's just really, really hard to find people who are exceptionally good-looking—like, naturally good-looking in an exceptional way—who are also exceptionally nice. Like, Here, I'm gonna go out of my way to do this nice thing for you for absolutely no reason, *I rescue birds from the highway* nice. I think to really get ahead in life you have to be one or the other—really good-looking or really nice. But if you have both or neither you're sunk."

"No way," I said. "I can think of plenty of really ugly assholes and good-looking nice people."

"I'm sure you can," he said. "But they haven't gotten very far. Really good-looking people *need* to have some sort of edge, otherwise they're just *boring.* Like their faces are symmetrical, computer-generated-type faces, and if they're sickly, generically cookie-cutter nice it's like they're automated or something. It's so *boring.* It's like the niceness takes the edge off your beauty, or undermines it to the point that you don't even notice it anymore. Think about it, when you meet a really, really good-looking person—like, we're talking top one percent good-looking—you're kind of waiting for them to do or say something interesting. And let's face it, nice isn't that interesting."

"Okay, Roni isn't exactly *making* it," I said.

Decker looked over to where a group of men had gathered around the tap where she was talking about one of the Real Housewives, even though I would bet both my ovaries none of the men had ever heard of the woman.

"She's getting paid to stand there," said Decker. "She'll be fine."

"She's not *that* hot," said Nina.

Decker looked at her like she had just told him the daily specials on the moon. "She's hot."

"Yeah, maybe, but she's like Denise Richards hot, not Winona Ryder hot."

"Girls," Decker said, shaking his head. "You sound like my sister. I mean, what does that even *mean*?"

By now Nina looked like she had been poked in the eye with the sharp point of those umbrellas that come with piña coladas. I don't think it was just Decker's admiration of Roni's physical assets. I could feel her studying the three of us as Decker waxed about his theory, calculating how it applied to us, and what it meant that Lindsey was both the prettiest and the nicest. Normally Nina was the keeper and setter of our dynamics, and it had probably never occurred to her that there were other forces at work.

"I think what she means," said Lindsey, "is that she's not a timeless beauty."

"She's more of a stiletto, hair-extension beauty," I added, getting Nina's grateful look, which was far rarer than the others she'd been giving.

"You girls can call it whatever you want to," said Decker. "She's hot."

"Okay, fine, agree to disagree," said Lindsey hurriedly, eager to move along before Nina started misbehaving. "But does that mean when you see a less-than-Clark-Gable-esque actor, like Steve Buscemi or what's-his-face *Sideways*—"

"Paul Giamatti."

"Sure. Does that mean they're super-nice?"

"Maybe *nice* is the wrong word. They have, I don't know, *character*. You can see it, their character, when they act. Like they're calling upon some greater truth behind the universe rather than, I don't know, what they're gonna have for dinner. They're wise instead of wickedly funny or cuttingly sarcastic."

We took a drink break to think about the last movie we had seen either of them act in.

"So what's your second theory?" I said, after replaying *The Big Lebowski* highlights in my head.

"I don't believe in moderation," he said, putting down his empty bourbon glass and picking up the beer he had ordered with it.

"Explain," said Lindsey.

"Everyone likes to tell you to apply moderation in everything. At least all the people I know. But I think the opposite. I don't eat foods that are bad for me in small quantities. I like to eat seven thousand calories a day and then run ten miles. And I don't drink in moderation. Obviously. I go on a five-day bender and then sleep for five days. I mean, not really, but there's not a lot of productivity happening in the five days after my five-day bender. And when I read a book, even if it's like *Anna Karenina* or something, I want to get to the end as soon as I can. Like, it's hard for me to do anything else until I know what the fuck happens to Anna Karenina."

He saw Nina open her mouth to speak.

"And *don't* tell me she throws herself under a train, because I know that. I read that book in two days."

"I haven't read that shit," said Nina. "I was actually going to tell you that's a theory I can get on board with. Moderation is for pansies."

He nodded, glad they were back on the same team.

"My theory is that it all evens out in the end—all the extremes, I mean—but watching the sunrise after fourteen beers is a lot more fun than going home after three beers to feed yourself a responsible dinner in front of the TV."

"Wow," said Lindsey. "You're really afraid to be bored, aren't you? Boring is like your Kryptonite, huh?"

"My mom says only boring people get bored," I said, realizing as I did how childish it sounded.

"Yeah, well, moms say all kinds of things," he said, and I loved him all over again for sounding as juvenile and square as I had.

"Wait!" Nina said.

"What?" Decker asked.

"What about you?"

"What about me? I just told you really the only two things you need to know."

"No. I mean, you're attractive and so far you're not the *biggest* dick I've ever met. I mean, you don't even know us and you keep putting our beers on your tab."

"I'm not that attractive," he said.

We all gave him *Yeah, right* looks at once.

"There are a lot of expensive grooming products I've been able to afford for the last few years that are real game changers."

"Sorry, dude. Nice try, but she's right," Lindsey said. "Your theory's shot."

"Fine," he said, shrugging. "Maybe I'm not that nice a guy."

After our field trip to the day school we had a long stretch without any pranks, so Max must have hit *some* sort of nerve. It was an unprecedented dry spell, by the end of which we were all willing to take bubble baths again, unworried about what our bubbles had been replaced with, and our necks stopped kinking up from looking over our shoulders so often, which only made it worse when the gesture became automatic again. Max, ever transparent, grew lighter, less pensive with every prankless day, and this had its own buoying effect on Nina. She recognized his happiness and, realizing that she was responsible, took a sort of pride in it. His brain no longer occupied with listing all the potential dangers of the prank war, Max was free to focus all of his attention on Nina and her ideas. Eager to compensate for undermining her greatest idea ever—the prank war itself—he declared everything else she came up with "excellent" or "gorgeous." It was like they were engaged in a weeks-long back-and-forth of standing in front of an open door, insisting the other go through first—determined both to put the other's happiness before their own and to make it known to the other that this was what they were doing. They were just so *nice* to each other.

Sometimes Nina even let Max pick what we did. Which meant we did things like play trivia baseball, in which you made your way around the bases to score, as in the traditional game, but you advanced by answering history, literature, and science questions. The harder the question you successfully answered, the more bases you sailed through in a single turn. It was the only game he routinely beat all of us at. We made detailed blueprints for a fort we never built, because Max estimated the materials to build it "properly" would have been four digits at least, though he assured us the geometry he had used in the plans was flawless, and urged us to keep them until we had the money. We even bought a piggy bank to start saving, though the only thing we stored in it was the folded-up sheet the prints were on. Sometimes, when Lila had too much homework, something that had never happened until that year, Max would even be waiting for us alone at the three crosses when we got there.

The three crosses were in memoriam of the Hendricks family. At the time of the accident that made them infamous, Judy Hendricks had three kids under the age of six, so you can hardly blame her for what happened. Plus the accident happened in August, and everyone knows what Florida Augusts can do to a person's mind. One presumably bright morning she took her three children to the playground next to the crosses. Her oldest, naughtiest child, Caleb, refused to get off the monkey bars and, to show him how little she cared about whether or not he listened to her demands to put his shoes back on and get in the car, she gathered up her other two children and packed them in the car and even reversed out of the parking lot before Caleb jumped down and started wailing for her to wait. Angry, by now, that her bluff hadn't worked earlier, she threw the car back into park before climbing out of it, or thought she did, but really it was in neutral. And because the playground sat at the bottom of a hill, the car rolled back down into the parking lot and into a metal lightpost that had been installed only weeks earlier after too many complaints about the illicit behavior that was being conducted in the park at night, the remnants of which cluttered the playground by day. The lamp fell on top of the car, crushing the two youngest Hendrickses. The third cross was for Judy, who shot herself with her father's rifle a month later.

Judy Hendricks became the patron saint of overworked mothers, of which there was no shortage in our neighborhood. Every child who lived within a twenty-block radius of the crosses could feel their mother's gaze travel subconsciously in the direction of the crosses on their worst days. An acknowledgment of the fact that it could always get worse or a search for empathy from the one mother who would surely understand, we were never sure. We were too young when the accident happened to actually remember it, so to us it was just an easy meeting spot, but Max found it unbearably sad and insisted we find a new place to congregate. Unenthusiastic about the prospect, the stop sign across the street with no tragedy attached to it was the farthest he could get us, just far enough that Max couldn't read the kids' names while he waited for us (he was always the first to arrive). Most of us forgot, though, so we met at the crosses as always, and he would call to us from across the street, waving excitedly as if it were a coincidence that we all found ourselves in the same place.

One day when I was running late after an errand my mother

insisted I do immediately, I went to the crosses as always, but the other girls had already migrated over to Max and his stop sign. Marie was with them, which was infrequent but not rare. She was a creature who seemed genuinely happy to be alone, but on the few days she did want some company we were generally it. This wasn't because she was an outcast of any sort. All the mothers in our neighborhood seemed always to be leaning forward, ready to mother her in her own mother's careless absence, and would have had more than just a mouthful of words should any of their own children be unkind to her. But she seemed, sometimes, too old even for us, so I can understand how there was very little appeal for her in children her own age.

As I started to cross the street I saw that Marie was standing over Max, braiding his short hair in a series of tiny braids in a stern, almost soldierly way, determined not to be defeated by the impossibility of her task. Max kept leaning back and looking up at her to stick out his tongue, his eyes widened in mock craziness and real delight. He adored her in a way that would have made it clear, even if we didn't know him, that he had a little sister of his own.

"Are you ready?" Nina asked as soon as my second foot was out of the street and over on their side.

Lindsey raised her eyebrows, clearly amused but not able to say why, because she kept trying to swallow her smile. And I knew there must have been a disagreement about whatever it was Nina wanted me to be ready for.

"Max wants to show us something," said Lila.

"Okay, what?" I asked.

"It's a surprise," said Lindsey, the glee in her voice even more of a giveaway than her illicit smile had been.

"Follow me," said Max, pulling up his bike and hopping on with more grace than I had ever seen from him, enough to convince me whatever he had for us might be good. Before he met us, Max hadn't been on a bike in years, never having been an outdoor kid, and you could still sometimes tell when he rode.

We went farther than we had ever ridden before, off the bike paths we knew better than the layouts of our own houses, closer to Max's house and his part of the state than we had ever been. We went single file, never talking, communicating only in the silliness with which we rode—sometimes without hands, sometimes without feet, the rogue appendages always held high to make sure their bad behavior was noted. Layers of clothing were peeled and wrapped around heads like sweatbands, and around waists and shoulders, making us a colorful brigade. We pedaled furiously, joyfully, calling to one another in whoops and arm waves and smiles thrown over our shoulders, and I loved not knowing where I was going more than I ever thought I would.

Just when I forgot there was any purpose to the outing other than the ride itself, Max turned off the path into what looked like shrubbery, into a clearing. There was a thick canopy above it, making it almost fully enclosed, giving us shelter from the sun and cooling the air by at least a few degrees. At the center of the clearing was what looked like a little pond, and just after it was a swamp big enough to make it a safe bet that there were at least a dozen things in it that could kill you.

"What is it?" Lindsey asked, nodding at the pond as she dismounted her bike for a closer look.

"It's a pool," said Max triumphantly.

"That thing is a pool?" I asked. "Why is it black? It's creeping me out. You can't see the bottom, or tell how deep it is."

"It's chlorinated. And clean. The owner just had it painted dark and had these rocks put all around it, so that it looked natural, so that it would blend right into its surroundings."

"I don't get it," said Lila.

"So you can enjoy the beauty of nature without worrying about snakes and gators."

"But it's not nature," I said, sticking my hand in. "It's chlorinated, like you said. And temperature-controlled, I'm pretty sure."

"But it looks like nature, and while you're swimming in it you can look out on the swamp, at the real thing. My dad's friend had it built. He said he found the bright blue pools next to these gorgeous swamps with all these fascinating creatures in them gaudy. He just hated that there was all this incredible wildlife next to these uniform, cookie-cutter pools. He said he always wondered what the animals thought of them."

"Ah, but what if that becomes a problem?" Lindsey asked.

"What?"

"What if the animals like it too much? What if they mistake this pool for their swamp home? How do you know there aren't snakes and gators in there now? It's too dark to see the bottom."

"Seriously?" Max asked, looking at Lindsey like she had just suggested man's first walk on the moon had been staged by the government, his least favorite conspiracy theory. "Do you know what the effects of chlorine would be on the internal environment of a snake?"

"Yes, Max," Lindsey said. "Actually, no, but I was kidding. I know there are no snakes in there." She said it without any malice. She found his guilelessness as endearing as the rest of us did. She had been teasing him only because that's how you said *I love you* in her family. She rustled Marie's hair and winked when Marie looked up at her, an acknowledgment of how silly boys could be.

"Why isn't this thing by the guy's *house*?" Marie asked. "It's in the middle of nowhere."

"He has another one there. This is just his favorite swamp, so he bought all the land around it."

"Rich people," said Nina.

Max looked over at her, an automatic gesture.

"No offense. I don't mean you, obviously."

I felt a little bad for him. Not for Nina's comment about a class of people he certainly belonged to, but because he didn't yet know that all of these questions and challenges were standard after a discovery or opinion stated by any one of us. The rest of us had to turn it inside out before we could agree and adopt it into the list of things we all valued and believed true, never stopping to consider that we could have more than one worldview among us. Our questions could be ruthless, especially Nina's, but once a piece of wisdom or a belief was in, it was in forever. This did nothing to fluster Max, though. He was a boy born for debate club. I had never heard him waver in anything.

"I think it's really great, Max," said Lila, smiling over at him. "Really. I've never seen anything like it. Hey, Marie, should we ask Dad for one for Christmas?"

Marie shook her head solemnly. "I already have my list."

It was unsurprising that she had prepared for Christmas like she did everything else.

"Okay, I get it," said Nina, not acknowledging Lila's comment, or even that the rest of us were there. She was looking directly at him. "I mean, I get what he's going for. But didn't he kind of ruin nature by building this thing? Like, if you wanna enjoy the swamp, look at the swamp. Don't make something that looks like it but without any of the magic beneath the surface. I mean, it just feels like a lot of work for something that, in the end, is just a swimming pool. Like, maybe swimming pools and swamps just don't belong next to each other at all."

"No way," he said, looking over to return her gaze. He started to turn back to look at the swamp but stopped short, as if he had just noticed something about Nina's face that required a second look. Or as if it were just then occurring to him how pretty she really was.

"My mom made me go out to Palm Springs with her for her sister's wedding. I thought it was absurd to spend half a day on a plane to travel from one unlivably hot environment to another, no matter who lived there. You know, like when you're on a plane for that long you should end up somewhere totally different. But she insisted, and when we got there it *was* different. It was a totally different kind of heat. A dry heat, where nothing green was ever meant to live. But it looked like Disney World—the greenest grass you've ever seen, grass that never would have grown there naturally and must have taken all kinds of intricate manufactured systems to keep it alive. And it was the first time I realized it."

"What?" Nina asked.

"How crazy it is, the places that man has made livable. Like the places not hospitable to life that we've managed to put houses and societies in. Like this pool—do you know how difficult it would be to dig a hole this close to a swamp, the kind of ground the pool was built in? And yet here it is."

Lindsey looked over at me. *Fascinating*, she mouthed. I opened my eyes wide in alarm, like, *Dude, don't get me in trouble*. Not wanting to be the one to ruin the unveiling of Max's eighth wonder of the world. It really was just a pool, but his reverence was inspiring. Even then, without having the words for it, I knew it was better to care about anything that much than not, and it was never something we had done. At least not something we talked about. When I think of Max now, that is always what I start with—his quickness to marvel at the world. And I think that, for all Lila and Max's shared car rides and teachers in common—as lavish as both their weekly allowances might have been—it was Nina who most loved and understood this capacity in him. Her watching him when he went on and on about the beauty of red canoes or the significance of which caterpillars have fuzz and which don't is the one context I can think of when she ever fully, willingly ceded control.

We stood there, waiting for him to go on or sum his little speech up, but Max was never one for gestures—for openings or closings or segues. He said exactly what was on his mind as it came to him without any fanfare or finesse. He never took much time in the presentation of his observations and declarations. Having said everything he had to say about man's ability to thrive in inhospitable environments, he laid his towel out a few feet from the pool, pulled a thick purple book from out of his bag, and sat down. The rest of us silently followed, arranging ourselves around the pool, pulling out the towels and the creased magazines and tattered copies of R. L. Stine novels we never went anywhere without, never knowing when the day might call for a swim. Not ready to let everyone settle into their private worlds yet, Nina looked over at Max's book, which he was already engrossed in.

"Max, why is your book purple?"

"I don't know, because that's what the publisher decided it should be," he said, not looking up from the page.

"No, I mean, what are you reading that is best summed up by the color purple?"

He held the book up, displaying Virginia Woolf in profile under the title *The Virginia Woolf Reader*. "Everything she's ever written."

"Thought you'd do a little light reading by the swamp, huh?"

He shrugged. "It was on the bookshelf in the hallway on my way out. It was the first one I saw, so I grabbed it—probably because the purple makes it so noticeable. So I guess it was a good choice by the publisher."

Knowing, probably, that this would not be Nina's last interruption and not wanting to miss anything, he flipped from the page he had been reading to the back. As he read you could chart his progress by the back-and-forth of his eyes. He read like he did everything else—with full commitment to it. His entire body was involved. He looked away from the page for a moment, out of boredom, I assumed at first, as he studied the intersecting branches above us, but then his face just folded. At first he looked like he had a sneeze that wasn't ready to be born, but I realized in horror that something on the page had made him cry. He made no attempt to hide it, or recover. I looked around for the others' faces the way I would look for an emergency exit after smelling fire, on instinct. None of us had seen our fathers or brothers cry, so there was no way to know what any of them would make of this.

"Max, what is it, what's wrong?" asked Nina.

"That's the saddest thing I ever read. I can't believe they published it."

"What?"

"It's her suicide note."

"Nasty," said Nina, but it was clear the idea appealed to her.

"It's the most beautiful thing I've ever read."

"What does it say?" she asked, reaching for the book flirtatiously. Only she would try to make suicide coy.

He held it away without pulling his eyes from the page, which he had starting rereading. "I mean, it's a suicide note, so of course it's going to be sad. But the really unbearable part isn't her description of how miserable she was."

"Okay, so what is it?" Nina asked, the only one, apparently, willing to take part in this bizarre conversation.

He didn't answer her at first, having gone back to reading, far more attuned to the letter itself than the conversation.

"Max?"

"What?" he looked up. "Oh, right." He went back to the page, looking for the scrap that had made him cry. "It's the part where she says, *I don't think two people could have been happier than we have been.* She says it twice, and it's such a short letter, and she was too good a writer to be inclined to repetition. She just . . . She must have really wanted to make sure her point got across, to have written it twice."

"Or maybe she was crazy," said Lindsey under her breath.

"You think, when someone like this dies, how sad it is that we'll never have any more work from them, but until now I've never thought about the fact that she was a person." He said this like the magnitude of what he was saying was self-evident. That whatever he was indicting himself for was obvious, and no small offense.

"Max," said Lila, looking up from her own book for the first time since the conversation began. "How have you never read that before? Mrs. Chambers does a huge lesson on Woolf. And that was, what, two years ago for you now?"

And it was this, the suggestion that he should have known something long before he did—letting some beautiful, life-changing piece of prose almost slip through the cracks—not crying in front of a group of girls, at least one of whom he was half in love with, that embarrassed Max. That suddenly made him aware again of the physical space he occupied on the planet Earth, after Virginia took him somewhere else. And you could feel him calculate it, all the facts he would never know. All the pretty suicide notes and the rousing speeches given by generals to men going into battle, speeches that made it almost worth dying for. All the poems that you had to sit down at the final lines of, even after you had read them half a dozen times, and the affectations and insecurities of the poets who had written them. And you could see it change him, and make him smaller—the fact that you could spend your entire life in search of these things and never gather them all.

"Oh," he said, his voice small. "I never took her. I petitioned to take physics and chemistry instead of an English class that year, since I already had a surplus of English credits."

A silence fell upon our little group that even the gators and the snakes and the bullfrogs respected. The water lay still, with no splashes or rustling. I was about to cannonball into the pool just for the sound of it, when Nina spoke.

"In the fourth grade, Mrs. Bat taught us all about the Holocaust. And I mean, she spared none of the details. We heard about the gas chambers and the shooting-people-for-falling stuff, the families being separated. The whole nightmare. And because it was such intense stuff, she sent out letters to our parents a few weeks before, asking them to prep us. To give us some idea of what had happened. That, like, an entire race of people had been taken out and why and all that. So it wouldn't be a complete shock. But of course Elaine had more important things to do. She swore she never got the letter, but whatever."

Nina had been calling her mother by her first name since before we were old enough to grasp the subversiveness of the gesture.

"So, anyway, my mind is *blown*, right? Like I can't even believe that this happened and I had never known. That I was, like, just then learning it. I felt like I had been lied to, you know? Like, how did something this terrible happen and we're not, like, still talking about it all the time, like, *CAN you believe this?*"

Max had been in his head, still turning over the tragedy both of Woolf's note and the fact that he had gone so long without reading it, when Nina started, but the more animated her telling became, the more of his attention he gave her. By now he was really looking at her, curious where this was going.

"So I started telling *everybody* about it. The bus driver. The cafeteria lady. Like, *Oh, my God, listen to this fucked-up shit that actually happened.* And every time I started I felt sure they were going to flip out about it, but all of them looked at me sympathetically, like, *solemnly,* and just said, 'Yes, sweetheart, I know.' And I figure that, while they know, they must not really know how bad it is, or they wouldn't be so calm about it. So one day my mom comes home to me telling our *Jewish* mailman all about the Holocaust, not a single detail left out—I may have even embellished them to make sure he really got the extent of it. Can you imagine? He was really nice about it, but my mom really ripped me a new one even though it's obviously her fault. I was forbidden to ever bring it up again to anyone. Ever. So, yeah, I was a little late in coming to the Holocaust, sure, but I've never forgotten it. And I never forgot the way I learned. In fact, I would say there are few historical events I'm as well studied in as the Holocaust."

"Um, how have we never heard that story?" I asked, though I already knew the answer. Nina wasn't fond of stories in which she was the butt of the joke. She liked to give the impression that she had been born knowing everything.

"I have," Lila said, not looking up from her magazine.

"That's wild," said Max.

It was clear that he was as amused by the story as the rest of us were, but I don't think he realized the magnitude of what she'd done for him. I'd never seen her make a fool of herself for anyone.

"Right?"

"I thought Anne Frank's diary was a novel for a long time," said Max. Quickly, almost involuntarily, like he had Tourette's.

"Ha!" said Nina. "That's almost worse than me. Her picture's on the cover, you twat. Even I know that."

I waited for Max's wounded, pensive look to return, but he only shoved Nina playfully—a gesture I had never seen his formality make space for—and they both started laughing.

"Can you imagine if it *was* a novel?" Max said. "And you were the girl whose photo they used for the cover?"

"You guys are so weird," said Lila. "I'm bored. Let's swim."

She dove into the pool headfirst, and when she surfaced she started doing the practical little above-water breaststrokes old ladies do.

"I'll race you," Nina said to Max. And they sprang up from the ground as if the earth had kicked them out, and threw themselves into unforgivably sloppy cannonballs that disrupted the swimming lane Lila had created down the center of the pool.

"Don't wake Marie!" Lila whispered hotly, nodding at where Marie was curled up in the fetal position on her towel, totally gone.

"Why not?" Nina asked merrily. "She'll miss all the fun!"

But Lila had already turned away from her, her old lady strokes taking her farther away from Max and Nina.

I looked over to where Lindsey had been sitting next to me to see if she would be the next one in, but she was already up, circling the perimeter of the pool in her slouchy, stretched-out mom one-piece that looked faded enough to have actually belonged to her mother. She dipped a toe into the water but then jumped all the way in, quickly, before she could change her mind about it.

Before we could coo over exactly how short Sam Decker was selling himself, and insist that he was far nicer than us, that his kindnesses were everywhere, and that we were sure he had private reasons that clicked perfectly into place with his decision to treat Abby Madison to the symphony of unanswered rings that would drive even a crisis negotiator to madness, Bobby came wandering over in a Florida Cabaret T-shirt two sizes too big, making it look more like a dress than a T-shirt, a fire truck the red of a freshly picked mosquito bite in his hand.

"What up, maniac?" Nina asked.

"I've asked you not to call me that," he said, placing the truck neatly on the bar table before him like he was preparing it for a presentation.

Nina was routinely meaner to Bobby than she was to the rest of us. She swore it was good for his character-in-progress, as she called it. She always said that if she had had siblings to be mean to she would have been nicer to everybody else, and we tried not to be offended that she didn't count us as siblings. Someone had to see the worst side of you, she said. She reasoned that, by drawing it out of Bobby, he would be free to show his better self to everyone else.

"Did you catch Nancy what's-her-face yet?"

Bobby had made the mistake of bringing his first-grade yearbook to the bar a few weeks ago and letting Nina hold it long enough to see a rogue heart drawn around a girl named Nancy. He had only let Nina touch it at all because she said she wanted to sign it. He seemed too smart to fall for this, but once we saw how few signatures he had gathered, we understood, and even Nina softened for a few minutes before growing more antagonistic in her resolve to prepare this boy for the world he would find on the other side of a childhood conducted under the unwatchful eye of Veronica Beecher.

"That would entail me chasing her," said Bobby.

Where Max was all eager youth and Sam Decker was the epitome of physical manhood in its prime, Bobby was a boy who had been born with the knowing cynicism of a ninety-year-old. One look at him and you knew he knew and understood things about the world that no one his age had any business knowing. Where Max had questions and wonder, Bobby had answers he wasn't ready to share, afraid, you could sense, to burden you with them. Where to Max the crosses had been an unthinkable blow, too sad to accept or live among, if you had told Bobby about them, he would have only nodded grimly, an acknowledgment that these things happen. Max's unpopularity had probably never occurred to him. He had been raised by two loving parents to have a healthy self-regard. He became friends with us for the company. Bobby knew exactly how many signatures were in that yearbook, and exactly what that number meant. Every time I spent more than a few minutes with him I was newly grateful for Nina and

Lindsey, even if they sometimes drove me to madness. I re-interpreted Nina's bossiness as a willingness to take care of things no one else had bothered to, and Lindsey's refusal to talk about things like what the hell she was doing with some-one like Carine's boyfriend and what could possibly be in it for her as an optimistic worldview.

"That's not what she said," said Nina.

"She lives two counties away and her parents don't drink, so she's never been here."

"Okay, Romeo. Believe it or not, there are other places you can talk to someone."

He turned the idea over with his eyes and then decided not to worry about it.

"Do you want to see my new truck?" he asked Lindsey, nodding at the fire engine, giving her permission to pick it up. Like most people, Bobby liked her the best. Nina was the one you looked at while you were talking, but Lindsey was the one you entrusted things to.

"Not bad," she said, picking it up to study it. "It's a hook and ladder. My favorite."

"You would have a favorite truck," Nina said.

"You know what my favorite thing to do with my brothers' Hot Wheels when we were kids was?" she said, ignoring Nina.

"What?" Bobby asked, looking, for once, like a kid.

"Make these crazy pileup collisions. Just, like, miles of cars backed up on each other."

"That's awesome," said Bobby matter-of-factly. "I have some other cars over there. Should I go get them?"

"Totally," she said.

"Wow, he must really like you," said Decker, who was clearly amused and charmed by Bobby, though he had become shy as soon as he got to the table.

"What do you mean?"

"A man never leaves his car with a woman. At least not his newest, best one."

"Whatever," said Nina, rolling her eyes. "Can we at least agree that it should be criminal to bring a boy like that to a bar like this? I mean, most kids are assholes anyway, so it doesn't matter, but you can feel the ick of this place infiltrating his pasty little pores."

"No way," said Decker. "My parents used to throw these *wild* parties when I was a kid. All the time. On school nights sometimes. I remember going to sleep to the sound of them, and just not being able to wait until I was old enough to go to parties like that. Most kids are afraid to become their parents, but I never was. I couldn't wait to be like them. They had these friends that they, they *loved* them, you know. And that's what growing up meant. Getting to hang out with your friends all the time way past when you were allowed to when you were a kid."

"That sounds okay," I said. "But didn't they have shit to do? Like, work and stuff?"

I couldn't picture the adults in our neighborhood having time for that kind of merriment. The lawn chairs were more group therapy than lavish party, and always ended in time to get five or six hours of sleep before early-morning shifts.

"Nah. My dad was a fisherman. When he was gone, he was gone; when he was there, he was there. My mom was the secretary to the principal where I went to school. She was the one you checked in with when you were sent to the principal's office. And she always made you feel better about it. No matter what you did, or allegedly did, she had a smile for you. She made it seem like she was on your side. I think the other kids always liked me for it. So it always made sense, her staying up late when she shouldn't be. She was one of us, just trying to get away with it, no matter what it was, and because she was an adult she sometimes did. She's still at it. You should see that woman make her way through a bottle of wine."

We could picture her perfectly. Before the reign of Abby Madison, he took her to all the award shows. She had a haircut that promised her clothes weren't from Chico's, or wherever else women her age were supposed to shop.

"So, man, you've had a charmed life all the way through, huh?" said Lindsey.

He tilted his head to consider this, like it had never occurred to him. "I have no complaints."

His face went from disinterested acceptance to that happy smile you give a puppy and kitten napping together. We all looked to the point where his face was turned and saw Bobby making his way toward our table with his giant cabaret shirt pulled up so he could carry at least a dozen mini-trucks over to us at once.

"He's back," said Decker. "Hey, my man, what you got there?"

Even if Bobby hadn't been born with the seasoned wisdom

of someone who had done all this before, the tone Decker used
was way off, suited to someone years younger than Bobby.

"Who's this?" Bobby asked Lindsey, unimpressed.

"This is our friend Sam," she said.

"He doesn't know what a Hot Wheel is?"

"He's *special*," Nina said conspiratorially, taking a rare break
from antagonizing Bobby to align herself with him against an
even more savory target.

"Hey, man," Decker said, totally game, his hands parted
momentarily from his beer in surrender. "It's okay, you don't
have to share. I know how it is with cars and girls, man. Each
of us to our own."

We looked over at Roni to see what she thought of the
movie star riffing with her kid—now treating him like he was
five years *older* than he was—but she was fixing her lipstick in
the metal of the beer taps.

Sal came slouching over just as Bobby turned his attention
to the work of laying all his cars out in a row as Lindsey had
suggested.

"It's too late for that, Bobby," he said in his most no-
nonsense voice when he was still two real-car lengths away
from our table. He wasn't doing it to be mean. For months now
he had designated the booth in the corner of the bar, the coziest
one, to Bobby's nightly ritual. Every night at around nine they
retired to the booth to watch two innings of whatever baseball
game was on one of the three channels Sal got on the antenna
TV he had installed there. Sometimes, when I wasn't at the
Shamrock and I heard a baseball score, or a snippet of a game
on the TV or radio, I would think of Bobby and Sal, watching

and not talking, together, the bar settling in around them. Bobby was always asleep by the end of two innings, and Sal got up to start the second half of his night. Sal had confessed to us once that he hated baseball, but that it was the only thing that put Bobby to sleep, and the only thing worse than watching a game that boring was watching it alone. He seemed to be afraid that Bobby would witness something he shouldn't if he stayed up too late, but after-hours the Shamrock usually saw only the same things it did in the middle of the day, however sad they were.

We knew from the way Sal treated Bobby that, should we need it, Sal would be every bit as fatherly and protective of us, which was probably a big part of why we kept going back to the Shamrock, though it was never something we discussed. We made a big fuss of being grown-up enough to go out drinking, the same way all the other people too old for school vented after long days at work, but by going to Sal's we got to be adults under the safety of his watchful eye. Sal didn't let bad things happen to people he liked, at least not until the night he met Sam Decker. Maybe it was because we learned that there were some things even Sal couldn't prevent that we stopped going to the Shamrock after that night.

Whatever the merits or limits of Sal's parenting, Bobby was too young to appreciate them. He stood up taller, suddenly on alert, at Sal's suggestion that he put his cars away.

"But I just got them out," he said.

"Next time start earlier," said Sal in a voice impossible to argue with.

"Don't worry, guy," said Decker, finally getting the tone

right, and winning Bobby's attention with it. "You won't always have to go to bed right when things start to get interesting."

A few days after our discovery of the swamp pool, Nina, Lila, Lindsey, and I were supposed to meet to make that year's Halloween costume. We always went as a foursome—the Beatles, or the queens of diamonds, hearts, clubs, and spades. We always met the Friday before Halloween to draft our plan and make our costumes. We knew we were getting too old for it, but we didn't have anything better to do yet, and we still liked the candy. No one wanted to be the one to call it.

It was my year to raid the thrift store down the street for clothing and jewelry to pull from. It had become a contest to outdo one another on this front, and the strength or weakness of any year's ensemble was understood to depend, largely, on the supplies we had available to us, even though some of our best costumes had been waiting for us in our closets, or required no more than a T-shirt and a permanent marker. I had made an extra run to the fabric store catty-corner from the Salvation Army, so I was struggling under the weight of neon pipe cleaners and purple and gold Mardi Gras beads, and bundles of fabric with corn and snowflakes and stars on them, in addition to other people's discarded clothes, and running late by the time I finally made it to Nina's.

Lindsey was sitting on the front stoop, and looked up at me without saying anything as I came unsteadily up the walkway. I slumped down next to her, letting all my bags go at once.

"Why didn't you go in?" I asked.

She handed me a note.

Heard about this gnarly haunted house in Max's neighborhood. Tonight is the last night we could go. Can't wait to see what you tricks come up with for costumes. Don't be predictable and get mad, k?

Love,

Your hottest friend

P.S. Lila made me do it.

"Dude, what the fuck?"

"I know," she said, betraying no signs of anger, or even irritation. Lindsey took no more than five minutes to get over anything.

"I hope they don't think we're making their costumes," I said.

Lindsey shrugged. That wasn't the point and we both knew it.

"You don't think they left without us because they know I'm afraid of haunted houses, do you?" she asked without looking over at me.

"No," I said. "Max can't like them any more than you do."

"Yeah, but he'll have *two* girls to comfort him. I'm pretty sure that makes it worth the risk even for him."

"Whose bosom do you think he'll cry and start citing the history of the haunted house into?"

It came out with sharper teeth than I had intended.

"Sorry, that was mean," I said. "Max isn't even the problem."

"I really like Max," said Lindsey. "He's the weirdest person I've ever met, but he's interesting. I feel like I'll never get bored with him around. I used to think, *I wonder how many more times we can do this before it gets old.* And I don't anymore."

"I know," I said. "That swamp pool was pretty cool. I feel like he lives on this entirely different planet that's been right under our noses, and now we get both. His planet and ours. Like we have dual citizenship or something. He's like the E.T. of central Florida."

Lindsey started rifling through one of the bags I had brought, probably just to return my favor of saying they hadn't left us because they knew she wouldn't be able to handle a haunted house.

"Do you think Nina is gonna let Max stick it to her?" I asked.

"Only if Lila will leave them alone long enough."

"Do you think she does it on purpose?"

"Lila?" Lindsey asked, looking up from a handful of Pez-dispenser necklaces I had considered my best find, though they now seemed cheesy and cheap, exposed under all the afternoon sun.

"No. Elvis. Yes, Lila," I said. "You'd think she'd take the hint. Every time they're together Max and Nina come just shy of dry humping, and Lila's the only one who doesn't excuse herself from the private conversations they're always having. You'd think she'd have gotten it by now. Like, I'm surprised Lila's not here with us. That we're the two alone."

"Are you really, though? I'd be surprised if they didn't share tampons."

I wrinkled my nose, but I was smiling. "Dude, you're so crass. You're such a boy."

"You know what's weird, though," she said, ignoring, as she always did, any suggestion that she was anything less than wholly female.

"What?"

"I don't think it's Max that Lila's guarding."

"What do you mean?"

"It's like she can't stand that Nina might like somebody more than her. It's like she's trying to distract Max from Nina so Max doesn't hog her or something. It's like she's hiding the good booze at a party or something."

"Maybe," I said, suddenly tired of trying to work through this riddle that had nothing, I realized, as I said it, to do with us. "You know what's annoying?"

"What?" she asked.

"They probably assumed we'd spend the afternoon talking about them once we found the note. And here we are."

"Should we go do something?" she asked.

The day suddenly lay empty and ugly before us.

"Like what?"

"Doesn't the ten-dollar all-you-can-scream thing start tonight?"

Every year the discount theater in our neighborhood charged ten dollars to watch as many horror movies as you could sit through. They showed them all through the night on all eight of their screens. They played everything from *The Shining* to *I Know What You Did Last Summer*, and no two screens showed the same movie at any given time, so when you finally had your fill, or needed to hear the click of a lock behind you, there was no blaming your exit on a lack of variety, or on account of having seen everything they were showing.

"Yeah," I said. "But don't you hate scary movies?"

"I'll live."

We stood up and turned our bodies toward the theater.

"Should we take this stuff with us?" Lindsey asked, looking down at it.

"Nah," I said. "Let them deal with it."

And we walked away without having to worry whose hand we would clasp at the scariest parts of the movie, leaving all the supplies I had bought slumped on Nina's front stoop as evidence that we had been there.

That guy's cool," Decker said, watching Sal and Bobby walk away. "He knows what's up. Can you imagine? Just hanging out at a bar all day long."

"Um, I mean, I can think of cooler jobs than that," Lindsey said.

"Wait, what do you guys do?" he asked.

"Not us. You!"

"Eh. Whatever. By the end I could've taken it or left it."

"What do you mean, 'by the end'? You have four movies coming out in the next year," I said. Nina gave me an *Easy, tiger* look. "I mean, don't you?"

"Yeah, but there was a point, right before things took off, when I was ready to pack it in. It felt like the end. I was ready to go."

"So what happened?" Nina asked.

"I was in this B movie. Actually, that's being generous. It was a C movie."

"Can I ask something?" I asked.

"Because you guys have been so shy till now?"

"Oh. Sorry. Never mind."

"I'm kidding. I obviously don't care. I like you guys. You're funny."

He said "funny" like it was an alleged, tentative concept that he was trying out. He finished the finger of bourbon left in his smudged tumbler in one shot, and held up the empty glass at the non-Roni bartender in a way that was remarkably inoffensive, as if they'd somehow managed to work out their own silent language without speaking.

Nina *actually* winked at him, and when I opened my eyes wide in exaggerated horror when he wasn't looking, she mouthed, *What?!*

"Go ahead," he said. "What's your question?"

"So, why do people even *make* C movies? Like, why do people make movies that are gonna go right to DVD?"

"Well, half the time you don't know. Distributors sometimes pick up movies long after they're made. You'd be surprised how thin a line it is between *Good Will Hunting* and *Swimming in Winter.*"

"What's *Swimming in Winter?*"

"Exactly. It was written by this earnest, good-looking smart kid—just as likable as Damon. And it was all set, for everything. The festivals. Everything. And now that guy's working construction. He couldn't book a commercial."

"That sucks."

"Yeah, it does." He shrugged, like it wasn't actually of that much consequence. "But other times they pretty much know it's gonna be a flop right from the start, because it's a shitty movie. And the studio has a writer or an actor on contract for X number of projects, and they figure if they're paying someone, they might as well use them, and they have biggish-name actors play certain roles in the hopes that Americans are dumber and less sensitive to bad acting and absurd plots and sappy dialogue than we normally give them credit for, and that putting in a few familiar faces will somehow prevent projects that never should have been undertaken from going right to DVD. And they'll make back some of the money they've already paid to the people they're forcing to be in the movie. Which, remarkably, sometimes works."

"Wait, should we be offended by that?" Lindsey asked.

"What?"

"The dumb-Americans thing."

"No. I already told you. I like you guys. And most Americans *are* dumb. Including the people who make movies."

"Dude, good thing *Blush* isn't here to hear that . . ." said Lindsey, eyebrows in a scandalous position as she looked pointedly away from the table.

Decker looked at Lindsey like she was the irritating afterschool friend who had just eaten all of his favorite snack. Like, *Dude, c'mon.*

"Anyway . . ." said Nina. "Weren't you telling us about your big break?"

Apparently Lindsey and Decker's looks had come too close

to the junior-high-style flirting that Nina had been relying on since she actually *was* in junior high.

"Actually, this is all relevant," said Decker, "because the C movie I was talking about, Jack Alfonso was in it, even though he's Doctor Oscar. And he was *not* happy about it. Everyone knew the script was shit."

"I *love* Jack Alfonso," I said.

"Yeah!" said Lindsey. "He's like someone's clueless but still somehow timelessly attractive father."

"Totally. Like, hot grandfather. Or one of those people you know is going to smell good in an I'm-not-trying-too-hard kind of way," said Nina.

"I have no idea what that means, but no," said Decker. "He's a total fuckhead. Like, *epically* so."

"No!" Lindsey said. "I don't know why, but I find that really heartbreaking. Like, somehow I would be less disillusioned if you had told me Barack was a dick and cheats on Michelle."

"I don't know, man. Politics is not my thing, but I do know that Jack Alfonso is one of the worst human beings on the planet. And he made no secret of how pissed he was to be there. He unapologetically kept trying to get the craft-services and costume people to go home with him. He didn't even bother to take off his wedding ring. I mean, I've seen some shady shit, but this just *took* it. And it made me really, really depressed."

"Why? So the guy's a dick," said Lindsey. "What's that got to do with you?"

"Because until you make it out there, it's a fucking grind. No health insurance, inconsistent schedule—just *days* of sitting around, feeling like your life's going nowhere, followed by having to leave for God-knows-where for commercial shoots without any notice, to work thirty-hour days. And that's all fine, because everyone still willing to do that thinks somewhere in the back of his mind that he's going to be one of the impossibly few people to make it. And here was this guy, who *had* made it, who was clearly completely miserable. And I watched him *really* closely the whole time we were on set, and by the end, I didn't even want it anymore."

"I mean, did you at least *talk* to him?" Lindsey asked. "Maybe he was just having a bad time. Like, maybe he just learned that his wife was cheating on him or his dog had cancer or something."

"Do dogs even *get* cancer?" Nina asked, as if Lindsey had just accused dogs of tax evasion or lying under oath. Like it was the dumbest thing she'd ever heard.

"I tried," Decker said, ignoring Nina to answer Lindsey's question. "I went up to him on the first day and introduced myself and offered my hand and he totally ignored it and said, 'Kid, don't be an idiot. I know who you are. No one would be on this set without me okaying it first.'"

"Wow," Lindsey said. "Okay, fine, he's a dick. Maybe there really is something to your attractiveness-slash-personality theory."

"Yeah, and keep in mind we played father and son in the movie, so it wouldn't have been the worst thing for either of us to get to know the other a little better. But after that I didn't even try. I don't think we exchanged more than three words when we weren't acting."

"Wait a minute," said Nina. "Isn't this the story of how you made it?"

"It is."

"So what the hell?"

Decker didn't know Nina well enough to know that she wasn't actually angry that his story wasn't tight and straight enough for her, she was just pissed that Lindsey was the one leading it astray. Her eyes had been a furious little game of ping-pong between the two of them during their private question-and-answer session. I looked over at Lindsey to see if she was starting to squirm under the agitation she was clearly the cause of, but she wouldn't look at me, which I knew meant she was even more upset by Nina's tantrum than I thought she'd be. I also knew she wasn't trying to flirt with Decker—one love triangle was enough. She just really wanted to know the things she was asking Decker. Nina knew it, too. She just didn't like to be upstaged.

Decker was unfazed.

"So on the last night of filming, everyone's shocked when he shows up at the wrap party. And he's in a visibly better mood—like off-the-charts better than he's been all shoot, probably because the craft-service girl was finally talking to him, and he thought he was gonna get laid. And he comes over to me, and he goes, 'Kid, you ever hear about the way it works over in Kenya, with the Olympic runners?' And I'm like, 'No, sir'—I actually called him 'sir'—'What about them?' And he tells me this story, right? He goes, 'So it doesn't work over there the way it works over here. With the trainers and the sponsors and the fancy running shoes. Over there the ranked

Olympians just run along the country roads that everyone else uses. And everyone knows the route the current Olympian in Kenya takes every day. They know exactly where he's gonna pass when he's out running.'"

Each booth at Sal's had its own individual stained-glass lamp hanging above it—the kind you associate with grandparents' basements and card tables. It was shining over Decker's face, giving his delivery the air of low-budget, experimental theater with bad lighting.

"'And it's every young tenant farmer in Kenya's dream to be the next Kenyan Olympian, because over there, there are really only two career paths—running and farming. And so each day, when he runs by, young tenant farmers along his route come out to join him—barefoot, remember—and run alongside of him, just to see if they can keep up. Most of them don't, of course, and they go back to tenant farming. But every once in a while—and this is very rare—someone does keep up. He stays with the Olympian for part of his run, and so he gets to try again the next day. You know, to see if it was a fluke or if he can really keep up with him.'"

"What a psycho," I said.

"Yeah, I don't get it," said Lindsey.

"No way," said Nina. "That's hot. *Runners* are hot. It makes me like him more."

"You're on drugs," said Lindsey. "It sounds made-up. And why does it feel, I don't know, vaguely *racist*?"

"I don't know about *that*," said Decker. "But it's definitely evidence of narcissistic personality disorder, because just wait for how it ends."

"Wait, what's that?" I asked.

"What's what?"

"The narcissism thing. Is that, like, a Hollywood thing?"

"Dude, the story," said Nina.

Even Lindsey looked at me dubiously.

"Right."

"So, anyway, he puts his hand on my shoulder, and he goes . . ."

We all leaned in, and he smiled, knowing he had us.

"'Welcome to the Olympics, kid.'"

"Holy shit!"

"No way."

"Shut up!"

"I know," he said. "And he offers me the role in *The Last Day of Vengeance* that really started everything. He had contractual approval on the tortured hit man out to get him, which in his world means he gets to handpick him."

"I'm confused," said Lindsey. "I thought this guy hated you."

"Yeah, I was, too," said Decker. "And I told him that. I was, like, *What the fuck?*, before I could even think of anything else to say. And I reminded him of how few words he had spoken to me over the last eight weeks."

"And?"

"And he goes, 'Oh, c'mon, kid. You think the Olympian makes it easy for the tenant farmers?'"

"Wow," said Nina. "Just, wow."

"I know. I still wonder what would've happened if he hadn't given me that job. He's a moody guy, like, *notoriously* so.

He just as easily could've left that wrap party without saying anything to me. If someone had cut him off on the way to that party, I'd be sitting in an office somewhere, or maybe working on some fishing boat."

"You'd have a lot less money," I said.

"But, man, Anchorage is beautiful. Especially this time of year. Have you guys ever been?"

"Yeah," said Lindsey. "We're real world travelers."

"Abby wants me to meet her abroad after this. She's gonna be in Europe for two more weeks, and I have three weeks left before I have to be on set for Criminal Lingo. I don't know, though, Anchorage might get me in the right place for this role."

"I can understand wanting to go back for a visit," I said, "but you can't seriously wish you had packed it in to go home for good instead of starring in a movie with Jack Alfonso."

"I don't know. I think I had come close enough that I wouldn't have spent the rest of my life bitter. Like, I had my chances, and it didn't work out. I wouldn't have wondered or asked What if? or whatever else regretful people run around saying, because I had given it a fair shot. And I was never unhappy in Anchorage, just full of plans."

"Yeah, Maggie," said Nina, her voice as cold as I'd heard it all night, even when we were talking about Lila. "Not everyone hates where they're from as much as you hate it here."

Nina had recognized and been suspicious of my wandering eye probably before I did, the way Nina seemed to know everything. One day we were watching TV and I was mesmerized by this stupid, cheesy commercial for Michigan tourism, and when they cut to the final shot of one of the lakes, I almost couldn't wrap my head around it, it was so enticing—like an ocean without the waves, which always felt more turbulent than fun to me, never mind the one tourist a season who inevitably never popped back up out of them after going in for a quick dip. I was so taken by it that I kept staring straight ahead at the screen where the lake had been when the next commercial came on, and Nina saw my wonder and said, "Dude, who wants to go swimming when it's zero degrees? It's cold as balls there all year round. And there's no sand. What are you supposed to do, lay out on the rocks?" She was like a parent in that you might one day know as much as her, but she would always have gotten there first.

"But don't you think that's part of why you *were* happy," I said, not acknowledging Nina. "Because you had those plans? Like, maybe the reason Anchorage was okay and you have such warm feelings for it is that you were dreaming about what was going to come next. And it was all still possible, because you were young. And if you went back, and it was all the same except it was *always* going to be that, and you knew for sure that none of what you always wanted is going to happen, and it isn't just the thing that comes before whatever is next, it wouldn't have nearly the same, I don't know, magic, if it ever did."

He shrugged. "I have no idea." He fingered the rim of his bourbon glass, turning it slowly. "Maybe there are only two options."

I jutted my chin out from my neck, prompting him to go

on, incredulous that he thought he might be able to stop there, without telling us what they were. He recognized my urgency and smiled.

"You either stay where you're from, thinking about all the things you wish you could change about it until that's all you see."

"Or?" I asked.

"You leave it and spend your whole life missing it like crazy."

"Dude, this is depressing," said Lindsey. "And I would definitely miss it too much. So I guess I'll have to be the first type. Though I can't think of that much I'd change."

"We know," said Nina. "I'll be impressed if you ever make it out of that house."

I was about to make Decker tell me which was the easier one, the least painful, but his phone started ringing again. He took it out of his pocket to silence it, and Abby Madison's perfectly symmetrical face rejoined our table.

"Dude, she must know by now that you're busy," said Nina. "I mean, does she really think the twenty-first time is the one you're going to pick up?"

Nina had once stolen a twenty from her mother's purse to buy a swimsuit she said she couldn't function without because it reminded her so much of the one that Abby wore in *Brighter Stars Than Ours*.

"She's persistent," said Decker. "She's worse at taking no for an answer than anyone I've ever met."

"But now you know Nina," I said. I meant to get back at her

for giving me shit about pressing Decker on Anchorage, but she looked pleased.

"I guess that's how she gets so many roles, huh?" said Lindsey, the only one still determined to be nice.

"Is this normal?" Nina asked. "I mean, does this *persistence* translate into thirty unanswered calls every day?"

"I think you have to stop calling it persistence at ten," I said. "Then it becomes something else."

The buzzing stopped for a few seconds when the call went to voice mail, but started again a few seconds later, when she hung up without leaving a message and tried again. Nina reached out to grab the phone from him, either to turn it off altogether or answer it herself—both equally likely with Nina. Decker pulled it out of her reach.

"Ladies, ladies," he said, though he was clearly enjoying himself. "I've got this."

We smirked at one another as he silenced it yet again and slipped it back into his pocket, less uneasy, by now, about being in cahoots with him on this. It seemed like less of a betrayal to this woman we had spent hours and days, maybe weeks, of our lives loving from afar, given that she hadn't even told us her real name.

Max's small half-plea worked only for so long. Nina tried, she did, but her scheming eventually got the best of her. A few weeks after Halloween, when Max was out of state with his all-male a cappella group from school, we had a rare girls-only sleepover, and she started the conversation we'd all been dreading. Say what you want about Nina—and most things have been said, when the entire population of Florida is taken into account—but she was never cruel, at least not to people she liked, a list of people Max was surely at the top of. She wasn't trying to torture him. She was still, I'm convinced, trying to win him over on this thing she loved, so that they could share it.

"Okay, guys, it's time," she said, sprawled out on her bed, flipping through an old *Kiss* magazine that was sticky and wrinkled from the number of times we'd all been through it.

"For what?" Lila asked from the floor, where she sat painting her nails a bright red color that made her look even more tan than she was.

"Day school girls aren't allowed to play clueless," Nina said. "Your tuition is too high."

"Dude," Lindsey warned, as much with her eyes as with the tone of her voice, when she turned from riffling through Nina's closet, even though she knew every item of clothing in it, along with the location of the stains and faded spots and the holes. Even then she was the good cop.

"Fine, but I know you know what I'm talking about," Nina said, finally sitting up.

"Are all of us supposed to know, or just her, because I'm lost," I said.

"It's Max's turn. To be pranked. I think he's gonna keep feeling left out until we get him. I think he's ready."

Lila opened her mouth to speak, but Lindsey held up a finger behind Nina's head, indicating that she'd take this one.

Because Lila was always the first to protest on Max's behalf, Nina was starting to think it was their own private issue, but the truth was, Lindsey and I could've used a break by then, too.

"Neen, I don't think Max is a prank-war kinda guy," Lindsey said. "I don't think he *gets* it."

"No way, he just doesn't want to be publicly humiliated. Which is why I've come up with a prank we can do at his house. We just have to find a way in."

"Jesus, Nina!" said Lila, surprising all of us with her anger and flicking little beads of red nail polish on her thigh when she looked up from the job abruptly. "Get a clue. If you fuck up his house, he's gonna lose it. He's not going to think it's funny."

"No. You're underestimating him," said Nina calmly, still flipping magazine pages and not acknowledging Lila's tantrum. "Baptism by fire. The sooner he gets used to this prank war, the better off everyone will be. What are we gonna do? Not have the prank war anymore?"

"I don't know . . ." I said, looking over at Lindsey, urging her to come up with a nice way to say that, yes, that was exactly what we were going to do.

"What don't you know?"

"It's getting *embarrassing*," said Lila, still clearly pissed. "I feel like I'm constantly in danger of being the girl who shows up to the school cafeteria naked, which normally only happens in people's *nightmares*. I'm always looking over my shoulder, like I'm in some sort of witness protection program, all so that I'm not soaked in someone's bodily fluids or tripping down a flight of stairs."

"Still smarting from that locker swap, huh?" Nina asked, unable to suppress a smirk.

"I mean, maybe we *are* getting a little old for it," Lindsey suggested tentatively, as if it were a new or passing thought. "I mean, I respect how creative everyone is getting, but every month it feels like the setup and the planning is taking more and more time."

"I agree," said Lila.

"Maybe you're just busier than you used to be," Nina said, as if Lindsey hadn't been the one to raise the issue.

There couldn't have been more than thirty seconds between Nina saying this and Lila's response, but some switch was flipped in that silence. I had never seen Lila's face look the way it did. And I knew if she was that angry, it was for things that hadn't happened yet. She was going to cave.

"Okay, fine, Nina," Lila finally said, a half second after I knew she would. "We'll prank him. But can we at least not do it at his *house?* That feels like such an invasion."

"Why are you being so protective of him, anyway?" Nina asked, her small victory not enough. "We're *all* friends with him."

"I just think making someone feel uncomfortable in his own home is crossing the line."

Lindsey made an *Eek* shape with her mouth in agreement.

"No way. People feel the safest in their houses. We'll let him stay in his comfort zone, so he feels more secure during the fallout. Plus, I wanna see his house."

"Jesus, is that what this is really about, Nina?" Lila asked. "Why don't you just ask him to see it? It's really not that great."

"You've seen it?" Nina asked a beat too quickly.

Lila sighed. "Of *course* I've seen it. He lives like five minutes from where we go to school."

"Perfect," Nina said. "You'll know your way around."

Lila threw her hands up in a mixture of concession and exasperation, not even trying to salvage her nails anymore. Nina turned to Lindsey and me with her *Look, guys, we got her* face all alight, but we both looked down at the gray carpet that used to be white.

I remember every detail of that night. What we were all wearing. How far down the curtains fell on the windows. Which lamps were on. I don't know if this means that, even then, I knew the prank we were about to pull wouldn't end well, that it would be the thing to end the prank war, which, though I never would have admitted it to Nina, or even Lila and Lindsey, I might've welcomed, if everything else didn't end along with it. Only one detail has changed in my memory of it. Something that was still true then, I just didn't understand it yet.

Lindsey was right. Lila wasn't trying to protect Max. She was trying to protect Nina. I think as oblivious as she pretended to be, she knew how much Nina loved Max—she knew because she knew what it looked like when Nina loved someone. She knew better than anyone. And as much as she hated the prank war, and maybe even Nina for inventing it, she didn't want Nina to lose the one thing she wanted the most any more than the rest of us did.

"We go next Saturday," Nina said.

. . .

O kay, so the million-dollar question," said Lindsey, looking around at us expectantly, like she couldn't believe no one else had thought to ask it.

"Yeah?" Decker asked.

"Why did you get your big break just in time? You think about it a lot, clearly. So what have you come up with? The timing's pretty crazy, right? So were you just, like, meant to be a movie star? Is that how it works?"

"Well, it's not karma."

"How do you know that?" I asked.

"I used to cheat. At Seven Up."

He was comically stoic when he said this. We let a moment pass to give his face a chance to collapse into a Gotcha! smile, but he didn't.

"What the hell is that?" Nina asked.

"You guys didn't play Seven Up? Maybe that's why all the crazy stuff happens here?"

"What do you mean, 'crazy stuff'?" I was surprised by the edge in my voice. No one had to convince me that Florida was a strange, maybe even slightly off, place that saw things other places didn't, but it was still mine. It was like the sticky, annoying little sister I was always telling to get lost. But whom I would break teeth and draw blood defending on the playground if anyone tried to pick a fight with her.

"Isn't this the state where the Scientologists gather?" Decker asked, oblivious. "In Clearwater?"

"You're the movie star, you would know."

He gave Nina a stern-teacher face for that, looking down his nose at her—if he was wearing glasses, they'd have slipped over the bridge—but he didn't abandon his tirade.

"And the recount thing. And I once read that the black market for illegal animals is the third-highest-grossing industry in Florida. Like, more people smuggle in illegal exotic animals than drugs. Those Burmese pythons that are big enough to kill alligators—you guys saw the YouTube video, right? They're not natural to Florida. Someone *brought* them here."

"So?" I asked, trying not to sound defensive now. Like I really just wanted to know why it mattered. Jay was obsessed with that video. It really was terrifying.

"So I think you guys would all mellow out if you brought Seven Up to the state. It's, like, my best memory of the first grade."

"What's so great about it?" I asked.

He shook his head solemnly.

"As with all perfect things, it's difficult to say."

"Okay, so what are the rules?" Lindsey asked. "Do you remember those, at least?"

He sighed and leaned forward—settling into the impossible task ahead of him—and we all automatically did the same.

"There are seven people picked to be 'it,' but when you're it in this game, it's a good thing. Not like being it in tag or hide-and-seek or whatever. And everyone who isn't it puts their heads down on their desks to cover their eyes. And each of the seven its taps someone's head. And then everyone sits back up, and the people who were tapped try to guess who tapped them. And if you guess right, you get to be it, and tap in the next round, and whoever tapped you has to sit down."

"That's it?" Nina asked, looking at me and Lindsey to see if we got it.

"How in the world would you cheat in that game?" Lindsey asked, probably mostly just to cover Nina's underwhelmed response.

"I would cross my arms on my desk when I put my head down, and they'd be half off the desk, and I'd only shut my eyes ninety-nine percent of the way, so I could see the shoes of the person who tapped me. So I guessed right every time, and I was it more than anybody else in the class. I became, like, a Seven Up legend. And people tapped me all the time, because they wanted to try to be the one to elude my master guess. And I felt so guilty, because I didn't deserve it."

"And you think that's why you have bad karma?" Lindsey asked.

"Yeah."

"There are kids who, like, torture animals. All kids cheat, or lie. All the time. Just to see if they can."

"I don't know, we took the game pretty seriously. Kids would routinely cry and shit. Because they weren't picked enough, or because they always guessed wrong. It doesn't matter, though, because my reign came to an end."

"How'd that happen?" Nina asked. "The method seems pretty foolproof."

"I guessed correctly this one time, as always. And got up to take my place as one of the its, and the teacher was like, 'No, sit down. You were peeking. Adam gets to stay up and tap someone else. And next time, Matt, make sure your eyes are all the way closed.'"

We all groaned in empathetic horror.

"Ad-am!" Lindsey said in mock dismay at the boy who had blown his cover.

"Brutal!" I said.

"Yeah," he said. "At the time it was pretty much the worst thing that had ever happened to me."

"And you think that gives you bad karma?" Lindsey asked.

"Yeah." He shrugged. "I cheated."

"Dude, that teacher has bad karma," she said. "She humiliated a seven-year-old in front of a room full of people. She couldn't have let you go up and then taken you aside and told you to knock it off later?"

"Yeah, I thought about that. Years after it happened, like out of the blue, it hit me—that she must have known for weeks before that that I was cheating, and didn't say anything. And she was probably just having a bad day and decided to take it out on me. She could've put a stop to it long before then."

He paused for a sip of bourbon and to think about it.

"You wanna know the really crazy thing about it?"

We all answered at the same time.

"Of course."

"Duh."

"Naturally."

"Blush magazine interviewed her. A few years ago, because she was my teacher. They billed her as my favorite teacher, and she talked about what a good kid I had been."

"Yikes," Lindsey said.

"Yeah. See what I mean? Bullshit. Even when they get it right—like that she was my teacher—they get it wrong."

"Well, the good news is you're fine either way," said Nina. "Your karma is determined by what you did in your past lives, not what you do in this life. Maybe you donated your trust fund to cancer research in your past life. Maybe that's what you have to do to be a movie star in your next life."

Nina had been a Buddhist for all of two months in the seventh grade. She had never been above adopting theories that served her own life, no matter how exotic or outdated or rare they were in our part of the world.

"I'm not an authority on much, but as someone who's met more movie stars than the rest of you, I'm going to go ahead and call it doubtful. And I hope your karma theory is wrong, because I shudder to think where that would put me in my next life."

No one spoke for a moment while we all did a silent tally of where what we'd done in the last decade or so would get us cosmically. It wasn't looking so hot for any of us.

"Either way," Decker finally said, "I don't think you change."

"What do you mean?" I asked.

"Like, across life. Or *lives*," he said, looking at Nina. "You can be shaped, but the color of the clay isn't gonna change."

"Good line!" said Lindsey. "Did you just think of that?"

"It's from *Tango at Noon*," said Nina, before she could stop herself.

"Nice," said Decker, looking genuinely flattered that she knew this. "But you're missing the point."

"Which is?"

"I think the fact that I cheated then probably says something about me now. Like, given the chance, I would cheat again."

No one said anything. Lindsey and I looked over at Nina. We couldn't tell if this was his way of saying he would cheat on Abby if Nina gave him the chance, and we wanted to see what she made of it. He started talking again before any conclusion could be reached.

"It's not just me. I remember the first time I went home with Abby. You guys think *you're* from the sticks—"

"Um, did we say that?" asked Lindsey.

"She's from keep-your-money-under-the-mattress Tennessee," he went on, undeterred. "Her mom's house was tiny. And it was just covered in pictures of Abby from when she was in pageants as a kid. She has a brother and a sister, and I don't think I saw a single picture of them."

He took another bourbon break, eyeing us over the rim of the glass to make sure we were getting it all.

"I mean, we obviously want to know anything you want to tell us about her. Because she's your girlfriend, not because she's famous," Lindsey clarified, looking at Nina evenly. "But what does this have to do with cheating?"

He was so eager to get to the punch line—to show us that there was one—that he slammed his glass down with more force than I think he intended.

"So she has the exact same stance—her feet turn out at the exact same angle—in *every* picture. And it's the same *Look how pretty I am and I don't even care* pose she uses now. And it's like, her mom was saving pennies to buy her inappropriate sparkly pants back then, and now designers beg her to wear their clothes, and the position she uses to show them off is the *exact same*."

Silence descended on the table as we all pictured seven-year-old Abby Madison in sparkly pants. I pictured all the worn T-shirts Jay had had since before we met that he refused to throw away. He claimed they were "part of his story."

"Yeah," said Nina, nodding grimly, playing an Abby Madison reel in her head. "I know the one."

"And her eye makeup!" he said. "She does this raccoon-eye thing. Smoldering eye—"

"Smoky eye," Nina said.

"Whatever. And I know everybody does it now, but she must've been the first one. She must've like, *invented* it. Because she had that, too, in the pageant pictures."

"Dude, the smoky eye is *hot*," I said. "I don't think most guys would complain."

That was a lie. When I was a junior, my mom and I drove two hours to Saint Petersburg to be in my mom's second cousin's wedding. I had met her only once, but they wanted someone young and in the family to do the second reading, and that left only me. Because I was in the wedding I got to get my hair done in the salon of the four-star hotel, and they had copies of *Vogue* instead of *Blush* and *Kiss*. When I got home, I tried to copy the eye makeup I saw on almost every page of those magazines. Jay had laughed when he walked up to meet me, before he realized that I wasn't joking, that it wasn't some stunt Nina had put me up to.

"I guess it's fine every once in a while," said Decker. "But she can barely go to the gym without it, and her eyes are her most interesting feature. Like, sometimes I don't get it, how someone who watches as much VH1 as she does can pull off the roles she does. But the, like, three times I've seen her without all that shit on her face I get it. They have secrets, those eyes."

"You make her sound like Meryl Streep," said Nina. "Or Gandhi."

Decker shrugged again. "She's a better actor than me."

"Let's play a game!" said Lindsey, trying to lighten the mood.

"Seven Up, anyone?" said Nina in the cheeseball voice we used to illustrate just how idiotic adults could be. She swung her arm all jolly-hey-ho-go-get-'em, punching Decker at the end. She looked like a little Italian elf. If I didn't know her, I would've found it adorable.

"We don't have enough people," said Decker.

"Dude, I'm obviously kidding. Never Have I Ever?"

"Oh, man, I *hate* that game. I've never understood the human impulse to tattle on yourself. To, like, *advertise* the things that no sane human being would ever willingly admit. I guess I played when I was younger. Maybe that's how you know you're old. When you decide to let your secrets be secrets, and you don't feel the need to brag about them."

"No," I said. "I think that's how you know you're really famous."

"It's okay," said Nina. "We've done things we're not proud of, either."

· · ·

There were no buses this time. Nina saw to that. We had agreed to meet at the flagpole in front of the school—a place we had never met before, not wanting to be in sight of the drab, dread-inducing school building, but which Nina assured us would be perfect. But five minutes after the appointed time, Lindsey, Lila, and I stood in a small circle around the pole, facing one another, and there was still no sign of Nina. She had been able to talk of nothing else but this very moment since the date for Max's prank had been set, so while she was generally the likeliest candidate for tardiness, we couldn't believe she wasn't there, ready to go.

"Dude, it's a good thing she's *not* here yet," Lindsey said, nodding at the day school logo across the chest of Lila's sweatshirt. "You had to wear that on her night?"

"It's the only black thing I own," Lila said, her body language a sigh. "And even if it wasn't, it's not like it's her *birthday*. We're doing her a favor here."

"I don't think she's gonna see it that way."

"You guys," I said, glad to have a reason to distract them. "Isn't that Jeremy Piker's car?"

They looked across the street to where I had nodded. Nina waited until the exact minute she had the attention of all six of our eyes before she popped up in the front seat.

"Bitches!" she called, not even trying to keep her voice down, even though she had insisted we all wear black and avoid any distinct jewelry or accessories, to call as little attention to ourselves as possible. "We're going in style."

"Dude, what did you have to do to get Jeremy to hand his car over?" I asked.

"You don't want to know."

Nina had been making herself comfortable behind other people's driver's seats since we were thirteen. You could track her love life by whose car it was she convinced you to drive down the block with her in during any given week, but we rarely left the neighborhood, and the cars' owners were never far away. In fact, those owners were very often the people she was showing off for.

"Nina, you're not sixteen," Lila said.

"Yeah, but I'm not ten, either. Besides, you guys ride with me all the time."

"Not on the highway."

No one said anything for a minute, and I had a small surge of hope adrenaline at the possibility that we might get out of it.

"I guess it beats the bus," Lindsey finally said, walking toward the car. Lila and I fell in line behind her and we all climbed in, Lila in the front seat.

"Do you know how many laws we're breaking?" Lila grumbled, buckling her seat belt.

"I don't know," Nina said. "You're the one wearing the Day sweatshirt. We don't have AP government."

"Jesus, do you just want me to take it off? Why doesn't anybody give Max shit? He goes there, too."

"Oh, relax, Lilac. It's when we don't tease you that you'll know you have a problem."

We all did relax a little when Nina used her old nickname for Lila.

"Fine," said Lila, a little less pouty. "But can you at least tell us what the prank is?"

Lila had been asking questions about the plan all week, but Nina had revealed exactly nothing.

"It's a surprise. Just trust me."

"That's the problem," said Lila. "I don't. I'm sorry, Neen. But I don't."

She may as well have slapped her. The silence that fell in the car wouldn't have been any more charged if she had. Lindsey clamped her right pointer finger over my left pinkie—an involuntary gasp of a gesture—the only acknowledgment anyone made of what had just happened. We waited for Nina to argue with her, but she only turned to give me and Lindsey her scariest *What the fuck?* look, which didn't help anything, because we were already on the road, and we all would have preferred Nina keep her attention on it.

"You can be as pissed as you want, Neen. But this is it. Last chance, or I walk home at the next stoplight."

"You've really gotten really uptight, you know that?"

Lila unbuckled her seat belt.

"Okay, fine. Food coloring. We're going to put food coloring in the pool."

Lila didn't rebuckle, but she did turn back to Nina to give her her full attention.

"Go on."

"I bought about a million little bottles of green food coloring. And about a hundred rubber snakes. And a blow-up alligator on top. If Max likes that swamp pool so much, we're going to give him one."

"Um, Neen?" said Lindsey tentatively from the back, like she was a schoolteacher talking to the slow student in her class at the end of a long day—good-natured, but fraying. "Isn't it also going to take us hours to put in enough of those little food-coloring vials to change an entire pool? I wasn't anticipating an all-nighter."

"Yeah, and what if it fucks up their pool?" I asked. "I could see the woman who raised Max being, like, meticulous about the shit she puts in there. And the, like, chemical levels or whatever."

We were getting bolder in our objections, now that it was clear that none of us were alone in them.

Lindsey and I sat waiting for Lila to lodge her own complaint. Lila had loved that swamp as much as Max did. Apparently Nina was waiting for it, too, because she kept looking over at her.

"Actually, I like it," said Lila.

I sagged into the back of my seat at almost exactly the same time Lindsey did. We were going to have to go through with it.

"It's simple, but effective. And it's outside, which is good." It was more than that, we knew. The prank was as much a nod to the swamp as anything else. An acknowledgment of how weird Max and his hobbies and passions and the strange things he gravitated toward could be, but also that they were worth celebrating in the only group activity in which Nina focused on anyone other than herself. If she really thought it was stupid, the prank war was the last forum Nina ever would've raised the swamp in. I was just surprised Lila was willing to see it that way. "And unless we screw up, no one's going to get hurt. It's harmless."

Okay, it looks like we all need another drink and I don't see my man Sal. I'm going up," Decker said. "What do you guys want?"

"I'll go," Nina said.

"Don't be an idiot. I have more money than God. Literally. I'm pretty sure I'm worth more than the Catholic Church at this point." He said this without any ego, like just the fact that it was.

He made it easy to accept his generosity.

"Dude," said Lindsey. "I mean, I know we didn't land on any one certain or rigid order of the universe or anything, but aren't you worried that he's gonna smite you when you say shit like that? Or, like, take away all your money?"

Decker thought about it for a moment before beaming a stoner's satisfied, placid grin at us.

"Nah."

"I'm not even religious," said Lindsey, "but you don't, you know, have to go looking for trouble. Or bragging or whatever. I'm pretty sure there's a commandment about humility."

"It's not even that. I was raised Episcopalian. My family goes to church on Easter and all that."

"So what the frick?" Lindsey asked, a stray curl leaping out from behind her ear for emphasis.

"I just think God has bigger things to worry about than a white guy in America with too much money."

He started to lift his glass to his mouth but stopped before he could discover that it was still empty.

"And no, there's no commandment about humility."

Lindsey shrugged.

"I mean, don't get me wrong," he said. "When it's three in the morning and I don't want my delayed flight to be canceled, or I'm down by one point in a game of pickup basketball, I'm not above throwing up a Hail Mary, but in general I think he's done enough."

"So you're more grateful than cynical?" asked Lindsey, ever the optimist.

"So not above thanking him in, say—"

"An Oscar speech?" Nina finished for me in a playful, sing-songy voice that was the adult equivalent of pushing him on the playground.

"Very funny," he said, eyes roaming the crowd for Sal now.

Nina started the chant, but Lindsey and I were quick to pick it up.

"Os-car SPEECH! Os-car SPEECH!"

Carine and the patterns looked over along with the rest of the bar. Nina made the finger at them with one hand and then pantomimed that she was crushing it violently with the other one.

"I mean, sure," Decker finally conceded, turning back to us abruptly. "I would thank God."

Our chant turned into wild, encouraging applause. He gifted us a tight, irritated smile, like, *Okay, good one, guys, move along.*

We didn't stop. He sighed like the kind of prissy girl Nina ate for breakfast.

"Okay, fine. And my mom."

More applause.

"And the guy who invented the In-N-Out Burger, because you know I'm gonna have to go there after I win."

Our applause mounted.

"Don't forget Jack Alfonso!" Nina shouted with her whole body, gleeful.

"Love that frickin' guy!" Decker shouted, finally giving himself over to the spirit of the game. He was on a roll now.

"And the kid who sat behind me on the bus who showed me my first Victoria's Secret catalog. I knew I was going to have to go big to get a girl like that."

"Well, maybe don't say that," I said.

But we kept cheering anyway.

"Don't forget Abby Madison!" Lindsey shouted.

"Eh . . . Okay, fine. Stacy Berliner!"

This was followed by applause and hollering so loud that Sal finally waddled over from the corner of the bar he'd been ignoring us from. When he saw that we were all smiling and that no one else seemed to care, he only waved his hand in dismissal and turned around.

"To My Man Sal!!!" Decker shouted at his back, banging his fist on the table for emphasis on every word.

We banged our own fists on the table in approval and whooped.

We had dedicated ourselves so completely to the task of creating celebratory noise that we didn't notice him stand up slowly, as if rising for the Pledge of Allegiance. I'm not sure if it was the alcohol, or if he was just that swept up in the moment, but his eyes were shining. "To the nights you don't go to bed, and the people who keep you up." He nodded down at us. "To the friends you've known forever, and the enemies you share who only make you closer." He raised his eyebrows suggestively, but even having reached this level of spectacle, and without having exchanged a single word with any of them, he knew better, by then, than to acknowledge Carine and the patterns with a look in their direction. "To the girls whose hooks you just can't get out of you"—here he patted the breast pocket where he kept his cell phone—"and the hometowns you talk about even hundreds of miles away from them. To the haunts you go back to again and again, and the ones you never return to. And to the people who offer you a bed and a meal and good conversation when you're only passing through to somewhere else."

We stayed quiet for a moment after he finished, in case there was more, even though he had pretty much covered everything by then. Then we waited for him to reach the punch line, or laugh to break the less playful tone he had wandered into, and to reassure us it was all part of the joke. We all realized he was serious at the exact same moment, and started clapping as one, and the smile he gave us then was more than enough to reward this bit of good timing. We could have listed half a dozen different smiles that Sam Decker called upon in his acting, complicated blends signaling several simultaneous emotions, but this one was easy. The simplest kind of smile. He was happy.

"Now we just need to win you an Oscar," Nina said.

"Nah," he said, batting the idea away with his hand.

"Or at the very least a fresh drink," I said.

"I'm on it," said Nina, standing up. This time he let her go.

"But, dude, awkward fact," said Lindsey, leaning in toward him like she was about to divulge a secret. "We don't have a bed for you. That booth is just for Bobby."

He laid his head on her shoulder for a second and they laughed into each other.

"I think just the beers and the good conversation will do it."

"Look, I'm obviously in for another round, and this is great, but there are better bars in Orlando," I said, trying to snap them out of the sleepy contentment they seemed to be settling into.

"Dude, what are you *talking* about?" asked Lindsey. "The Shamrock is the balls. We come here every weekend."

I had never lobbied to leave the Shamrock before, but I suddenly wanted everything to match the electric buzz that Decker's presence had created at our table, and in our lives. The friendly, chatty exchange of information that our conversation had been up until that point now felt like a waste of the opportunity we had been presented with. Maybe I had reached the point of drunkenness where you talk just to hear yourself and reckless ideas take shape, but it occurred to me that if even a movie star joining our table couldn't change the routines and settings of our Saturday night, maybe we were doomed to a life where nothing ever changes. Not the scenery or the seasons or the things you did to pass the hours, no matter who you passed them with. The suggestion in Decker's speech that the Shamrock was a place we would return to in an endless cycle seemed to cement that it was.

"I just mean, you know, Orlando also has bars you can't wear T-shirts to, with, like, doormen and ten-dollar drinks," I said.

Lindsey looked down at her T-shirt. I hadn't thought about the fact that she was wearing it when I suggested we roam.

"What?" I asked sheepishly, even though no one had said anything. "Those drinks are delicious."

We had been drinking watery, two-dollar beers all night. The idea of ten-dollar drinks with fruit flavors sounded ridiculous even to me. "I just don't think it would kill us to try something new," I said.

"I hear you on that," Decker said. "But if you want a new or novel experience, there are other things we could try."

"Gross," said Lindsey.

"Dude, don't be a pervert," he said, smiling like a pervert was the most charming concept he'd come across in a while. "That's not what I meant."

"What are we talking about?" Nina asked, bending to drop off the four beers she was expertly managing.

"Switching bars," Lindsey said.

"We just got more drinks!"

"You know these will be gone in no time," I said.

"No, I like this one," Decker said. "You know I like this one."

"But you might like other bars here, too," I said. "For all you know, Orlando's bar scene is, like, far and away better than L.A.'s, and you've been missing out all these years, and the chance to see what you've been missing out on is finally here, and you're still missing it."

"Dude, your FOMO is *really* starting to get out of control," Nina said.

"What's FOMO?" Decker asked.

"Fear of missing out," Lindsey and Nina said at the same time, both looking at me.

"Jesus!" I said.

"Whatever," said Decker. "I'm staying here. But you know what we could do?"

"What?" Lindsey asked.

"*This* is what I was talking about before," he answered, making pointed eye contact at her. "When you were being a pervert."

"Okay, I'm listening."

"We could bring a little more of Orlando to us."

"What, like kids running around with sticky fingers from twelve-dollar lollipops, chasing around middle-aged men in cartoon costumes?" Nina asked.

"Yeah," I said. "And the ocean's a good hour away."

"No, I was thinking we could take the party up a notch."

"This is what, like *seven*?" said Lindsey, holding up her new beer. "What did you have in mind?"

"Something a little harder."

"What, like pot?" Nina asked. "I might have a little in my glove compartment."

"You're getting closer . . ."

"Ha! That could mean so many things," said Lindsey. "None of which we can help you with."

"Yeah," I said, relieved that Lindsey had shut down that line of inquiry so Nina and I didn't have to. "You're talking to some honor-roll, most-likely-to-succeed *ladies* here."

"Wait, really?"

"No, but thank you for that," I said.

"I mean, if you want I could make some calls," said Nina, ever determined to be in the know, even after Lindsey had gotten us off the hook.

"Don't worry about it," he said. "Who needs it, right?"

The magazines that taught us the things we knew about Sam Decker had changed more than just what sort of person's face became as familiar to us as the faces of our family members and loved ones, and what we thought about in the minutes before we went to sleep, and how many movies we went to go see each month. The people in those magazines were captured doing the most ordinary things—things like getting manicures and eating fast food, biking with friends and going for runs. It made us feel they weren't so different than us, which was, of course, ridiculous. They were movie stars. But in our minds, in the streams of consciousness we kept even from one another, if they were like us, then we were like them, susceptible to the eyes of the world at any moment. I used to walk down the street sometimes with five-dollar sunglasses on, waiting for the world to marvel at how normal I was.

Those magazines changed the size of the handbags we carried, and the angle at which we tilted our heads up to invisible cameras not following us. They made us think that our lives might be worth watching, because the lives that we watched weren't so terribly different from our own. They made us think that people like Sam Decker would want to be friends with us, because we had so much in common—we loved dogs and playing in the park, too. Once, when we passed a girl who was wearing cowboy boots with cutoff shorts and oversized sunglasses, who was letting her roots grow out to show the dark brown hair she had started with in a way that only a *Rumor* or *Kiss* reader would know to credit as fashionable, Nina said, "*Someone's* been reading a few too many trashy rags," but the truth was we all had, and the same thing could be said about any one of our outfits or hairstyles, the expressions that we used, and the postures that our bodies fell into at rest.

I wonder now if those magazines weren't also part of what made me want more than I had—why I couldn't shake the image of that snowy field, or that calm, waveless lake—and why I was so maniacally unsatisfied with the things I did have. Jay was good and handsome by almost every standard. It was those magazines that made me believe our small town wasn't the insular small town of movies and shows, but just one of countless places to leave from or arrive at in the comings and goings happening everywhere, on every one of those magazine pages. Any given issue might have pictures of a single star in both London and Dubai. It also took the mystery out of where these people were from and who they had been before they were the center of the glossies. I imagine it was possible to believe that Audrey Hepburn was born on the set of *Breakfast at Tiffany's*, but there was no forgetting that Allison Cash was from Denver or that Mimi Peterson was from Detroit—our magazines had pictures of them in these places at least once a year, or the recipe for their mother's stuffing, which they still made every Thanksgiving. It felt like everyone was only ever one eyeblink away from being somewhere else—somewhere even more glamorous and charming, where they would smile even wider. It felt like we were all one reality show or contest away from joining the faces on these pages, and this made us wish for things it might never have occurred to us to want otherwise.

Or maybe just me.

We stopped reading those magazines a few months after the night we met Sam Decker. Maybe it was because nothing ever felt as real as it did to us when he was sitting across the bar from us. Maybe it was because he had discounted them. Maybe it was because, as kind as he was to us, as humane and human as he was, it was apparent, too, how different he was. The magnetic force of the room changed when he entered it—we felt people's bodies turn toward him, even if they couldn't have told you why, opening up and inviting him in the way that no room had ever opened for us.

I like to think it was also partly because there was a hole in those magazines where Sam Decker's picture used to appear—there was not enough magic in Hollywood after he left. But I think it is at least as much because it showed once and for all that for all the golf he played with his father on Father's Day, and as many times as he was seen having to go through the airport security line that plagues us all, he did things that the housewives in Minnesota and the cheerleaders in Iowa who left the beach copies we scoured never did. He had been moving away for some time, it became apparent to us after that night, in bottles and milligrams, and long, lonely trips to the bathrooms of the restaurants we watched him step into and out of, and sleepless nights engaged in losing staring contests with the ceiling, and we had been too busy marveling at his favorite frozen yogurt toppings to notice. We preferred caramel, too. As much solidarity as we projected onto him, there were some things he did outside of sidewalk cafés and airports and red carpets and the streets of the city where he lived—things he did outside of our omniscient gaze—filling holes we thought all the hobbies and likes and habits we shared with him would fill, and that it was a lonely, sad black magic that drove him until it didn't.

The ugly reveal of how empty, in the end, those magazines were, of how easily we had been fooled, might've crushed any wanderlust they had created in me.

But I was already gone.

No one spoke the rest of the way there. We didn't realize we *were* there until Nina stopped the car. She knew exactly where to go, and I wondered if she had made a practice run by herself. I wasn't sure why the thought made me sad.

Max's house wasn't huge, but it might've been better if it had been. It was modest in size, but it was elegant and tasteful. It wasn't an assembly-line house of cheap, overnight construction, the way so many of the new condo developments were. The kind with stainless-steel appliances but plaster walls a six-year-old girl could've punched a hole in. Max's house was stone and brick, and it looked like it had been around for decades. These were people with nothing to prove. People who were accustomed to their money.

Once we realized which house was his, we were horrified that we hadn't parked farther away.

"Shouldn't we at least park behind some bushes or something?" I whispered.

"The less suspicious you act, the less suspicious people are gonna be," Nina said. "There's no reason for anyone to assume we *shouldn't* be here."

"Yeah, except this piece-of-shit car," Lindsey said. "Nobody ever intends to do anything good in a car like this, as evidenced by the fact that Jeremy Piker owns it."

"Well, we're not going to be in here for very long, anyway," Nina said, "as long as Lila did her job."

Lindsey and I, who were both leaning forward, scrunched together through the small opening between the driver and front passenger seats, turned in synchrony toward Lila. We were expecting her to demand to know why all the hard shit was always her job—why she, Nina, had only bought a couple of packs of food coloring, while Lila was expected to figure out how to break and enter—but she didn't. She looked placidly out the window, appraising the house with mild disinterest, as if it were passing scenery.

"It's gonna be even easier than you think," she said. "There's a screen door that leads directly into the screened-in porch where the pool is. We'll be able to go right through it. People who live in neighborhoods like this don't lock their doors."

And there it was. The first piece of evidence that Lila had provided for us, that we hadn't imagined, or invented to mock her with, that she was different from us. She knew what people in neighborhoods like this did.

People like us.

Lindsey and I didn't say anything, didn't dare even to look at each other, and waited for Nina to say something, to call her on it, playfully or not, but she didn't.

"So are we going or what?" Lila asked, turning to look at us.

We were girls so unversed in this sort of midnight activity that it didn't occur to us to crouch or dart between the trees or travel in the shadows any more than it had occurred to Nina not to park right in front of the house. Our bodies didn't yet know the language of illicit behavior. Our knees didn't automatically bend at the sound of twigs cracking underfoot, and our default posture wasn't a slouch to make ourselves as small as possible. We were poor, and maybe a little easy; we weren't honor students, and we would probably never work jobs with health benefits, but we weren't, until then, bad girls. We made our way out in the open, single file, like the girls from the Madeline books that our parents could never afford and made us check out of the library instead, or like we were at the mall, avoiding walking abreast so we all had equal view of the store windows. It occurs to me now that someone must have seen us—the houses in Max's neighborhood weren't very far apart—and that the way we were moving is probably what stopped them from calling someone, or trying to stop us. Girls who cause the sort of trouble we did don't arrive out in the open like that. Everyone knows it's the trouble you don't see coming that gets you.

We walked to the back of the house, to the screen door of the patio. Lila was right. It was unlocked.

"Oh, my God, this is going to save us so much time," said Nina, surveying the length of the pool. It was meant for just one family, rather than a whole row of houses like the pools we were used to, so it was smaller. "It's not going to take nearly as much dye as I thought. Though I hope getting this tarp off isn't going to be a problem." She kicked the brown piece of plastic covering the pool.

This confidence on her part didn't seem to make anyone else more eager to get started. We all just stood behind her, awaiting further instruction.

"We should divide into teams," she continued. "A dye team and a wildlife team. Someone's gotta blow up the inflatable alligator. Use as many of the rubber snakes as you can, but don't go overboard. We don't wanna clog the filters. I'm pretty sure that's the only way we can fuck the pool up."

I saw Lindsey's eyes go wide with horror at the thought.

"All right," Lila said, sticking her hands in one of the plastic bags. "Let's get started."

Suddenly, without any noise or warning, the light above the door that led from the house to the porch went on. Everyone froze.

"Shit! Nina, I'm sorry, but this is too much," said Lindsey, her hands up in surrender. "I was game to give it a try, even though this is *crazy*, but someone is clearly awake, and home, and we're *definitely* going to get caught. This is stupid."

Nina looked at her expectantly, as if awaiting a translation of what she had just said.

"I'm waiting in the car."

A small dog came leaping out of a doggie door I hadn't no-ticed until its owner filled it, distracting from Lindsey's grand exit. From the perk of his ears and the bounce in his posture, it seemed he was there to play. He'd never encountered an intruder in his life, but his welcome was a noisy one. Four joyful little yaps.

"Okay, I'm out, too," I said. "If this thing keeps yapping, every person in that house is going to be out here before you get through the first bottle of dye. There's no way we're gonna pull this off."

When the door to the house opened, we all ducked behind the patio furniture closest to the screen door, getting the dog even more excited. He thought we were doing it for his bene-fit. Whoever opened the door didn't walk out onto the patio, only called through the narrow gap he had cracked it.

"Bruiser! Quiet!" It was a male voice, agitated. He said it like he assumed that the dog was barking at nothing, and I felt a little bad that the dog was being reprimanded for doing his job. When Bruiser—a name he must have been given ironically—barked again, the voice demanded he come inside, and he com-plied. I waited until he had gotten through his doggie door before I turned to go.

"Wait! What are you doing?" whispered Nina.

I looked to Lila for help.

"I told you, I'm going! We haven't even started and it's a disaster!"

"But he left!"

"You're delusional. We gave it a try, and it's not going to work. We can try something else. Later."

We both looked at Lila.

"Are you going, too?" Nina asked.

Lila didn't say anything for a full ten seconds, not looking at either of us. It was an active concentration—it looked like she was solving an equation in her head rather than zoning out. Finally, she let out a loud, irritated sigh, and Nina, knowing what this meant, raised her hands in silent victory.

"I knew it!" Nina said. "You're the best."

"I'm on their side, for the record," I heard Lila say as I started crawling for the door. "I just know that if I leave you alone out here you're going to destroy the place."

I don't want to be an artist or a jewelry maker or a singer. I don't paint or build furniture or write poetry. I don't have a head for numbers. I want to work at a souvenir store in the Grand Canyon or be a waitress in a coffee shop in Seattle. I want to rent a trailer in Austin and drive it to L.A., and eat pie in every city along the way. I am not unhappy being poor.

I've been friends with exactly one nerd in my life: Trevor Jenkins. But I use the term loosely. *Friends*, not *nerd*—Trevor Jenkins was definitely a nerd. Some overworked secretary in our scheduling office accidentally put me in college-prep chem lab junior year, and by the time I realized the mistake all the other classes were full. It turns out there are plenty of students at our school who wanted to take regular, don't-pull-a-muscle science classes, but not that many who want to take college prep, which was, by the way, as high as it got there. There were no honors or AP-level classes offered in any of the subjects.

When I walked into class that first day, three of the four tables were full of the twelve kids who traveled in one hive. Whose lives weren't even that much lonelier on account of their being smart, because there were just enough of them to establish their own hierarchy. So they didn't have to bother with the larger, school-wide hierarchy, which they sat at the very bottom of. There is something unnerving about an obese or acne-riddled sixteen-year-old without any immediately detectable insecurity issues, and this, too, they used in their favor. It felt, sometimes, like they were waiting for you to put them down in some subtle way—maybe not even intentionally—so they could make it clear what they thought of the kind of person who would judge someone as gifted as them on superficial criteria. Trevor sat all by himself at the fourth table.

He was watching an episode of *The Sopranos* on his iPhone without making even the smallest effort to conceal it. Everyone at our school used their phones when they weren't supposed to, but everyone had their own particular method for not drawing any attention to themselves by doing so. Some people wore hooded sweatshirts with hand pockets sewn onto the stomach, in order to store their devices there. Some people slid them in between notebooks, while the least motivated students (including Nina) cut out pages of their textbooks for convenient electronics storage. When I walked up to Trevor and asked if anyone else was sitting at the table, he shushed me, not looking up from his phone, making it even more obvious what he was doing and how little he cared. Already feeling defeated by the fact that there would be only two of us working toward answers most tables would have four people collaborating on, the very real possibility that this class would stand in between me and a high school diploma felt more real still.

"I guess it'll just be us, then? I wonder if they'd rather we both go join other tables? If, like, they prefer groups of five to groups of two?"

"I doubt they give a shit," he said, still not looking up. "Our teacher didn't even bother to show up. He just left copies of this problem set, which is a joke. I already did the first half. I left the second half for you."

He slid the paper across the lab table toward me, still looking at the phone.

"So if there isn't any teacher coming, why are they still here?" I asked, looking at the table closest to us.

"Because they're idiots."

"So why are you still here?"

"I'm just finishing the episode."

"Is Adriana dead yet in the episode you're watching?"

This, finally, made him look up.

"Yes, but what if she hadn't been?"

"I just wanted to make sure you had eyes," I said. Which only made him look back down at the screen.

"Just do the second half of the problem set. We're supposed to turn it in on Monday."

I meant to at least attempt my half of the problem set, I really did. The weekend sometimes just has its own trajectory, along which the plans you had feel utterly inconceivable when it comes time to execute them. And as the weekend pulls you pleasantly along the current it's set on, you can't imagine what you were thinking when you made the plans you did, and then, suddenly, come Monday morning, you're just as confused as to why you didn't do whatever you were supposed to when you had the chance. It's as close to a double life as normal, average people ever come. It's not that I *forgot* about the problems while I was walking the stray puppy Nina had found that week and hid from her mother for two full weeks before driving it three and a half hours to the closest no-kill shelter, or making pot brownies with Lindsey when this idiot twelve-year-old on her street told her he would give her two hundred dollars for a batch, or paying for one movie and then sneaking into a second and third with them both, sitting in the theater long enough to actually need a refill on the unthinkably large tub of popcorn, a second helping of which is normally outside the realm of human possibility. It was always in the back of my mind, making everything less fun, and by the time the sun set on Sunday, I was nearly immobile from panic. But even then, wanting desperately to solve the problems, I knew I'd have no idea what to do first if I did go all the way upstairs to my bedroom and take the time to unzip my book bag and open the folder where I had stashed them. Trying to save myself from that empty feeling I knew I would have when I saw those problems staring blankly up at me, like a pervert on a playground, I never took them out. And I voluntarily went to bed, an accomplice to the atrocity that not doing anything would make my Monday.

It was the first time I was ever early to class. I thought if I could be there, ready to explain what happened before Trevor had time to settle himself, he would be doing other things while I was talking and might not hear how empty whatever I had to say was. At first I thought it was working. He didn't seem concerned enough to look up from the backpack he was unzipping—probably to get out his phone to watch another episode of *The Sopranos*—until I got to "which is why I didn't do my half of the set." And then, like the weapon used for the last mob hit you ever saw coming, a look crossed his face and then disappeared so quickly that it took a moment to process, but I saw it: He was physically elated at the fact that he had more problems to do. And even though he went on to tell me what an idiot I had to be to not be able to do the first day's homework for a class like that, and asked me if I knew what the word for a female idiot is, I liked him. Because he hadn't left the second half of the problems to make my life more difficult or even because he wanted to get back to his show. But because he thought I might like to do them.

"Give me the sheet," he said.

I wordlessly complied, and after three minutes of attention more rapt than even what he had shown Tony Soprano, the sheet was finished.

I never saw him outside of the classroom, never mind the building, but after that, I considered him a friend, if only because we both gave the other something they wanted. He got to have an entire lab table's worth of homework all to himself, and I got my only A in the only college-prep class I ever took in high school. I have no idea where he landed after we graduated. If he's the brightest burger flipper in the country, or if he's one step closer to cutting into people's brains or curing autism. But I think about him often, because he taught me that it wasn't just my short attention span and my addiction to MTV years after everyone else had stopped watching it that conspired in the low

B's and high C's and even the stray D's that marched across my report card. I saw something in Trevor Jenkins's eyes when I handed him that unfinished set of problems that I had never felt. For numbers or language or anything you can find on the periodic table. And I had to see what people were really capable of before I could truly embrace my own limits.

Which is fine by me. I just don't want to live in central Florida anymore.

Back at the car, Lindsey and I buzzed with the kind of relief you feel physically in response to getting out of the most hopeless situations—when a blizzard closes the school on the day of a midterm you didn't study for or your lab partner proves a genius; when your dentist decides the cavity he had you come back in to have filled isn't bad enough, on closer inspection, to require drilling; a sealer will be enough. The kind of small miracle that happens only a handful of times in a life. I felt the endorphins of a runner's high. I hadn't realized how much I'd been dreading the prank until I didn't have to do it anymore. The ease with which we'd absented ourselves—it had taken only a single phrase, and Nina hadn't even been mad—made every problem seem solvable, and made it clear that it had only been our mishandling of the situation that made it a problem in the first place. All we had had to do was say "no," a word we were going to have to use more often. And the solidarity with which Lila and Nina had stayed was like watching your parents who were on the brink of divorce share a tender moment— hands clasped across a white-tablecloth dinner, or a shoulder massage at the end of a long day. And of course, things always seem less dire when they're happening to other people. When we had been in on the plan, it had felt like breaking and entering. Now that we were safely off Max's property, we saw that it was really only a little bit of ink. Everything, we were suddenly sure, was going to be fine.

We didn't talk about any of this in the car, of course. We were teenage girls. We talked about the liquid earwax that was always flowing freely out of Garrett Henchler's left ear, and whether he and his best friend, Aaron, were concocting a substance that looked like earwax or if it was real. The pride with which they went pointing out the problem and the fact that Garrett was a perfect physical specimen in every other way made us certain it was fake, but we couldn't decide why they would spend so much time and energy on something that would make them less appealing. When that ended in a draw, we took up whether Jenna Lipman's mom was sleeping with Tommy Clooser's dad, which is what everyone claimed, and how awkward it would be if they had to move in with each other, since they'd been dry humping in the supply closet in the school gym for months by then.

I was just about to tease the limits of my new good fortune with a yawn, and by wondering out loud what was taking them so long, when Lindsey's face changed. She was looking out the window I was leaning against, the one closest to the curb outside Max's house. It was the look on the horror-movie heroine's face when she spots the killer behind the person she's talking to.

"Oh, fuck."

Four

B obby must have had less caffeine than normal that day, because Sal came back to our booth after what couldn't have been more than a single inning. "Okay, girls, name the animal that went extinct almost exactly a hundred years ago, and in which museum the body of the last one is currently on display."

This was our favorite part of the night.

"The passenger pigeon, in the Smithsonian. Her name is Martha," said Decker, before we could even gather our heads and begin the long think-tank process of coming nowhere near the right answer.

"Gross, they gave her a *name*," Lindsey said. "Why does that make it seem more morbid?"

"I guess I should tell my brother he's got to get his kids watching that Mickey Mouse show you were on, huh?" Sal said, clearly more impressed than he was disappointed at having been unable to stump the table.

"You have nieces and nephews?" Nina asked, incredulous.

"Yeah, why?"

"I don't know. I guess it's just weird to think of you with brothers and sisters. I've always kind of assumed you came out of the womb as a fully grown man."

"You're out of luck," I said, to avoid having to think of Sal covered in amniotic fluid. "It's been years since that show was on."

"Eh. It's fine," he said. "Those kids watch too much TV anyway. They're worthless."

"I knew there was a reason we had never heard of them," Nina said, vindicated, as if anyone had been arguing against the strangeness of Sal having siblings.

"For you," Sal said, nodding at Decker and ignoring Nina's comment, "a drink on the house for the right answer. What're you drinking?"

"Awesome. I'll have a bourbon," Decker said with all the earnest enthusiasm he might have had if he didn't have enough money to buy his own bourbon distillery.

When Sal disappeared behind the bar to fill the order, we all turned to Decker.

"What?!" he asked.

"Dude, how did you know that?" Lindsey asked.

"When I was in D.C. to promote *White House Winter*, the curator of the Smithsonian gave me a private tour of the exhibit on extinction they were preparing before it was open to the public. So Martha and I go way back."

"But you haven't made a movie on extinction or a movie set in a museum," I said, earning another *Don't get carried away in your public display of Decker knowledge* look from Nina.

"You'd be surprised," he said. "People want to impress. I've seen blueprints for buildings that were commissioned for millions of dollars before ground was broken on them, and I've been given tours of flagship stores for brands that only sell women's clothing. I never ask. People come to me."

"No offense," Nina said. "But why do they want your opinion? You're a good actor and everything—I mean, obviously—but why would you have anything to say about dead birds and architecture?"

"You know, I've spent a lot of time thinking about that," he said. "And I think they want to show me how good they are at their jobs. Like, *Okay, you might be one of the biggest movie stars, but I've got the market cornered on geology,* or whatever the fuck you call the study of things that lived a long time ago—"

"Um, not that—" Lindsey said.

"And I'm not even saying that they like my acting—I find that as long as you say your lines correctly most people are fine with a performance, it's the critics that try to make it something more than it is. But they just trust, from all these movies I've been in, that I'm good at what I do. And they want to show me that they're good at what they do, which, I mean, in a way I respect."

"But isn't it sometimes awkward?" I asked. "When they're, like, looking at you, expecting you to see the beauty and tragedy and meaning in what is essentially roadkill, and all you see is a bird corpse?"

He looked at me like we had just figured out that we were from the same small town, or had the same distant cousin.

"You have no idea. I would far rather spend an hour with a *dying kid*—"

Lindsey and Nina drew back in horror at the prospect.

"Dude, I know, but that's part of the job, too," he said. "But that's easier for me—I leave feeling better than I do after spending an hour making some middle-aged scholar or businessman feel like his life's work isn't good enough to impress me because I'm not a good enough actor to make him believe that it does. And sometimes I don't even want to be there. I mean, that day at the Smithsonian I was exhausted. What I needed was a jar of Vaseline and some pay-per-view—"

"Gross," Nina said, making it clear that she didn't really think it was.

"And other times I feel really grateful."

"For the pigeon corpses?" Lindsey asked.

"Because I know there are people who *do* want to see these things—who have read about them or heard about them—who will never get to see them, and I'm sitting there thinking about the waitress I had at lunch who I wouldn't mind seeing naked, when I'm standing right in front of them."

He was really getting worked up now, and the pronunciation of his words had grown a little soft. The complimentary bourbon that one of Sal's waiters had dropped off was already gone.

"School was never my thing. Part of why I got into acting was that it was all I thought I was qualified for, and somehow I've managed to cobble together a first-rate education, from things that even people who go to Harvard don't have access to, and it makes me feel guilty."

"Can't you just say no?" I asked. "I mean, if you don't want to go *and* you feel bad that they're going out of their way. Can't you just save both of you the trouble?"

"I would love to. But the same eager-beaver agent who abandoned me in Orlando of all places—no offense—says I need to take advantage of every PR opportunity we're offered. He always does that—uses the plural pronoun even though he never ends up going with me. He would make me go to a Wendy's opening in Antarctica if *we* got the invite. And there are always like thirty people, tops, because the people throwing these things want to get off on how exclusive they are. Maybe Abby's right—she's been trying to get me to switch to her agent for months."

"She really is a bossy pants, huh?" Nina said. Now it was my turn to give the look to her.

"Have you ever talked to a shrink about this?" Lindsey asked. "Because I have no idea what you should do about it, but I'm pretty sure a therapist would have a field day. One of my brothers goes to a shrink, and he has a lot to say about guilt."

"Once," he said. "I spent an hour talking about how I worried I would never have a marriage as solid as my parents'."

"And?" Lindsey asked.

"And what?"

"Did it make you feel better?"

"At the end of the hour she asked for my autograph."

"No way," said Lindsey.

"Way."

"Can't you get fired for doing something like that?" I asked.

"Yeah, *imagine* the press. 'Sam Decker Gets Starstruck Therapist Fired.'"

"Yowzah," Nina said.

"Yeah, pretty much."

"What about Abby?" I asked, to another look from Nina. "I mean, she must have some experience in this, too, right?"

"No," he said, "because people like Abby like to fawn over the bird corpses. They ooh and aah and are all 'That pigeon is *so* amazing, it makes me *so* happy I practice kabbalah,' or whatever it is, 'and I just don't understand why more people don't go to see it—isn't that so *sad*,' like she's some enlightened Buddha that had his stomach stapled, and I'm like, 'No, Abby, I don't think it's sad that farmers in Iowa and teachers in Detroit aren't shitting their pants over taxidermy, and the only reason you know about it is because you're in B movies. And you'd never find these things if they weren't thrown in your face.'"

"Have you tried telling that to her?" Lindsey asked, nodding at his jacket pocket, which had started, once again, to vibrate.

We had all grown so accustomed to the Abby Madison vibrations that kept our table humming along that when I first heard the buzz of my own phone against my thigh, I assumed her buzzing was getting more invasive as her desperation grew. It took me a moment to realize it was my own phone, and that Abby Madison, who somehow still didn't know me after all this, didn't have my number.

It was a text from Jay:

WHERE U AT?

. . .

They forgot to put the tarp back on. I guess it has to be part of your plan in the first place for you to forget, which I'm not sure it was. But either way, that was their fatal mistake. Nina was four bottles of food dye in when the dog came back. Not aware of any danger—only that the dog would now surely give them away—Lila and Nina took off, and had just reached the screen door when they heard the house door open. They assumed it was the adult male who had been yelling out the door earlier. In fact, it was Max's seven-year-old sister, who walked out on the patio to find the dog she had picked out and named floundering in the water. The fact that he couldn't swim did nothing to diminish his love for the pool, which was why the tarp was there.

Max's sister jumped in to save him, but, already an unsteady swimmer, she was pulled down by the weight of her night-gown, which she wasn't used to in the pool. Her father got to her in time, but just. She spent a week in intensive care. The dog didn't fare as well. It wasn't until Max's sister was safely out of the water and whisked away in an ambulance that any-one thought to go looking for him. By then he was all the way down at the bottom of the pool. They found him sucked up against the drain.

We had no way of knowing any of this that night. When she cursed, Lindsey had only been reacting to Nina and Lila flying toward the car—running full speed from the back of the house, clearly excited, buzzing with some sort of news that Lindsey and I didn't yet know. They were both so beautiful—Lila's blond hair waving all over the place, reinforcing the chaos of the moment, Nina's young, able legs pumping high-school-track-star fast. They were giggling even as they ran out of breath, and they kept charting the other's progress as they made their way, like they were racing. Or like they didn't want to leave the other behind. The bout of giggles that each shared look sparked made it clear that they had conspired over whatever they were laughing about. I remember feeling, when I saw them, the full weight of how young we were, and that we wouldn't always be. It was one of those rare moments when you're not sitting around waiting for something to happen or reflecting back on something that already did, but simply marveling at what is. When the present, the middle child of tenses, swallows the ever-dominant past and future, and your entire life floats within a single moment. I remember thinking, *This is what it is to be young. You will tell this story later.*

They came for Nina the next morning. Nina and Lila never came face-to-face with any witnesses. Jeremy Piker swore up and down that they never asked him any questions—they didn't trace the getaway car back to him only to have him serve us up. He wasn't a particularly pleasant person—my first distinct memory of him is a sneer in reaction to his little brother wiping out on a skateboard he had lent him, and he always told everybody who would listen which girls' shirts his hands had had a chance to roam under. But he wasn't cruel—he would never, for instance, have tried to knock his brother off the skateboard, or let his hands continue roaming when the owner of the shirt asked him to stop—and he didn't care enough about us to lie to us. All of which meant, of course, one thing.

Max must have given them her name.

We understood, kind of. She was his sister—his little sister—and you don't even stay in the hospital for a whole week when you have a baby, or your appendix is taken out, which were the only other reasons we had encountered for a stay there. It was touch and go for a while. The trip to the hospital might have been the least of it. And Max loved animals. The angriest I ever saw him was when Lindsey killed a spider that was creeping on the nacho tower we were enjoying in Nina's front yard. He listed all of the ways spiders contributed to our ecosystem, and he was so obviously affected by it all that Lindsey didn't even go back to eating the nachos until he had finished, which would mean more to you if you'd ever seen her eat nachos.

What we couldn't understand was why the lone cruiser that pulled up in Nina's driveway just before dawn that Sunday didn't go on to make stops at Lindsey's house, and mine and Lila's. They wouldn't have had to go far. For days after they came for her, we kept waiting for them to come for us, but they never did. Not even to question us or confirm whatever story Nina told them. We never knew how close they were to discovering the varying degrees to which the rest of us were involved. Nina never said, even when she came back. She was remanded to the juvenile detention center where she would serve her one-year sentence less than a week after it all happened, and our parents agreed it would be better if we didn't visit her there, so she didn't really have much chance to say.

Max knew us well enough by then to know that none of us ever did much alone.

For all the trouble that night caused, on the way home from Max's house, Nina was electrified by the chase. Once we were out of the short, intersecting roads of his neighborhood and out on the open road she rolled down all the windows and blared her favorite Doors album and gave up the howl of joy that other girls in other lives give to the world upon being announced homecoming queen, or getting into college.

"That was crazy!" she said. "I thought for sure someone was going to stop us! I can't believe we got away."

"Yeah, barely," said Lila, still panting in the front seat.

"No complaints from you!" Nina said, clearly too happy to be angry. "You didn't think the doggie door was worth noting in your recon?"

"Whatever," Lila said.

"*Of course I've been to his house. He lives like five minutes from where we go to school. We go there all the time,*" Nina said in a voice that, it would have been hard to deny, sounded exactly like Lila.

Lindsey and I had nothing to add. We gave in to the music and the feel of the air on our faces just a little. We were going to make it home.

"But when you think about it, it's kind of *good* that we screwed up," Nina said, almost babbling now. "I mean, it's kind of like Max *won* this round or something. And people are always more inclined to like things they're good at, right? I can't wait to see what he comes up with for this."

She was so animated, so cheerful, so *sure* that everything would be fine that she left no room for us to doubt it. We all slept soundly that night. But that certainty was only the arrogance of youth, which lasts only as long as you can avoid seeing, a certain number of times, an adult doing something they've expressly forbid you not to—even if it is mostly harmless—like pick your nose or talk critically of someone who's just left the room. Before you've watched someone in generally good standing deliver something you know to be a lie without any hesitation, or stammer, sounding convincing even to you. Before you realize how much effect an arbitrary detail like the placement of a plastic tarp can have on the course of a life, and that the order that is projected upon the world by the people who teach you that there is one is really just for show. It's the same arrogance of youth that leads to donuts in icy parking lots and chicken fights in murky waters with rocky floors. Things that are mostly harmless except for the scattered few for whom they aren't. We couldn't tell you if what decided the category you fell into was luck or fate or good planning any more than we could have told you why Sam Decker was a movie star and we didn't have savings accounts, but we all knew—in the gut, without talking about it—that no matter how many rules you followed and how slowly you burned through your second chances, or how meticulously you'd counted the number of times you could flip a coin and have it land in your favor, everyone got slapped with the realities of life at some point—a standard new-shoe blister that turns into an infection you almost don't survive; the one-night-stand pregnancy test that reads positive; the night you enjoy too much of your favorite not-quite-legal substance that has always gotten you through in the past; or being sent away from all the people you love because of a dark sense of humor that, until the day it stops working, only ever made people like you more.

To be fair, it's the same arrogance of youth that allows for swan dives off suburban roofs into suburban pools by teenagers with bodies so beautiful even they can't quite believe them—bodies built exactly to do foolish, unsafe things like that—and for the first sip of alcohol in the back of someone's mom's car, which almost never tastes as good as you think it will, but that you go on to recall almost reverentially, with pride that you were doing exactly what you should have been doing at that age. Not according to the law, but the elusive recipe for marinating a person that comes out on the happy ground between interesting and broken. It's the arrogance of youth that would cause anyone to believe they might find success at the other end of a one-way ticket to Hollywood, giving an entire generation of girls the pleasure of their first crush, which even after it fades they'll remember for the rest of their lives and giggle about with the other old women they shared these feelings with. It is the arrogance of youth that drives most of the wild, devilish stories that make your grandchildren like you more than they like their other set of grandparents— stories that are wicked without being evil.

And it's only yours to lose once.

So what's this *Criminal Lingo* thing you're starting in three weeks?" Lindsey asked, probably trying to lighten the mood after the pigeon-corpse tirade capped by unanswered rings that carried with them the disappointment of the caller on the other end.

"Eh." He wrinkled his nose, as if the question had been accompanied by a nasty smell. "I don't really know."

"Dude," Nina said, "you've already told us everything else. You're seriously gonna draw the line here?"

"No," he said. "I just haven't read the script rewrite yet, and apparently it's totally different. Like different end and everything."

"Aren't you curious?" I asked. "What if they, like, kill off your character in the third scene now?"

"Yeah," he said. "I'm not worried about it."

"Why?"

"I'm the only name in it. It's a low-budget indie."

"Oh, Jesus," said Nina. "Like some *Blue Valentine* bullshit or something?"

Decker looked at her skeptically.

"What, you're surprised I saw *Blue Valentine?* I see *a lot* of indie movies; I just saw this one a few nights ago, which is why it was the first one that came to mind." She started to take a sip of her beer and then stopped, the thought she had too pressing to wait for a swallow. "They put all that shit on pay-per-view now so that even the peasants can watch it. And, you know, pay for it."

He laughed. "You make it sound like a conspiracy," he said. "Isn't it a *good* thing that it's easier to watch good movies?"

"Don't you mean *films?*" Lindsey asked.

Nina ignored her. "It would be if that shit was any good."

He laughed again, totally unoffended. "Okay, fine," he said, his palms up in surrender. "Tell me what the problem is with

Blue Valentine. Maybe I can go back to Hollywood as your ambassador and make some crucial fixes."

"Good," she said. "You should."

I was about to jump in and try to coax the conversation back from her before she said something truly unforgivable, but just then my phone buzzed with another text from Jay:

HEADING INTO THE CITY WITH THE GUYS. MEET UP?

I could feel Nina looking at me, pissed I wasn't giving her big moment my full attention. Only ever able to worry about one thing at a time, I ignored the text and looked back up.

"I'm waiting," Decker said.

"Okay, maybe it's not even that it's so bad, in a vacuum, but it's supposed to be this elevated, like, art film, so much better and serious and wise than those movies with little blond architects and fashion editors running around hip cities in four-hundred-dollar high heels after the beefcakes you know they're going to end up with, and those high school movies about the war between the popular kids and the nerds, but really they're all the same."

"They're not. I promise you," Decker said.

"They are."

"Okay, fine. How?" Decker asked.

"Okay, take, for example, the movie *She's All That*."

"I love that movie," Lindsey said.

"Yeah, no shit. You made us watch it like nine thousand times."

"It wasn't *that* many."

"No, I didn't even mind because that movie is really fucking good. But I remember everybody was all like, *Oh, yeah, I love how they have this gorgeous girl and they put her hair in a ponytail and put glasses on her and are like, Oh, yeah, look at how ugly this obviously gorgeous person who is always going to be the hottest person in any high school is with these terrible glasses.* Like it was such an obvious conceit. But then they do the exact same thing in *Blue Valentine*. I mean, the only thing that changed in their relationship between when it was a hipster fairy tale and when it became this screaming nightmare is that he starts wearing horrible fat-man glasses and grows bad facial hair."

Decker laughed, one sharp crack of a *Ha*, but he kept listening. He didn't even look away to take a drink, just kept running his thumb up and down the side of the bourbon glass, the up-and-down motion of a nod.

"Even when things are shit he's obviously a great dad. Funny as hell. He doesn't even get mad when she lets the dog out and gets it killed. He's still got those fucking biceps, and she looks at him like a Bible leper. And please, any man who knows how to kiss a woman the way he does when she's waiting for him outside the moving company in her adorable plaid shirt—no questions asked, right, he's just so happy to see her—still knows how to do that when he gets a little soft. Plus he's, like, obviously the best person in the movie and, what, he loses some hair and grows a bad mustache and she won't fuck him? That's why God invented the fucking razor."

Decker was shaking his head by now, but he was smiling with more teeth than he had the entire night. He was loving every word.

"And I mean, at least in *She's All That* it goes in the right direction. The, like, *hair* transformation or whatever. And the glasses swap. Plus there's that baller dance scene. But somehow that movie is simple and so transparent, but when they do it in *Blue Valentine* it's a fucking Oscar parade."

"No one won an Oscar for that movie," Decker said, his bourbon-rubbing thumb pausing in recognition of this observation.

"You know what I mean."

"Okay, but what about the end? When he goes totally apeshit and freaks out."

"Oh," she said, her maniacal politician posture deflating just a little. "I didn't see the end."

"Dude!" he said. "That's cheating! Total foul! *Technical* foul."

Decker was the only one surprised. That was just Nina, we knew, always willing to take a hard stand on a subject she came to casually, one she really didn't know that much about.

"Whatever, I got a sense of it," Nina said. "And I don't care what he did at the end, I'd still fuck him."

"Okay, what if I promise to keep the same haircut and eyewear for the entirety of this movie, and you promise to watch the end of *Blue Valentine*?"

"Eh. If I have time."

"I'm just saying, if you don't see the ending I think you might be missing the point."

"No way," said Nina. "You're missing the point. And so are those movies."

"Which is?"

"People don't change. You can put a pretty girl in glasses,

but she's still got a twenty-six-inch waist. And you can put the hero in a fat suit, but he's still a good guy."

"I don't know," I said. "I mean, I feel you on the glasses thing, but people *can* change. Like, in *theory*."

"Yeah," Decker said. "I'm with her."

"No," Nina said. "You said so yourself. You'd still cheat, all these years later, at Seven Up. And Abby still uses her pageant pose."

"Yeah," Decker conceded, unconvinced. "But by that I meant how crazy it is that those small things—habits and tics—don't change when everything else about a person does."

Nina didn't say anything, but shook her head into her beer.

"You're young," he said. "Once you've been out in the real world for a couple of years, you'll see."

I braced myself. *The real world* was a trigger phrase for Nina, and tonight was no exception.

"Jesus," she said. "I hate it when people say that. Seriously. What *is* the real world? Like, I get it. You've been to Togo, West Africa, and Cannes or whatever. But I don't get how any of those places are more real than this bar."

She was gesturing the way she did only when a concept had really planted roots in her.

"Or how anything that happens there says more about anything or how it means any more than what happens here."

We had always believed, before Nina went away, that someone other than us would realize that she was destined to lead the universe, even if she would only get it into trouble, lead it into ruin. Not because of any career or calling—she was too unambitious and restless to go to college, even before she went away, and too smart, too scrappy to be a model. She could never have taken direction the way it would have required. She just had a wit that, if the world was to be trusted, would somehow find its way into a fur coat and a series of regular lobster dinners. I think we all relished the thought, because we knew some of this good fortune would make its way down to us, but we also dreaded the inevitability of it, because we knew it would separate her from us.

It was part of why we distrusted Lila's good fortune. It was supposed to be Nina.

We knew in similarly vague and intangible terms, once she got back, that this was never going to happen. That Nina was always going to live within a one-mile radius of her mother. And when she went on tangents like this she was declaring to everyone that this was okay.

"The world always has been and always will be exactly what you make it," she said, finishing strong. She turned to me and I averted my eyes, pretending not to notice she wanted my attention in particular. That I was beginning to waver in my complicity in this illusion that there was nowhere else in the world that might suit us better, and there was nothing we might want that we didn't have, was unforgivable. "You can find whatever you really need wherever you are."

There were pieces of our friendship with Lila that might've been salvaged. We were angry and confused at the disparity between their punishments, but, because Nina was gone, we had no way of knowing what exactly happened when that police cruiser showed up in Nina's driveway. We couldn't be sure that Lila had confirmed what everyone already assumed— that girls like Nina were a bad influence on girls like Lila, and that Lila had only been in the wrong place at the wrong time. When bad things happen to girls like Nina, people like to say they had it coming. There was an equally good chance that Nina had insisted—the way only Nina could—on handling the situation and taking the fall, and that the grand result was only proof of her being a good friend, not Lila being a bad one. And it was impossible to ignore, of course, that even though we had stayed in the car, we had been there, too. About a month after Nina was sentenced, though, we heard from a boy who had been in Marie's class before she transferred and who some- times stole cigarettes for us from his mother's purse that Lila and Max had started dating.

Because she was one of only four people outside my family who knew my middle name and I had been there in the third grade when Nina had told her what sex actually entailed and she cried on and off for the rest of the day, when Lila called late one Saturday afternoon a few weeks after Nina went away, I agreed to meet her.

We met on the bridge we called Frankie Lane after Lind- sey's grandpa, dead almost a decade by then. A widower him- self, he had stayed with Lindsey and her family for a few weeks after his daughter-in-law died, another well-meaning male crammed into a house already full of them, one that really only needed a woman's touch. He had taken Lindsey and her brothers to the bridge every day to look at the alligators that congregated underneath it. He took a liking to one of them and started feeding it cold cuts and other treats, and named him George. Lindsey's father had been endeared by this tradition—one he knew only from secondhand stories, since his work schedule prevented him from going himself—until, on a rare day off, he had joined his father and children on their ritual outing and discovered that the gator was not the average six- or seven-foot gator he was imagining from the stories he heard, but one of the biggest alligators he had ever seen firsthand. A full twenty-foot stunner whose tail alone could have knocked them all out in one swipe. Horrified at the evident joy his children got from going right up to the edge of the small bridge's railing and dropping food to their new pet, and sure from the ease with which they did it that they did it regularly, he forbade any more trips there. Lindsey was too young when it happened to remember any of this, but it had become one of her favorite stories, and ours. In junior high we had started going to look at the alligators, and to see if George was still there. He wasn't, but plenty of other alligators were, which was enough to keep us coming back.

We used this meeting spot for outings we'd just as soon no one else know about—it was farther from home and less vulnerable to passersby. For a movie at the dollar Cinema Savers we would meet at the crosses, but it was Frankie Lane that would gather us before parties thrown without an adult chaperone. I had hoped, by suggesting we meet here when she called and said she needed to talk to me, to convey just how sordid I considered the issue at hand.

Lila was already there when I pedaled up, still sitting on

her bike, doing nothing to shade herself from the sun that sat straight above her, making everything too bright to look directly at.

"Hey," she said, turning around to smile at me, like we were here for a bike ride, or to hang out, like any other day.

"Hi."

"It's been a while since we've been here. I wonder how many of these alligators are new," she said, nodding down at them. "I can't remember why we stopped coming here, do you?"

I didn't look down at the alligators but at her new designer jeans, and the haircut I knew she hadn't gotten at the Supercuts by our house.

"I guess they live a long time, though. Maybe these guys will be here longer than any of us," she said, ignoring my silence, or trying to fill it. "Maybe we should start coming here more often. Max is right about the crosses being depressing."

Any hope that this meeting would be productive vanished at the physical reaction I had to her saying his name.

"Why did you call me?"

"Right," she said, shrinking into the timid, apologetic posture I had wanted from the start. "Look, I know it sounds bad. I can only imagine what people are saying."

"Yeah, it's pretty bad." I said it in the emptiest voice I could muster.

"I can't stand to think what *you guys* are saying," she said, fiddling with the handlebar streamers she'd had since she got the bike for her tenth birthday. Lila's dad had had Nina ride past the patch of sidewalk where Lila, Lindsey, and I sat eating cupcakes, talking about how annoying it was that Nina was always late. I wondered how long it would be before the bike was replaced, too. When I didn't answer right away, she looked up at me. I could tell she was hoping we could laugh it all off. That all of us were too tightly bound to one another, and for too long, for any of this to have any lasting consequences.

"We're careful to only say things that are true," I said. "Which is why I'm here. Set me straight."

She squared her shoulders back and took a deep breath, ready to launch into whatever speech she had prepared. She opened her mouth but then changed course.

"Wait. Where's Lindsey?"

"Her brother had a softball game."

"Oh," she said. Lindsey had enough brothers that one of them always had a softball game. There were enough to go to that she could afford to miss one, and she often did.

"I'm not screwing her over," she said in a rush, suddenly realizing how dire her standing was with us. She said it like it was poison that she was trying to get out of her body as quickly as possible, which maybe it was.

"You already did," I said. "When you let her take the fall. We all did."

"Wait, Nina didn't tell you?" she asked, leaning forward, really looking at me for the first time, confused and eager to set the record straight.

I was embarrassed that I had no idea what she was talking

about. Even after all that had happened, Nina still belonged more to her than to me.

"She told them she was the only one there. It was her decision. I didn't even ask her to do it. What's the point of all of us getting in trouble for this?"

"Fine. But how can you stand to be around Max when he just handed her over like that? He had to know she didn't mean any harm."

"It's not that simple," she said, shaking her head and looking down at the ground, trying to convince the concrete. "The police were involved. If he said he had no idea who might have done something like this, he would have been lying. You know him. You know he doesn't know how to lie. It wouldn't even have occurred to him. And . . ."

"What?"

"It's his little sister. You can't really understand if you don't have one."

I hated her then for bringing Marie into it. It felt like she was trying to take her away from us, too.

"Well, I guess there's just a lot I don't get, isn't there?"

She shook her head sadly, making no indication that she understood I was being sarcastic.

"But none of this actually matters," I said. "I really only have one question for you."

She didn't say anything, knowing what it was.

"Are you or aren't you?"

When she still didn't say anything I turned around and started riding away, feeling how inappropriate my getaway vehicle was. It felt like we were in territory way too adult to be navigated with a bike you got in junior high, but I kept my chin up as I pedaled.

A few months later, Max would disappear, along with the rest of his family, starting rumors that upstaged the ones about what happened that night, and whatever was going on with Max and Lila. It was like putting a real supermodel next to the prettiest girl in a small rural high school. Between the two of us, Lindsey and I heard everything from them having moved to Texas as part of the witness protection program, to them having been taken out in a mob hit after Max's father tried to skim some off the top from the men who had invented the trick. We might've asked Lila what happened—she would've known better than anyone—but we hadn't been talking to her for months by then.

That day, Max was still very much around, and I wondered, as I picked up speed, if he was somewhere close by, waiting for Lila to finish what was surely going to be an unpleasant exchange. The possibility made me angrier than I got when I rode past Nina's empty house.

There were only thirty yards between me and her when Lila called after me, panicked at the sight of my back. I must have been getting smaller and smaller as I pedaled away.

"It's not what you think," she said.

I stopped my bike but didn't turn around.

"Okay. Fine. What is it?"

"I'm not doing this to her. He's just the only thing I have left of her." She was desperate now. You could hear it in her voice.

"She isn't *dead*. She's coming back."

"But it won't be the same. You have to know that."

And even though I did, I started pedaling again, and didn't look back.

By now Abby's "persistence" had reached a feverish, maniacal peak. The calls were coming with almost no pause between them. Decker's batting them away after only a ring or two did nothing to dissuade her. We had to wonder if getting wasted in the earliest hours of the morning was something that people did in Italy. We couldn't imagine behaving this way in any context other than extreme, I-might-need-my-stomach-pumped intoxication.

"Never do long distance," he said, finally shutting the phone off altogether.

We all nodded attentively, like he was giving us advice we were going to need imminently—how to make our voices travel across the stage we were about to step onto, or how to get around the defensive men we'd be facing.

"If that Jay guy tries to open a franchise out of state," he said, nodding at me, really wound up now, "let him do it without you. It doesn't even have to be out of the state. Don't even try to make it work from here to, I don't know, *Miami*."

And then, as if Jay were running a race with Abby Madison and she had just passed the baton to him, my phone went from the isolated blasts of a text's buzz to the steady hum of a ringing phone set to vibrate, and I knew he was calling me. The fact that Jay was eager to be present at the scene where he was a topic of conversation, with the very person I was trying to keep him away from, paired with the fact that my own phone problem had exploded at the very moment Decker had taken control of his, was starting to make me panic. All this was set, of course, to a 1950s musical doo-wop background, which seemed, suddenly, fresh and timely from Decker's enthusiasm, rather than the vintage throwback we always thought of it as. It gave everything at the table a surreal quality. I felt like I was floating, or like the universe was shrinking—had, in fact, started running out of characters and settings along with decades and musical styles, and that it was only a matter of time before all the ones left were in a room together. The alcohol, and the movie star among us, and the persistent buzzing that felt like a mechanized mosquito, was starting to make me feel like I was dreaming. The conviction in Decker's speech—still going strong—drew me back to him.

"Long distance makes everything more difficult. I don't know how we could ever have kids when we can't even find a night to have dinner on the same continent."

I stiffened at the word *kids* at the same time that every atom in my body shifted all the nervous energy it had been training on the threat of Jay coming here to Lindsey and Nina. Children were a concept we'd never discussed, even in the hypothetical.

"Whoah!" said Lindsey. "Who said anything about children?"

"C'mon. It's not a secret that after two years women start looking at rings, and e-mailing them to their friends, and dropping hints and making a point of fawning over other newly engaged couples, and talking about them when they're not around. And what's the point of getting married if you're not gonna have kids? I mean, both of my brothers had knocked their wives up less than a year after they had gotten married."

"Yeah, but I bet your brothers don't have their faces on buses," said Nina. "Doesn't that buy you even a little time?"

"Yeah, I guess. But it starts to feel, at some point, like you're falling behind. All the guys I went to high school with, my brothers, even the guys I used to cater with and bartend with—they're all doing it. And sure, it looks, for the most part, pretty miserable. They've gotten fat, and the lack of sleep, man, it's like a second nose for as subtle as the effects of that are. But, you know, they also love their kids like maniacs. Like the way a four-year-old loves her new puppy. Guys who you never would've guessed would care about anything other than getting laid and making money. And, you know, it's just something I always assumed I would do. It's just, you know, something you do, unless you've made a conscious decision not to, which I never did."

"So, dude, go knock Abby Madison up," Lindsey said. "She'd be superhot pregnant. And I'm pretty sure you guys can afford it."

"Babies are in right now," said Nina.

"I don't know, man. It feels, sometimes, like everything that happens out there is fake. Not even in a superficial, plastic kind of way. I'm not having some no-one-has-a-soul existential crisis. I've actually met a lot of really nice people doing what I do. People I like and trust and relate to. I don't mean plastic fake in a bad way, is what I'm saying. It just feels totally divorced from the way every other human every other place does things. And there's just such little overlap between that life and life everywhere else. And, you know, that's fine for me, and maybe it's fine for Abby, but we chose that, you know? And God knows it has perks. Like perks you guys can't even imagine. No offense. But it feels unfair to bring kids into the world and make them live in some weird, sci-fi-ish isolation chamber from the rest of the human experience. I see four-year-old birthday parties at the Ivy and I literally want to go have a vasectomy."

"What's the Ivy?" I asked.

"God, as if I could love you girls more. Please never learn the answer to that."

"No, seriously," I said. "What is it?"

"It's not even anything great. It's just a restaurant where people go to get their pictures in the magazines that you girls seem to love so much."

I could see the other girls notice how much he sounded like someone's dad with that last part: *that you girls seem to love so much.*

There were things Sam Decker didn't know, and couldn't explain to us.

"So couldn't you just *not* throw your kids' birthday parties at the Ivy?" I asked, partly to make it seem like I knew the answer to his problem to make up for the fact that I didn't know what the Ivy *was.* "Throw them in the backyard, or every year you make it a tradition that you go to Anchorage for their birthdays. I don't know. It just feels like you have more control over these things than you're making it sound like."

Maybe I just hoped.

"Yeah, but the thing is, I'm pretty sure Abby would want to have them there."

"I mean, don't *all* kids rebel from their parents at some point? Don't they always eventually find *some* fault in the way their parents did things?" Lindsey asked. "Your kids can spend freshman year of college talking about how horrible all those birthday parties at the Ivy were and about how they're going to be a carpenter or a math professor."

"Yeah," said Nina. "Angst is hot. They'd probably get laid a lot."

"I don't know," he said. "I never went to college."

"Yeah, us either," said Lindsey. And we all raised our glasses.

Abby Madison canceled the European leg of the *Existential Madame* publicity tour when she got the call. She did it right away—the news was announced almost simultaneously with news of Sam Decker's death—like she didn't even have to think about it, which seemed, to us, to mean something. We felt guilty. It was something we would have told him, just hours ago, if we had known. Instead of snickering every time her name and face flashed on the screen of his phone the way we did all night, confirming for him, I'm sure, how absurd she was. How ridiculous it was to the three girls he was with, this concept of conducting a failing love affair across continents. Girls who had never left Florida.

Despite the frequency with which her name crossed people's lips, on television, and in bars and into cell phone mouthpieces across the world, she eluded everyone for weeks after he died. The dozens of photographers camped outside her house had failed to capture a single picture of her. This only made his L.A. memorial service, which would be televised on E! and VH1 and even, in part, on some of the news channels, that much more newsworthy, because we knew she couldn't skip it. It was a full month after he had died, and so many people were expected to come that it had to be held in the L.A. Coliseum.

She was already on the stage when the service began, next to his mother and the siblings we felt like we knew, and a head shot of Decker big enough for everyone in the crowd to see, an early one that made him look young. Some humane producer had agreed that they didn't have to walk onto the stage, red-carpet-style, putting even more focus on them, making the whole thing even more of a circus. So they were already onstage when the cameras started rolling. She was sitting so still, staring so roboti-cally straight ahead, that at first we thought maybe there was AV trouble, and the picture was frozen. She wore giant black Jackie O glasses, and by wearing them she took her place as another symbol of glamorous tragedy. The beautiful wife the more beau-tiful widow. She was even better than those who had gone before her, though, because she was the Hollywood version, and everyone knew that was bigger and shinier, with higher stakes and a bigger budget. The black lace dress she wore was tasteful, conservative—the fashion blogs and glossy mags respectfully, demurely praised her for it for months after—but it didn't hide her figure, and her legendary curves called to mind the chemis-try that must have laid between her and Decker, so much stron-ger, like everything else, posthumously.

We didn't recognize her from the girl in the bar—the desperate, needy one whose calls and texts punctuated our night.

About thirteen minutes in, just after the second speaker took the lectern to the right of her seat, she did something we never expected her to do. Something Jackie O, who stayed behind the veil, never did. Right in the middle of a C-list costar talking about how big Decker's heart had been, she took her sunglasses off to fish something out of her eye, and changed everything. With that one gesture, a light downturn of the wrist, her grief morphed from the most coveted fashion accessory in America to a violent, deforming scar. The kind that looks like it hurts long after it actually does. Her grief had aged her—she looked haggard—but also made her small, vulnerable, like too much clapping after each set of remarks about Decker could have blown her over. It had been a month. We'd have thought she'd have it together enough to wear makeup by then. Without it she looked, suddenly, like a person. A sad one. She was only five years older than us.

That moment she showed us her eyes was like the moment the album you're listening to across a long, scenic road trip, or while watching the sun set into the Gulf of Mexico, cuts out. And you see, suddenly, how dependent, how wrapped up in the music whatever you're marveling at was, and how different it is without it. Not worse, maybe, but something else entirely, with entirely different forces at work. Something that will break your heart in an entirely different place.

We were not the only ones to notice Abby Madison's decision to take off her sunglasses. The already hushed, precious air became more sacred still. The collective breath the stadium held was so noticeable that the speaker stopped talking. And it felt like, for all the online blog tributes and all the slideshows of Decker's career, that unplanned moment of silence was the truest, most pure acknowledgment of what had been lost. Even if it lasted only a handful of seconds.

When she showed us her eyes, we saw them: the secrets Decker had been talking about. And it made everything he had told us that night feel that much more true. Her eyes confirmed that that night had really happened. That it wasn't just a dream we'd all had at the same time. It brought us right back to that table in a bar we used to go to, and reminded us that we had lost something, too.

She did not acknowledge the interruption she had caused but to put her glasses back on and nod, so imperceptibly that some people argued against its having been given, this permission to commence whatever small consolation and pretty words people had planned. Permission not only to continue, but to keep the words pretty, and focus on the glamour of his career and the drama of his exit, instead of the black, ugly absence that stood after he finished making it. That was the burden she would bear so that we did not have to—it was a burden only someone who loved him could bear. One of therapy bills and panic attacks, and feeling alone in rooms full of people you had known for years. Of having lost some central joy in getting to do the job you had beaten millions of other starry-eyed girls to get to do, sacrificing, along the way, other joys, like summer camp and sleepovers and prom. Of sitting in America's most expensive and exclusive restaurants, across from men most women would have murdered their husbands to sit across from, drowning in the noise of all the ways in which they would never measure up. It was a burden, the beleaguered, barely there, this-is-all-I-can-manage nod made clear, that no stadium could hold.

I had my own reasons for hating Lila Tucker, not least because she let me pedal away that day. I wanted her to know how mad I was, and how lucky she was. How lucky we all were to have a friend like Nina Scarfio. I wanted her not to take for granted the things she seemed to be that day. I wanted her to find a way to make it up to us. I expected weepy phone calls and small gifts left in unexpected places. Surely the daughter of the Crayola Unbreakable could find a creative way to say I'm sorry. I would have forgiven her if she asked to be. But after that day I didn't hear from her. I had to wonder if this was the opportunity she had been waiting for all along.

Lindsey and I still saw each other, of course, but life without Nina was like living one long, continuous Monday morning, or the first day back at school after a long holiday break. There was a lot of watching movies we'd already seen in dark rooms without talking. We were more polite with each other than we had been, and left each other's houses earlier. I felt tired more than anything, and I could tell from her glassy eyes and sluggish gait that Lindsey felt it, too. It felt like we were waiting for something, and when Nina came back we realized we had been.

It was during that year that Nina was away and we suddenly didn't know Lila anymore that I met Jay. By the fall of

Lila's second year at the day school I had been seeing him for a few weeks, and had already grown tired of him. According to both the movies we had watched at the sleepovers we no longer had and all the unsolicited advice on males that Nina was always giving even though she'd never had a proper boyfriend, there were certain things you avoided doing in the early stages of a courtship. Bored as I was, I had decided to do them all, just to watch him squirm. I had come just short of complaining about the explosive diarrhea I had had the night before or leaving a used tampon in the toilet in my attempts to alienate him and humiliate us both.

It was Halloween the night I decided to cut him loose. Or force him to cut me loose, really. It was the first Halloween that I didn't dress up for. Even the year before, when Lila and Nina had stood us up for our costume-making session, we had thrown something together at the last minute. We were the four corners of the country—Florida, Hawaii, Washington, and Maine. We just dressed like the people who live there do—flannel for Seattle, a lei for Hawaii, fisherman sweaters for Maine. Nina got to be Florida, of course.

That year, I had eyed the slutty nurse and bunny and maid costumes at the ninety-nine-cent store, but I couldn't think of anything sadder than a girl with no friends treading on the appeal of a body not quite finished yet. Sitting in Jay's backyard, I could hear the whoops of trick-or-treaters, and wondered how many brand-name candy bars they were getting, and if they were fun-sized or full. I decided to tell him everything. If I couldn't scare him away, clearly the extent of my friends' depravity would. And the fact that I didn't even care. That I maybe even thought it was funny.

He didn't say anything when I finished. I didn't realize I was crying until I brushed a strand of hair out of my face and it came back wet. I waited for him to ask me questions—whatever happened to the little girl; if the dog died right away or suffered—but he didn't have any. All he said was, "That's really fucked up." Simply, like it was just the fact that it was. He didn't offer any words of comfort, or try to assure me that everything would be okay. In a world where people who loved each other the way Nina and Lila clearly had could lose each other so young, before they even went anywhere or made any real decisions about the way their lives would go, there wasn't a lot to say. And the only thing to do was not try to make it right, but to go to movies where Sam Decker made sure that justice was served and that all ended well. That all the girls got in trouble for drowning the little girl and her dog or none of them did. Or maybe he stepped in before it had the chance to happen at all.

In the silence that settled after Jay made his declaration—the smartest thing I'd ever heard him say—all this seemed implicitly clear in a way it hadn't before.

I remember it smelled like laundry, because our lawn chairs were right next to the pipe that released the steam from the dryer in the basement. When I look back on it, I remember seeing my breath when I spoke, but I probably couldn't. It is rarely that cold in Florida. It was a chilly day, not cold, but cool enough that you had to wear an outer layer when the sun started to set. It was unseasonable weather, and I took it as another sign that everything would always be wrong—a little off—from then on. When I think about it now, it occurs to me that I was finally getting a taste of what the weather might be somewhere else at the exact moment I was committing myself to the boy who made it unlikely I ever would. Because that was the moment that I decided that there were worse things than ceasing my commitment to torturing this nice boy who seemed to have a preternatural acceptance of the hard truths the rest of us were only starting to understand.

Five

S al shuffled back over to our table for the third time that night, showing us even more attention than he normally did, even though we knew by then that we were one of his favorite groups of regulars. He had clearly just pulled up his considerable slacks, which were always slumped just above his butt crack, or just under his rather womanly pectorals, because his giant belt buckle led the way like a figurehead at the bow of a ship.

Decker's face was so boyish in its happiness, spotting his new friend, that I suddenly wanted to hug him for reasons totally divorced from the length of his IMDb profile.

"More trivia, my man? What do you have for me this time?"

Sal shook his head somberly. "I wish, my man, but no. We have business to deal with."

We had never heard Sal call anyone "my man" before.

"Okay, fine," said Nina, "he's on more than just *The New Mickey Mouse Club*, but you already have your picture."

"I have no idea what you're talking about," said Sal, "and right now I don't care. How do you girls know those girls over there?"

We knew who he was talking about before he looked over at the corner that Lila et al. were huddled in. They smiled back at us with irritated, smug half-smiles. I knew Nina wanted to throw a bottle at their heads even more than I did.

"Why?" Nina asked. She studied Sal's face like she might find the answer there, too angry to just wait for it.

"They told me you girls trashed the bathroom and I went in there and it was a mess. Wet toilet paper everywhere. A phone number written on the stall with permanent ink. And I told them I been talking to you girls all night. You haven't gone to the bathroom once."

"Have we really not?" Lindsey asked, genuinely amazed. "That can't be good for you."

Sal gave her a warning look.

"Then they told me they wanted to buy you girls drinks, but that they wanted me to bring them over there first. They wanted to write a note to go with them. I told them I'd deliver the message for them and they said forget it."

"Cunts," said Nina.

"Hey, man," said Sal. "I don't want no trouble. I told them to leave you girls alone. That you're nice girls. I told them if they keep it up they're gonna have to leave."

"Yeah!" I said.

"Kick 'em out!" said Lindsey at the same time.

Nina was too busy slaughtering them with her eyes to join in the campaign.

"Hey," said Sal, snapping to get her attention back on him. She dutifully complied.

"I mean it. No more of these antics."

"We didn't even *do* anything!" Nina said. "Like you said. We've been here the whole time."

Sal gave her a *Yeah, right* look that we wouldn't have thought he had in him, not having any kids.

"Listen," he said. "They're only two booths away from where Bobby's sleeping. If you won't do it for me, do it for him. For all of us. Those girls have never seen Bobby fresh off a nap. They have no idea what they'd be in for."

Bobby was not a morning person.

"I'm going to smoke this cigar," he said, holding it up. "When I come back, everything's gonna be good."

"Of course," said Lindsey.

"Jesus," said Nina. "Way to hold your ground."

Lindsey only shrugged, knowing she wasn't actually the one Nina was mad at.

"Okay, c'mon, what's the deal?" Decker asked as Sal walked away. "It's more than just that one thing. The lizard or whatever. Do you routinely battle with them over guys? Like, are they coming after me next? Am I going to be taken hostage?"

The fact that they might *not* be coming after him was too rich to not laugh at, especially given the fact that there was no standard, by this point, by which we were not entirely, hopelessly, dry-mouth-in-the-morning plastered.

"Uh, yeah, that's totally it," said Lindsey, breaking into slap-happy, I-can't-remember-what-we're-laughing-about laughter. The kind that isn't really reliant on the joke, but feels good in and of itself. He joined in, even though he had no idea what was funny in the first place.

"Or you," he said, actually pointing at me even though I was less than a foot away from him and eye contact would've done it—he was even more shitfaced than us. "What's-his-face? Jay? Did you steal him from them?"

The idea of Jay in any sort of verbal exchange with Lila or Carine or the patterns sent Nina and Lindsey into another round of hysterics, the source of which Decker was once again mercifully clueless.

"And what about that girl?" he said, nodding at Lila. "Those other girls look pissed, but she's like the mom or something. She has the look of a lady in church, she just needs a bonnet."

She did look Sunday-service placid, but not in a doting or reverential way. She looked bored. Like, middle-of-the-homily bored. It was like the rest of us were playing a game—guessing how many marbles or pieces of candy were in a jar, and she already knew the answer but couldn't say, and she was half tired of waiting for us to catch up with her, and half amused at how far off our answers were. I wondered what it was she thought she knew that we didn't, certain that she couldn't have been more wrong.

"I mean, maybe she's a little overdressed," I said, "but I wouldn't call her a church lady."

She got out eventually, of course. A year passes, even when you are eternally young. She came back with as little fuss and ceremony as she had left with. One day she was just there, at the three crosses. Lindsey and I weren't even meeting there; we were on our way to the movie theater. I would say it was good timing that we happened to be walking by just then, given how much less frequently Lindsey and I saw each other that year than we had every other year of our lives, but it occurs to me now that Nina could have been out there any number of nights before the one we finally went strolling by. She looked comfortable where she sat on the ground, between the second and third crosses, like she had settled in, had been there for some time but didn't even mind because she had time to spare.

Lindsey and I stopped dead in front of her. For a second no one said anything, we just looked down at her while she looked back up at us. Lindsey and I half turned toward each other and then pounced on her, whooping as if one of us had just scored a goal against an opponent that made it unlikely.

"Bitches, don't start," she said, but it was clear from her voice, muffled under Lindsey's armpit and my chest, that she was happy.

When we finally rolled off, we sat on either side of her, one for each of the crosses.

"Where are the others?" she asked, as if we had all agreed to meet ahead of time.

The few times Lindsey and I did talk about Nina—always in dark rooms, watching movies, so we had somewhere else to look—it was always the same thing we wondered: if she would want anything to do with Max when she got back.

She saw Lindsey's eyes and mine look for each other again. "What?"

We both opened our mouths at the same time to speak, but our flapping jaws only underscored the fact that we had nothing to say.

"Is he still pissed? I just need five minutes. I'll be able to explain everything."

"Nina," I finally said, starting with her name just to buy more time. "Max is gone."

"What do you mean, 'gone'?"

"He doesn't live in Florida anymore," Lindsey said. "Or if he does we don't know where he is. They sold the house."

"We drove by," I said unhelpfully, trying to prove that we hadn't just resigned ourselves to rumor. We had looked into it the way she would have.

"He's not at the day school anymore."

"Was it us?" Nina asked, resting her arms on her knees and looking at the ground between them. "What happened, I mean?"

"Nah," I said.

"I mean, I doubt it," said Lindsey.

But we didn't know for sure, and she could tell.

"Wouldn't Lila know? I mean, he didn't just *disappear*."

"*Don't* look at each other," she said in the pause that followed, clearly exasperated at the possibility. "Just tell me."

"Things got weird after you left," I said, tossing the leaf I had been twisting more violently than I intended to.

"What do you mean? What's she been doing? Is she doing it now?" She turned from one to the other of us, trying to decide which of us had the least offensive answer before settling her attention.

"I don't know. I mean, we don't see her."

"*Lila?* You don't see *Lila?*" Her back-and-forth became more frantic now. Like there was a choking man on the ground in front of us and she couldn't figure out why no one was doing anything to help him.

"She was dating Max," Lindsey said when it became clear I wasn't going to.

"But Max is okay, right? We're sure he didn't, like, *die* or anything."

"No," Lindsey said, and sighed. "I'm pretty sure we would've heard about that."

"Nina, did you hear her?" I asked, suddenly pissed that she wasn't. "Max and Lila were dating. And I'm pretty sure he's the one who, you know . . ."

"Weird," she said, but whether she meant that Max and Lila had dated or that this had been enough to make us stop seeing Lila, she never said. She could simply have been so caught unaware by these turns that she could only manage to repeat back to us the word that we had used.

We all looked out across the street, not saying anything, watching the streetlights go on one at a time, trying not to look at the stop sign that Max preferred to the crosses. In the rare instances when Nina didn't know exactly what to say, she changed the subject while she figured it out, expertly continuing in a totally separate conversation as she sorted and sifted. She had no idea I knew she did that, but I could always see the work going on behind her eyes.

"What movie are you guys going to?" she asked, turning to me.

"How did you know?" Lindsey asked, mystified.

"Your pockets," she said, nodding at Lindsey's thighs. "They're bulging with candy. You cheapos never spring for actual movie-theater candy."

She was onto us, always.

After that, none of us mentioned either of them, and Nina, for the first time in her life, didn't say much of anything. She seemed totally uninterested in everything around her, like she was too tired to care, or like they had drugged her in juvie and we were all still waiting for it to wear off. But I would catch her, sometimes, looking over my shoulder, or pausing right in the middle of a thought or sentence, to look out on the horizon, and I knew she was waiting for Lila. Not convinced, somehow, that she was staying away on her own accord. She never came out and asked us, but you could feel it punctuating trips to the DQ for Blizzards and even our long sessions of lounging in one of our bedrooms: *But there was no fight or anything, right?* Or *Who told you they were dating?* It was the questions that haunted us more than even Lila's absence. Just as Nina would never put these words to air, she would never come out and say that, as badly as she wanted to see Lila, Lila had to come to her. She had been willing to take two people's worth of blame for that night. Could even, maybe, understand Lila's indiscretion with Max—she was loyal above all the other things she surely was—but she was also proud. Too proud to go seeking out thin excuses from someone who should have been falling over herself to produce them.

Lila never came. We never stumbled upon her at the crosses the way we had Nina, or at Frankie Lane, or at the abandoned swimming pools we still used as our own. She had no way of knowing that Nina was out, at first, but word must have eventually made its way to her, even at the day school. Whether she had found a way to morph her guilt and desperation into anger or simply never thought of us was one more thing I never knew.

In those first days back, spent waiting, Nina seemed nervous. She seemed expectant at times, and empty at others, but never angry. And every time I noticed that absence of anger, I thought again of that day on the bridge when I made it clear to Lila that the only thing that mattered was whether or not she was dating Max, and here, now, the only thing that seemed to matter to Nina was that she come back. I hadn't told any lies to Nina. I had told her we stopped seeing Lila when she started dating Max, but I wondered, sometimes, if I had given Lila just enough of an opening, if it had been on my watch that she ran. Strangely, it made me feel included more than anything else. Like we all had an equal hand in this mess. Nina for being too stubborn to walk away from an idea everyone had told her was bad; Lila for searching for Nina in all the wrong places when she went away; me for proving my loyalty to Nina by sending away the one person she most wanted to see; Lindsey simply for always letting other people lead the way, for smoothing things over instead of preventing them, for reacting, always, instead of acting. It was the last thing we did together—sinking the ship we had taken years to build.

I posed what I did, I think, just so I could introduce Lila back into the conversation. I thought being allowed to say her name might release something. It had been the thing to get us into this mess, why not the thing to get us out? Maybe two wrongs canceled each other out after all.

I told Lindsey first, giving her only the rough edges of the prank I had drafted.

"Really?" Lindsey asked. We were in the hallway at our lockers between second and third periods. The idea had come to me in the algebra class I was taking for a second time and really should have been focusing on. Instead I let the idea build and gel, expand and collapse back into itself throughout class, and decided to pose it right away. I was eager to know if it was as good an idea as it had sounded in my head. "I kind of think that's the *last* thing we need. Things are finally calm again; we don't have to worry about Nina anymore."

"Seriously?" I said. "That's the line you're going with? She can't have been much worse off in juvie than she is now."

"I guess I just don't get what the end goal is here."

"Maybe Lila's staying away because she feels *bad*. And this can be, like, the thing that evens the score. Each bad deed cancels the other."

"You don't think she's gonna be pissed?"

"I mean, probably, but what are we actually doing? Ruining some stupid party with girls she probably doesn't want to be friends with anyway. Once she knows we're back, she's not gonna need them anymore. At the very least, she can't ignore us anymore."

"And if she doesn't see it that way?"

"What do you mean?"

"If she doesn't want to be back? I mean"—she turned from

the locker she had been piling books into haphazardly—"what if it isn't guilt?"

The anger that crippled my muscular system at this possibility must have shown on my face, because she softened her theory.

"I just mean, what if she's happier now? It's been a long time. She's had time to settle."

"Then fuck her," I said. "She deserves it, then."

From the same source who had informed us that Max and Lila were dating, we had learned that Lila was rushing the day school's equivalent of a sorority, the Day Owls. Ostensibly it was a community-service organization—the Owls visited old ladies in nursing homes and baked cookies for prisoners—but from one look at the pictures of the girls in the group that we found online, it was clear that they were at least as pretty and popular as they were good-hearted; their average body fat had to be below one percent. It was the kind of organization designed for girls like Carine and the patterns.

Of course, we were eager—greedy, even—to learn the details of how Lila had been passing the time without us, and disappointed in the answer. Worst of all was the news that Lila had been designated the leader of her rushing class, which meant she was in charge of throwing the party at which it was announced who had been accepted into the Owls. From a single call to the school placed as the mother of one of the bitchiest-looking Owls in the picture, we got the name of the caterer who was doing the event. (We claimed her daughter was deathly allergic to those fried Asian noodles they put in

salads, and that we needed to call the caterer and hear for ourselves, right from the source, that they didn't plan to use them.)
From there, it had not been terribly difficult to track down
Jeremy Piker's best friend's older brother, who worked at the
temp agency that staffed the catering company and, susceptible
to all kinds of bribes, agreed to let us crash a catering squad for
one night.

Our plan, once we infiltrated the party, was to spike the
punch with a vicious amount of vodka. While all of the Owls
surely drank in unflattering, unladylike quantities off campus,
to get drunk at an official, school-sanctioned event meant to
showcase their contributions to the community and a "commitment to the legacy as it soars into the future," whatever the
fuck that meant, would be unthinkable. At the very least, Lila
wouldn't get in; best-case scenario, the Owls would be puking
up and down the school hallways.

When we finally told Nina we were reminded how bad off
she really was, because when she heard the word prank, before
she heard what we had in mind, and who our victim was, she
unwilted for a second. It was like a neighbor had finally
remembered to water the flowers he had promised to take care
of just before they died for good, just before you had to throw
them out. And it reminded us of what she had been, and
proved that we had not only imagined her the way she used to
be. The legend of Nina was real. Which by then only reminded
us again what we had lost. Once she understood the scope of
our plans, she retreated back into herself. She occasionally
chimed in a word or two here—a fact she remembered about
the layout of the school from that first locker prank, a sugges-

tion on where we might buy clothes that resembled catering uniforms for cheap. She never looked up from whatever she was doing when she said these things, though, and we got the sense that they were automatic. That for her sitting in on our conversations was like hearing a group of small children struggling to name the color of the sky. There was no way not to produce the answer when it was so ready, but there was no triumph in something that easy.

As we had on the day we drove to Max's house, we agreed to meet at the school flagpole on the night of the party, across from where the car we had borrowed and were still not old enough to drive would be waiting for us.

It never occurred to us that she might not show, but Lindsey and I knew as soon as we arrived that she wouldn't be coming. Never one for subtlety, Nina had masking-taped her note to the flagpole. It was waving in greeting, visible when we were still a good twenty yards away from it. As we made our way across grass bent at severe angles, flattened from years of student tread, I knew that whatever was waiting for us wasn't going to be good.

After I read it, I sat down on the base of the pole, dumbfounded, my catering cummerbund dangling like an arm or a leg hanging at an unnatural angle, one that meant it was broken. Lindsey started to take down the note, methodically pulling away the thick tape so we didn't have to litter or deface anything on top of everything else, the only one who would think of something like that.

Couldn't quite, it said.

Lindsey and I had no way to know if Nina was only scared

to get caught again—if it was a lesson learned—or if she loved Lila that much. She didn't become an altar girl after her time served, of course. When Regina Bresford started a rumor that Lindsey was a lesbian a few months later, Nina poured pudding in her gas tank, and later still she punched Danny Raker right in the middle of the prom dance floor when he grabbed her ass without asking, even though she would have said yes if he had, hard enough that he left without any parting words, cupping his jaw in pain. When I think about it now, I think about the cat I had years after all this happened, one who was capable of incredible jumps, from one piece of furniture to another nowhere near it, who would still, sometimes, sit at your feet and mewl to be picked up and put on the bed or the couch next to you. Who could have made the jump and a million that were far more difficult, but, for whatever reason, didn't always feel like making it. Wanted a break every once in a while.

Lindsey and I didn't wonder about this on the way home from the flagpole. In fact, we didn't say anything, but when we got to the turn in the road at which we would have had to take a left to go home and a right for Nina's, we both took a right without saying anything.

What I can tell you is that the scrawl was different in the second of the two lines of the note, almost as if two different people had written them. The first line was all Nina—loops and pure abandon, for everything, including what her penmanship might look like to anyone but her; the second was smaller, printed out in block letters. It was more determined, bolder, more final and declarative. It was easy to read, even in the dark.

Let it go.

Decker was wearing a watch. Judging from the thick leather cuff it was attached to and the massive size of its face, we had assumed it was for show, but now that his phone was off, he actually used it to check the time.

"New York and Florida are in the same time zone, right?"

"Um, do you seriously want us to answer that?" Lindsey asked.

"Yes," he said, muffled, since he had laid his head down on his arms, which were folded on the table in a distinctly Seven Up–like posture.

"Okay. Yes. Why?"

"I have to be on set in four and a half hours."

"Fuck that," said Nina, taking another gulp of beer, the only one still drinking at this point. "I thought you were gonna tell your agent to shove it anyway. You are way too big for the frickin' Disney Channel."

"No way, man. It would be such bad press if I bailed on a show for kids," he said, shaking his head into his arms now. "And I'm already here."

"Isn't it gonna be bad press to show up still wasted to a kids' show?" I asked.

"There are ways to get my energy back between now and

then. And with a few pieces of gum, kids don't know the difference."

"Just don't go to sleep," said Nina. "If you go to sleep now, it's a lost cause. No sleep is way better than three or four hours at this point."

"Now, that I would agree with," he said, pointing at Nina without picking his head back up.

The Regents' "Barbara-Ann" came on—a song that, judging from previous reactions to previous songs, would've topped Decker's best-of-the-sixties list, a list he had surely crafted at some point or another—but he didn't move. I thought about poking him, but before I could Sal walked back into the bar, still chewing on the end of his cigar. As if Decker could sense him coming, he finally lifted his head up, his entire body a weary smile.

"Sal, my man!" Decker shouted when he was still twenty feet away. "Livin' the dream."

Sal nodded at him and pulled his pants up again when he got to the head of our table.

"Next time you go out there, man, you gotta take me with you. We'll smoke those cigars and you can tell me more trivia. I'll impress you, I swear."

"Who would watch these girls, then?" Sal asked, clearly flattered to be invited into a huddle with this man of some repute, even if he wasn't sure what it was. "One of us has to do it. We're the only ones with any sense."

"That's the truth," he said. "I watched them while you were away. Those other ones stayed in their corner."

"Dude, we're not *farm animals*," Lindsey said, incredulous even in her drunken state.

"One of these days, I'm gonna go back home and open a bar just like this there," Decker said, ignoring her. "I'm gonna hire my brothers to work there, I'm gonna have inside jokes with all the regulars. I'm gonna raise my frickin' *kids* there."

"Dude, in a bar?" Nina asked. "That's probably worse than the Ivy."

I would've had my own case against his plan, but just then my phone buzzed again, signaling another text:

YOU AT THE SHAMROCK? I'LL COME. I'M NOT FAR.

When we got to Nina's all the lights were on in the house. We walked in without knocking to find Nina on the couch, an entire sleepover's worth of snacks before her. The remote poised in her hand.

"What the fuck took you guys so long?" she said. "I've had this cued up for almost an hour. You're lucky I didn't start it."

"What are we watching?" Lindsey asked, picking up a handful of salt-and-vinegar chips at the same time that she dropped in the nearest chair.

I looked over at her like, *Seriously?* She chomped violently on a chip in response.

"We're watching *Dirty Dancing* and we're drinking every time someone kicks their leg above their waist," Nina said, nudging the bottle of peach schnapps on the coffee table in front of her. "We have orange juice and Sprite in the fridge to mix."

I opened my mouth to ask her why she'd changed her mind. How she wasn't dying to see Lila just one more time, at least long enough to demand answers. The prank was mine, yes, but it was only to summon Lila. To poke her back awake to actual life. The rest was up to Nina. But she actually seemed *happy*, sitting there in the neon-orange T-shirt we all had an identical version of, a glass of God-knows-what in the mug she'd painted at Lindsey's twelfth-birthday party, when we all got to paint one mug and Nina had painted what was obviously a phallic design. She had done it to get back at the lady who ran the place and who had told her she couldn't use more than four colors. The purple penis was turned gleefully away from her and toward us. It was, suddenly, like she had never left. Like she had decided to excise that year of her life right out of the story, right along with Lila. She refused to speak of Lila from that night on, even when we found ourselves across from her in bars. She stopped waiting. Once she decided that Lila was gone, or gone enough that it wasn't worth risking pushing her even further away, to the point that obliterated not only all the things that might have lay ahead, but all the things we had shared, there was no going back. And certainty was the currency Nina ran on.

I wonder, now, if in needing her to be back I did her a disservice by corroborating the chunk of our past she'd cut right out. I'm not sure, though, that I would have gotten to keep her otherwise, if maybe pretending wasn't part of the deal. So while I wonder, I don't regret.

"My mom had to take me to the grocery store with her today. She's not allowed to leave me alone at the house for three months, which is awesome. I put a ton of extra shit in the cart. So we have the stuff for pigs in a blanket if you want. But I'm not making them."

"Fair enough," I said. "I'll go at the boring part."

"There isn't one!" Lindsey said, already moving closer to the TV.

Nina gave me the private look we had for all the things Lindsey did that made us think that, in another life, in the one where she kept her mother, she would have been a total drama-camp queen.

"I swear to God, Lindsey, if you start singing along I'm going to shave your eyebrows when you fall asleep. And you," she said, turning to me. "When do I get to meet the *boyfriend*?" She said the word the way she might've said *cunnilingus*.

"Jay?"

"You have more than one boyfriend?" she asked. "I'm impressed. Seriously, though. I have big plans for us this year. I need to make sure he's on board."

I would've worried about how quiet he would've surely been in her huge, neon presence, but I was too relieved that there would be someone else's plans to follow again. And while I wasn't exactly proud of Jay, I had been a little wounded at her refusal to even ask who he was when I dropped his name casually, unwilling to accept one more change.

"Whatever you say," I said.

"Oh, shit, I almost forgot. Elaine went to the nail salon and copped a bunch of magazines. She always pretends like she bought them, but I know she's totally filching them from the salon. Some of them are even marked with the salon's name, which probably means they're onto her. We should get our fill before they ban her from the premises," she said, wandering into the kitchen and then out again with a small stack of magazines. "Get it while it's good, ladies."

While Lindsey and I were running around occupying ourselves with the tools of Nina's previous life, Nina had been taking stock of the materials available to her, I saw, the way every master craftsman did. She had been calculating what was left, really. Now that she had made her measurements, she was ready to do what she always did. To charge out into the world she had found waiting for her at full speed—recklessly, even—doing the sort of things she did best—spiking movies meant for little girls, making new couples squirm, indulging in the hot goods procured by a parent always meant to be more of an accomplice than a guide. This charge would happen in a world Lila was no longer a part of, so she could not be in the line of fire.

"I call the one with Jackson Garrett on the cover," said Lindsey, whipping around from the TV, which she had scooted up to so that there were only six inches between her face and the screen.

"You would," said Nina, tossing it to her even though we both knew Lindsey would be so engrossed in the movie that it would take her hours to make it through the magazine. She passed me the second-best issue and opened the one beneath it.

"Oh, Jesus," she said. "Why is everyone wearing leopard print? Is Russian hooker, like, a trend now?"

It was with that comment, somehow, that the transformation was permanent. Lindsey looked back at me and smiled. It was like our parents just told us they were getting back together.

We stayed up until three that morning, but the cereal and the underwear stayed where they belonged.

Even though I could barely feel my legs by that point in the night, when I read Jay's text, my panic was physical. Jay being at the Shamrock would completely shatter the illusion that we were somewhere else. Somewhere far away from the lives we'd all have to go back to soon enough. The idea of Jay and Sam Decker meeting was the most horrifying possibility I could fathom, and for some reason, Sam Decker is the person this made me irrationally angry at.

"I don't buy it," I said.

"What?" he asked, looking at me with roaming, unfocused eyes, ready to laugh at whatever joke I was setting up.

"You're not going back to Alaska any more than I'm going to Hollywood," I said.

"And how do you know that?" he asked, suddenly less sloppy—he sat up a little straighter, the way he might've if a cop had pulled him over in this state. Ready to answer questions, but not necessarily honestly.

"Because you would've done it by now if you were going to," I said. "I'm sure you wouldn't even have to buy whatever bar you want to. They'd be so happy to have you back they'd probably just give it to you."

"Maggie," Nina said. She had eyes I hadn't seen since I almost let slip where we were really going to be when we said we had an overnight orientation for driver's ed sophomore year.

"Well, look. It's not that simple. I pay my mother's mortgage, and all of my siblings'," he said. "And they don't exactly live in the house we grew up in, if you know what I mean."

"You don't actually have to move back. That's not what I mean. I just mean that I think you'd probably hate your life just as much if you'd never left. Being poor and ordinary isn't exactly the joyride you seem to be imagining."

Lindsey tried to help, as always.

"I mean, it sounds like you're a little sick of the pace of your life, right? But it isn't all bad. You're not, like, *alone* or anything. You have Abby, who must know what it's like. I mean, I know you haven't exactly been thrilled to talk to her, but that's just because we've had a lot going on over here, right? I hate talking on the phone or checking in with other people when I'm having a good time, even if it's someone I like. And like you said, the phone is pretty horrible. I mean, she really wanted to talk to you. That's gotta count for *something*, right? You guys are gonna share an *agent* soon."

As if she had any idea what that meant.

"Is there a question in there?" he asked, but he was smiling, with mischievous, squinty, I'm-just-fucking-with-you eyes. Lindsey was irresistible when she rambled.

"Not really. I mean, no. I mean . . . it's just . . . My dad always used to say, really the key to life is just finding someone good to be on your team. To, like, help you through it, right?

And they used to go at it like cats and dogs. I mean, at least that's what my brothers say. I mean, I'm sure there were times when they didn't take each other's calls. But everyone knew how much they loved each other. And *you guys*. I mean, I can't even imagine that. You guys have, like, an *empire*."

"Oh, Jesus," he groaned. "You sound like *her*."

We all froze at the way he said *her*. It was not the way Sam Decker was supposed to refer to Abby Madison. Not picking up her calls was one thing; this was another.

"And that word. It's exactly the word she uses. *Empire*. Has she been saying that shit in magazines? Is that why you said it? I truly can't figure out what having an empire means in the twenty-first century. Just a joint checking account?"

"But you guys are in love, right?" Nina asked, in the first and only case I can think of in which she advocated for love. "I mean, it's Abby Madison. We've all seen her in a bikini; how could you *not* love her, right?"

"Well . . . the thing is . . ." He put his head back down in his arms.

We tried to be polite in our silence, but none of us blinked and I'm pretty sure at least one of us had our mouth open, too frozen with expectation even to make the simple gesture of closing it.

"Well, we're not strictly together anymore," he said, looking back up to face us, the red veins in his eyes more visible than they had been a minute ago.

"But she's been calling you all night," Lindsey said.

"Yeah, she's not exactly happy about breaking up. Or maybe she is. I don't even know."

"I don't get it," said Nina.

"She's really just calling to make sure I don't let my publicist announce it before her press tour for *Existential Madame* finishes. She wants me to go to meet her for the end of it. One last photo op in Venice."

"The city of love," said Lindsey.

"That's Paris," he said.

"Okay, fine. Of romance, at least."

"I guess it would be a poetic end," he said.

"It's the perfect place to get back together," Lindsey said.

"It might be," he said. "If I had any intention of going."

He studied us when he said this, a petulant child waiting to see how big the reaction to his antics was going to be.

"Um, you should *definitely* go," I said. "Like, now."

"And why's that?" He looked right at me when he said it, not quite a challenge, but almost as if he really wanted to know.

"Because it's Italy. And Abby Madison is probably going to win an Oscar this year. And you're sitting in Orlando in a bar with only two beers on tap with three girls who barely graduated from high school, and only one of us is going to put out, if that's what you were thinking."

"Ha! That's not what I was thinking. How many times do I have to tell you? I like you guys."

"That's nice, but you should still go."

"I've been to Italy. The beds are really small," he said, suddenly sober, and a little sad. "They don't have central air, and it's almost as hot there as it is here this time of year. All of the channels are in Italian, and the only sport they show is soccer, which everyone knows is the worst sport. They only sell Coke in these tiny little bottles, and their beer selection is bad."

The thought of Sam Decker enjoying a pleasure as simple as Coca-Cola made me want to cry.

"So have some wine," I said.

"I can't have red teeth. You never know when someone's gonna take your picture."

I would've found this unforgivably self-indulgent, even for a movie star, but I had seen enough pictures of him—pictures he clearly didn't even know were being taken—to know that it was true.

"So have someone bring beer you like with you. You're Sam Decker."

"I think it's cool," Nina said, seeing her opening. "You should do whatever the fuck you want."

She flagged Sal down and motioned that she wanted four shots. He brought five—one for him, too, which made Decker happy again, and we all took them.

"To doing whatever the fuck you want!" Nina said, right before we all threw them back. Even I finished it in one go.

"Well, I guess we know which one puts out now, right?"

As if it hadn't been clear the whole time.

"Dick!" Nina said, but she slapped his arm when he said it, and her eyes were more active than I'd seen them in years.

"I gotta hit the john," Decker said. "But we've still got—"

He looked down at his watch.

"—four hours until my big Disney comeback. Don't go anywhere."

. . .

He was gone a long time. I have no idea if he was already shooting up then, or if that was a late-night activity, long after we were gone. At the time it didn't even occur to us. He may have already been high when he walked into the Shamrock. We were girls who knew what we needed to about the things in our immediate orbit, but nothing about things like that. After, we thought about it all the time. He went to the bathroom a million times and spent the minutes there a million different ways in the days and months, even years, after that first time.

It was not lost on us, even then, at nineteen, when there were so many bits of wisdom still strewn across the world, waiting for us to pick them up—in ugly, lonely, gray-streaked dawns, and the early-morning cries of our unborn children; in solitary hotel rooms of our own, shades drawn well into the day, and Shamrock bars in third-tier cities the world over— how tragic it was that he died alone. This was a man who couldn't part his hair differently without people demanding a press conference to fawn over him for it.

Lindsey had been in the hospital room when her ninety-two-year-old, generationally racist grandmother died, cursing through her last breath, and had spent a considerable amount of time deciding the exact shade of the goo that trickled out of the old woman's mouth right after. Nina's pet Lab and the fifth lady at all of our sleepovers for as long as any of us could remember had been surrounded by all four of us, plus Nina's mother, when the needle that would stop her heart went into her left paw, and we could all pinpoint the exact instant when she went from here to gone even though the vet had said it would be a gradual shutting-down process of the organs. The pressure in the air just changed. When a boy the grade above us slit his wrists in his parents' bathtub the only thing anyone talked about for weeks was the exact language that Jenny Blume had used to break up with him the day before, and the song that had been set to repeat when he made the cut, and after.

We cried about these things alone and together and wrote about them in the journals we had grown too old to call diaries, and used the glamour of these tragedies to rescue us from the slow tick of the clock that culminated in coffee breaks from jobs we had not yet been working at long enough to have acquired a taste for coffee, but not nearly as hard as we cried about the fact that no one had been there to record these details about the night Sam Decker died.

We were shocked, in the weeks that followed his death, that we could not find them in the magazines that so faithfully cataloged how many pairs of sneakers he owned, what his favorite day of the week was, and how many children he wanted to have. We turned to them for answers about how our own night ended, expecting them to fill in the holes of the single biggest event that any of us had ever lived through, and they didn't even have the courtesy to make something up. There was no mention of the Shamrock in any of the coverage of his death, and this felt to us like a lie of omission. If what had happened to us had happened to other girls in other cities, we would have wanted to know the color of the chipped nails that they clutched their glasses with just a little bit tighter when they saw him across the room, and what those glasses were full of, the exact rates their hearts had climbed to when he slid across the cheap, cracked vinyl of their booth.

We would have been willing to tell.

It never occurred to us until later how many other people had stories from that night that they would tell for years—at high school reunions and on first dates, as if it were the story of how they lost their virginity or decided to pursue the career path they did. The Ecuadorian hotel maid who, recognizing the unlikely resemblance between Decker and a son she had not seen in years, had wiped the bead of blood that had pooled just under his nose before she called the front desk; the first-class stewardess on the flight to Orlando who had fed him peanuts and pretzels and probably plenty of champagne on the way to the city where he would die; the apprentice at the local funeral home who would have to explain to his aging boss the significance of the scruffy man they were about to embalm. For years we would argue over whether he smelled like bourbon or mint or clean sweat and who he made eye contact with first, but it never occurred to us to wonder about the last text he sent to Abby Madison, or if he finally picked up one of her calls—if he gave her the small indication of hope she was looking for from him that night—or how she chose the black lace dress she wore to his funeral, photographs of which made it all around the world, to Anchorage and then Italy and back, and became, for a generation, the unequivocal symbol for tragic love—even to us, who knew better—and would stand in our minds as the only dress she ever wore.

Because the one thing we could agree on was that, after that night, Sam Decker belonged only to us.

Dude, what the fuck," Nina said as soon as he disappeared into the bathroom.

"What?" I asked.

"We get it. You hate your life. It's miserable. So why are you still here?"

"What does that mean?"

"It means don't take your fucking preteen angst out on Sam Decker."

"Dude, easy. He's still gonna fuck you," Lindsey said.

"Oh, and that's a problem, Dr. Adultery?"

"Really? Now you're gonna judge me for who I fuck? And thank you, by the way, for pointing out that I'm someone's *second* girlfriend to Sam Decker, of all people."

"Listen to yourselves," I said. "You're right. Clearly I'm the miserable one. Because you guys are both really happy."

"Oh, Jesus, back to this again. Look, man, don't put your shit on me," Nina said. "I'm actually really good at teaching housewives how to Jazzercise. It's not fucking brain surgery—it's not even a real word—but I'm good at it. And I happen to like it. And my class is so full that the gym just added a second one. At least I'm not sitting around pouting about how my life turned out, doing nothing to fix it."

I looked at Lindsey, waiting for her to take my side again, because she always did. But she didn't tell Nina to back off, and she wouldn't meet my eyes.

"Don't look at her. She's fine, too. Stop trying to project your misery onto other people and bring us all down with you."

"Oh, so you think Fred's a good idea, then?" I asked.

"Of course I don't. But she doesn't need a real boyfriend. She doesn't even want one. She's not crawling out of that man cave she lives in anytime soon. Testosterone is like her oxygen, and she could never find enough of it in a pool of nonrelatives. No offense," she said, looking at Lindsey.

Lindsey raised her eyes a millimeter above the spot they'd been studying to indicate that there was none taken, maybe even to acknowledge that it was true.

"Look, if you're unhappy—"

I was pissed at her, but I still would have liked to know what she thought I should do, because I *was* unhappy. It had never been more apparent to me than it was that night. I never found out, though, because just then Lila and Carine and the patterns came back, and with even more purpose than before. Lila was trailing behind them, I'll give her that, but she was there.

I'll always wonder if they would've come back if Sam Decker hadn't been there that night. If they hadn't wanted to prove to him, too—confident that the rest of the world already knew—that they were better than us. If a defeat in front of him wasn't just that much more humiliating. Maybe if it had been just us, they would've let us go. They usually did. Whatever they had to say to us could've waited. None of us was going anywhere. That was the whole point of their attack. We were girls you always knew where to find.

"Look," Carine said, only inches from Lindsey's face. "I get it, you're fucking. It's really cute. But summer's almost over, and we both know he's not taking you with him back to school, so let's not pretend this is more than it is."

"What exactly are you asking me to do?" Lindsey asked, defeated and clearly tired. It really was getting late.

"I'm asking you to tell me where he is."

"Dude, I'm right here. With you. How would I know that?"

"So you mean to tell me he hasn't been calling you or texting you?"

"I'd be happy to say he had if it was true."

"Look, the fact that he's not with either of you right now probably means he's fucking somebody else," said Nina. "And if anyone had any sense, they'd be ganging up on him instead of distracting each other from the fact that he's probably balls-deep in some ninth-grade homecoming queen."

"Are you fucking kidding me?" asked Lindsey.

"What?" Nina asked.

"You really think now's the time to point that out to me."

"Jesus," Nina said. "You didn't know? Where did you think he *was*?"

"I don't know. Sanibel."

"Wow," Nina said, nastier than we'd said anything to one another in a while. "Well, I can't help you with that."

"Oh. That's convenient. Every man for himself now, huh?" Lindsey said. "When did that start? Were you going to let us know?"

"No, not every man for himself. I would just like to go to a bar just once and not have that horrible woman look at me like she's going to bite my lips off and use them as a douche," Nina said, gesturing violently at Carine. "If you even *gave* a shit, I would cut a bitch, but you don't. You only like him because you know nothing's ever gonna come of it, so you can sleep in the twin bed you had your first impure thought in, taking care of other people, so that you don't ever really have to *do* anything."

"You're right," Carine said, turning to Lila at the exact moment we forgot they were there. "She is trash."

Everything stopped then. When I think about it now, that moment is more of a portrait than a memory—Bob and Jax raising their heads high enough, for the first time that I can remember, that we could see their eyes. Sal, half sitting on one of the bar stools, leaning into the scandal mounting at a pace that even he had trouble keeping up with, but trusting us enough, despite what he had said, to see where it went before he got involved or, worse, kicked us out. At some point during the exchange we hadn't bothered to lower our voices for, little Bobby had come wandering out, squinty-eyed and confused, and that's when I knew we had gone too far—when the tower of bed hair on top of his head first came into view. Roni was standing protectively behind him, her arms wrapped around his tiny chest in a maternal gesture I wouldn't have been able to picture her making before I saw it, wondering, it was clear, who we thought we were to make such a scene in this, their home. I understood, seeing her cold, demanding face, that she had never been anything but pleasant until now. So maybe Decker's theory was wrong after all.

"I didn't say that," Lila finally said, though it was unclear if she said it to Nina or Carine.

She turned so that she was facing Nina and said it again.

Nina stayed frozen, but her eyes were wild, occupied. They

searched every inch of Lila for the answer to a question Lindsey and I and probably Paisley and Polka Dot couldn't begin to guess at. I had never seen such busy, desperate, demanding eyes. Lila must have read them better than I could, because she said, "His family changed their name to Balander when they moved to New Mexico. His father was involved in some sort of scandal at work, which is why they left. It had nothing to do with us. He came back to Florida for school. He's at State, just twenty minutes away. His e-mail is just Max Balander at Gmail. I'm sure he'd want to hear from you."

Nina is the most unpredictable person I have ever met. The kind of unpredictability you find only in someone who truly doesn't care, not someone who only wants to seem like she doesn't. I always wanted to know what she was going to do next, but never so much as I did then, in the face of the one thing that maybe ever mattered to her. But just then Sam Decker came gliding out of the bathroom with liquid hips and four-hundred-dollar jeans that most of the women in our hometown would never have been able to squeeze into and that bomber jacket of his grandfather's, pointed at Nina the way he did at the heroine of *Madeline's Last Laugh*, and said, "Lady, it's time." And they left before any of us could demand to know what for.

Six

The next morning, when the news broke that Sam Decker had been found dead in his hotel room by a maid who went in to clean the room after checkout time, we all kept waiting for the others to call, but none of us did. I still can't say why. We had never gone a day without speaking. Even the time Lindsey crashed my parents' car a full two years before we were old enough to drive, and my father demanded that Lindsey's father pay for the damages, insisting he wasn't interested in raising other people's daughters, and Lindsey's father, still small from the death of his wife, had only shrunk in his doorframe and nodded, and my father, suddenly realizing the impact of his words, left without saying another, and paid for the repairs himself. Or the time Nina left the homecoming dance with Jimmy Reagan the year he took me, even though she had been the one to help me do my hair before the dance, and stole one of her mother's favorite dresses out of her closet for me to wear, and had even bothered, later, to say she didn't realize I might have liked him.

The reason for Nina's silence was clear. There were very

few details available about the scene of Sam Decker's death—at
that point, they didn't even know that it had been a drug over-
dose, only that they could rule out foul play—but the one fact
of interest all the news sources were reporting was that hotel
cameras caught him returning home alone at four o'clock in
the morning, which meant she probably didn't want to explain
how he'd lost her, or why they'd parted. Why she wasn't there
at the end. It meant that even if they had screwed they had
done it somewhere public—the beach, his souped-up rental
car—and even for her, that was worse than not doing it at all.
Later, after we slowly made our way back to each other, we
started to compare notes about the night—things we wished
we had asked him and things we were glad we had said. We
searched every pause in the conversation, every evasion and
every reveal, for some omen that what had happened was
going to. We mused at what Carine and the patterns must have
thought when they heard the news, and we talked about if he
seemed happy. If his pouty complaints and discontent or the
smiles he gave us across the night—still burned into our
memories—and his willingness to laugh even at himself were
the truer thing. Eventually we tired of the other details, but
never that one. He was angsty, sure, but sometimes that was
the very thing that propelled you, we knew, and got you where
you needed to go. The thing to *make* you happy. Maybe he was
on the road to that bar in Anchorage after all. Maybe knowing
you wanted it was the first step.

Lindsey and I figured Nina would eventually, if left unprod-
ded, give us the final piece of the story that we had not been
there for, but she never did. I couldn't decide if this was because

she was mortified or because it meant something to her and she wanted to keep that piece of Sam Decker for herself.

That morning, the sound of air empty of a telephone's ring and a door not knocked upon felt cryptic, like Sam Decker had taken everyone with him when he left, but it never occurred to me to be the one dialing, or knocking. I wondered if what I came to think of as the standoff would have happened if he hadn't died, and all the ways in which the fact that he had would curse us. It's probably better, for me, at least, that we weren't speaking, though, because I'm not sure I would have done what I did if we were gathered on Nina's bed talking in fevered whispers about the night Sam Decker died.

At around seven that night, I went out for some air, just to hear the sound of people talking, intending to go to the diner down the street for coffee. And that's when I saw it. She had wrapped the note and the check around a rock, which only underscored the fact that she hadn't used the rock to make any noise, or draw my attention, the way rocks are often used to do. She was letting me come to it when I was ready, but she had put it in the middle of my front step so that there would be no missing it when I was.

I should have recognized the penmanship. Having the handwriting that most resembled a parent's, Lindsey was always the one who forged the things that needed forging. I didn't, though, not right away. Maybe because she and I were never the girls writing the notes, but the ones waiting for them, needing them for our cues. She must have recognized this, too, because she bothered to sign her name at the end of it, the way Nina never would have.

The note was only one line, but that was enough. The amount the check was for would be, too.

This town's no good since Decker left. Might be time to blow?

Like a coward, I hid in the bathroom after Nina and Decker left the bar that night. I didn't want to see Lindsey any more than she wanted to see me right then. We both knew that being around each other would only remind us that Nina wasn't there and make us feel guilty for not being better friends, and we weren't sure exactly what that entailed in a situation like this. Especially when we were both as pissed at her as we had every right to be. It felt a little like Nina had demanded everyone get naked at once, and then disappeared at the exact minute Lindsey and I had discarded our last piece of clothing. We were retreating to separate corners to rebuild our dignities or, at the very least, get dressed. We were losing face to the patterns maybe, but they felt, suddenly, more irrelevant than they ever had. They had served any purpose they ever would.

I stayed there, crouched in the stall closest to the tampon machine, long enough that I actually had to use it. The sight of the tampon machine had made me nauseous on the way in, a reminder, as it was, of why I wouldn't be needing it, but when I sat down the stall started to spin, and I put my forehead on the side of the stall just for the cool of it. I was drunker than I had realized, and I thought about turning around to get sick. So maybe it wasn't the tampon machine's fault.

They were almost pretty—the two ribbons of red that spiraled through the toilet water like food coloring. I still don't know if it was the end of the beginning of something, or just a really late period. I had gone off birth control three months before, deciding the monthly cost would be better spent on beer and gas money—it was one of the reasons I had assumed I was pregnant—and I hadn't been entirely regular since.

Whatever it was, it felt more tragic, there in the middle of a dirty, mostly empty bar, than it would have anywhere else. And I was pissed at the universe that it had waited until the exact moment I ran out of friends to give me the very thing I fell asleep praying for every night, knowing, as the universe probably did, that getting what you wanted sometimes hurt as much as having to deal with what you didn't. It was a little sad, like all endings are, and I felt a door that had been open close. But I was mostly glad. I waited until I stopped crying and used the tampon machine, grateful for it now, and took pleasure in the predictable swing of the door on my way out.

I had no car and no way home, and the size of my headache left no limit on the level it would reach the next morning, and my tongue was nearly stuck to the roof of my mouth, it was so dry. But all I could think was that, just like that, I was on my own.

I left the morning after I found the rock. In the end, it was as easy as that. I think I just needed one of them to tell me it was a good idea. I called Lindsey from the road, no more than twenty minutes out, ending at least that part of the standoff. I started to dial Nina—then, and again a half-dozen times over the next three months—but somehow never got through all ten of the digits. Not only because I was still a little mad at her—we had never been in a fight like that before, raw and exposed and public, and she had just left—but because I wasn't sure of the Nina I would find on the other side of that night.

She had caused her share of the trouble that night. She had used us to measure herself against for Decker, which didn't feel any better than when she did it with ordinary boys—someone had to be on the bottom of the heap for her to be on top. But even though she was nobody's victim, and even though she got to leave with a movie star, a grand prize beyond even her wild imagining, I knew that the night had been harder on her than it had been on the rest of us. It wasn't just being the one to escort him to his grave. It had finally all caught up with her. The one thing she could never outrun or outwit or argue against using even her most practiced Nina logic, and she had spent all the years since losing Max and Lila convincing herself she could.

I finally called her from a motel room in Kansas, maybe because *The Wizard of Oz* was her favorite movie. She used to put it on at the end of the sleepovers she kept us up at, finally falling asleep mouthing Dorothy's lines. Or maybe I was just lonely. I had associated the West with mountains and horses and ranches, but really the thing they had more than anything else was space. I was heading to Denver in a few days, but only for a little while.

She picked up on the first ring, as if she'd been waiting for me. Her voice was strong and clear, so I knew she was in the kitchen, the only room that got real service. I could picture her, a plate of lukewarm leftovers that she hadn't had the patience to heat all the way through half finished in front of her—the Tupperware she took it from still out on the counter with the Saran wrap she and Elaine used when they couldn't find the right lid crumpled in a ball, which drove her mother nuts. The bright yellow tile behind her would've set a cheerful tone that would've been dulled only a little by the chips and cracks in the tile from years without any renovation or even mainte- nance. Her feet would be up in the chair next to her, her hair in a messy bun, and she'd be leaning in to the phone like she was eager for whatever news was on the other end of the line, though she never would have admitted it. I decided to keep it light.

"So on a scale of one to ten, how much do you miss me?"

"You, huh?" she said, like my arrival on the other end of her line had been inevitable, sooner or later, which I suppose it was. "Calling for news from home?"

"I don't know," I said. "Do I want it?"

"Eh. You know how rare real news is around here. Less likely than a snowstorm."

"Has the Shamrock gotten over all the excitement we gave them?"

"Couldn't tell you. Lindsey and I have been sticking closer to home lately. Less drama around here."

"Yeah," I said. "That makes sense."

"The only problem that presents is that we sometimes run into Jay, who of course always asks about you."

I sighed. "He knows as much as you do."

"Yeah, but we could never admit that."

I could hear her moving on the other end of the line, realizing that this wouldn't be a short conversation. Settling in, getting comfortable, making whatever was in the Tupperware less salvageable still.

"He brought a girl to Charley's the other day," she said.

I thought she might've been trying to hurt me, but I also knew it was at least as much because she considered it disloyal not to tell me.

"Oh, yeah? Lindsey didn't mention."

"She is such a pussy," she said, probably just because she was hurt I had been talking to Lindsey and not her, a fact I'm sure she already knew. "I might've had to cut a bitch," she said, showing she meant no harm. "The new girl, obviously, not Lindsey. But when Jay introduced us and she said 'Hi' I realized she had halitosis, and figured she had enough problems."

"Well, that's good to know," I said, suppressing a laugh, but hoping it wasn't true. "Thanks for telling me."

I pictured Jay holding doors and pulling out chairs, for the right sort of girl now, and smiled.

"Have you seen him?" I asked.

"Dude, did you leave the planet in addition to the state? He's dead."

"Nice try, Nina. You know who I mean."

"Yeah," she conceded, after a pause. "I did."

"And?"

"I e-mailed him one night, a few nights after the Shamrock. Wasted, of course. And we met at a diner halfway between his dorm room and my mom's house the next afternoon. It was the exact halfway point—you know how precise he can be. And we had a few laughs, but he got ketchup on his goddamn upper lip that stayed there the rest of the meal. He's the only person I know who wouldn't have been able to feel that."

I bit my own lip to keep from laughing, knowing it was true.

"Was it good? I mean, was it awkward? Back to the scale of one to ten."

"I mean, it was the middle of the day, and we were sober—his idea again—but it was okay. I guess it was about a seven, but then at the end he brought it up a little, his score."

"Get some," I said.

"No. He said—how did he put it? He said, 'It's weird, isn't it? Before today all that felt like a million years ago, but seeing you here, it's like no time at all. I feel like I just saw you yesterday.'"

"Poetic."

"Right? That's some Sam Decker/Abby Madison shit right there," she said. "Their characters, I mean."

"Yeah. I knew what you meant."

"And then he said—and this is the only thing that made me think I might want to see him again—he said, 'Except now we're of age.'"

"I don't get it."

"Yeah, well, you wouldn't, would you?" she said, a new hardness in her voice. I thought we might finally be at the place where it all caught up to me, too. Not just the Shamrock. All of it. After all, I had been there that night, too. I had left when Lila had stayed. I started thinking of the best way to end the call, one I could live with when I looked back on it all. I started to panic at the blankness I drew, when she started talking again.

"We were gonna get married."

"Back then?"

"Yeah. We were gonna wait until we turned eighteen. When we were 'of age,' as he put it. Like it was some sort of goddamn Victorian novel. He had the exact day count."

"Wait, I'm still confused," I said, my voice a register higher than it had been. "I never heard a word of this."

"He used to slide me a piece of paper with the day count on it, every day," she said, ignoring my surprise, talking to herself.

I remembered the night we played hide-and-seek, and what I had seen in the bushes. I had thought it was a big, milestone event, but it was actually a daily ritual. Which somehow only made it feel more sacred.

"But you didn't even *see* each other every day," I said, arguing, really, with myself, putting it all together.

"Yeah, we did. He used to park his car across the street after he dropped Lila off at home and wait for me. Usually when I snuck up on him in the car he was studying. Even when he was being bad he was good."

I heard the pride in her voice and knew this was a thing she had loved about him, though she never would have admitted it.

"Jesus," I said. "I had no idea."

"I know. I didn't want you to. It was the only thing like that that had ever happened to me, and I wanted it all to myself."

She must've known that was going to sting, and spared me having to answer.

"I think that's why I was so crazy back then," she said. "You know how I can't stand to wait. If it hadn't been the prank war, it would've been something else."

I could hear her chewing her nails, her fingers muffling her words a little, which she did only when she wanted to convey a word or emotion other than the one she was actually feeling.

"You weren't so crazy," I said. "Or if you were, we all were."

"When I got there—to the center, for my term—I kept waiting for it. The daily count, I mean. It was almost fun, thinking about all the ways he would think up to get it to me. I wasn't mad at him, I never was. It was almost a month before I realized I was never going to get anything from him."

It was the most she had ever said about her time there.

"I don't think he would have mentioned the of-age thing if he were still pissed, though."

"No," I said. "I don't think so, either."

"Are you ever coming home?" she asked, and I knew we were done talking about Max.

"No," I said. "At least not for a while."

"Yeah." She exhaled slowly and I knew she had lit a cigarette. It was usually only a matter of time after the nail thing. "I figured."

"But hey, if you and Max get married, I'll come home and sing at your wedding."

"Jesus, reason enough to leave that boy alone."

"Okay, fine. No singing. But I'll be there and wear a dress that doesn't show you up."

"I don't know about all that," she said. "But let's just say you come home no matter who I marry."

"Obviously. But never say never."

She coughed, but more to fill the silence than on account of the cigarette, I knew. She was a pro, by then, at those.

"I like Max, is all I'm saying," I said.

She still didn't say anything, and I could picture her cigarette ash getting longer on the other end of the phone, and how the lights were probably dim enough for the orange-red tip to glow. She would've turned the lights down so they didn't wake her mother, who would have had to get up early the next morning. Elaine definitely would have been in bed by then, unless she was out on a date.

"Yeah," she finally said, her voice echoing across the empty kitchen. Or maybe it was shaking. I was too far away to tell. "I guess stranger things have happened."

After I picked up the rock that night, I kept walking. I scrapped the diner idea and headed for Jay's. I had never made any big decision in my life without consulting him first. Not because of any wisdom I smelled on him, but because he was always there.

All the lights in his parents' house were off when I got there, but he was in the driveway, leaning over the guts of the used car he had spent two high school summers saving for. In general, he spent one hour buried under the hood for every five hours he spent driving it, but he loved it anyway. I stood there for a minute, watching him before he noticed me, marveling at how natural he looked in that position.

He smiled when he finally looked up and saw me, serenely, like he had been expecting me there, or I had been standing there all along, but knowingly, too, like we were in on some sort of inside joke. Like we both knew the line I had come to deliver, which maybe we did.

"There she is. I was wondering what you had gotten into that made you disappear like that. I can't wait to hear all about it."

He hadn't texted or called at all that day, after my night of unreturned calls and texts. He knew when to give me space, which was another reason I didn't appreciate him nearly as much as I should have.

"I'm sorry," I said. "It was a strange night. Truly. I'll tell you about it sometime, but it's going to take a while, and I don't think this is the night."

"It's okay. A little mystery only makes a person more inter-esting to other people." He wiped the wrench in his hand on a dirty hand towel and sat back against the car. "And I figured you were with the girls."

"I was."

"So what's up? Are you hungry? We could go out."

I looked down at my shoes, realizing I hadn't rehearsed so much as an opening sentence. I blurted the first thing that came to my mind, realizing as I heard it that it was true.

"I'm tired, Jay."

"Okay," he said, nodding. Glad to have a clear problem to solve. "Let's go inside. We can order food and watch TV. There's a Sam Decker movie marathon on just about every channel. You know, since he died." A look of panic crossed his face and he froze. "Wait, you knew that, right?"

"Yeah," I said. "I know."

His shoulders fell in relief.

"I know how much you loved him."

"Yeah. He was one of our favorites."

"So should we hit the couch?"

I shook my head.

"That's not the kind of tired I mean. I think that would only make me more tired." My eyes filled with tears, knowing that once I started this I wouldn't be able to stop it.

"Okay," he said, not looking at me. He could never stand to see a girl cry, for as long as I'd known him.

"Everything seems to make me tired these days. Work, and hanging out after. Eating out and staying in. Even drinking with the girls. It all makes me feel old. Like there's nothing I haven't seen or done before."

"So maybe you should go do and see some things you've never seen or done before."

He said it like it was the simplest thing in the world. Like tying your shoe or stamping a letter.

"Yeah," I said, smiling at him, but also really crying now—steady tears, little sniffles, snot dripping from my nose, the works. I was so grateful, I almost fell in love with him. It was almost enough. "Maybe."

"You know," he said. "When you didn't call or text me last night, I got this feeling. Like you were gone. Not in a bad way. Hurt or in trouble. Just gone."

"I'm sorry," I said again, not sure of what else to say.

"No," he said. "Like I said, it wasn't bad. I was happy for you. And it felt, a little, like—I don't know—like you weren't in any one place, but everywhere, you know? Part of the atmosphere. Like Santa," he said, laughing at himself a little. I laughed, too, and nodded.

I stuffed my hands in my pockets and looked back down, not sure how to end a conversation like this, or if it was okay to hug him. I had spent so much time thinking about what it would be like to see him every day for the rest of my life that I hadn't bothered to consider what it would be like not to see him again.

"I did love you, Maggie. For what it's worth. Do."

"Yeah," I said, looking back up at him, knowing I owed him at least that. "I know that."

"I'd do anything for you. Even if you leave and then come back. Like, a long time from now."

I nodded to show him that I knew that, too.

I thought for a moment of the glow of Sam Decker's skin, and the watt of his smile—what an achievement it had felt like to be the cause of it. It already felt far away, farther away than countless Saturday afternoons spent giving myself over to the purple velvet of the movie-theater chairs as the light went dim and Abby Madison and Sam Decker took over the world. I knew then that, for the rest of my life, that night would feel very far away, sacred and distant at once, like a piece of music played by someone you love that reminds you of something you can't place.

"It was never like the movies, though, was it?" I asked. "You know, that crazy kind of love that everyone's always after."

I didn't say it to be cruel. But to suggest that maybe our movie loves were still out there, for both of us. I was not a sentimental girl. I didn't often make statements like that—talk in riddle or post inscrutable but suggestive music lyrics to my Facebook feed like so many other girls, about imperfect love and inefficiencies of the heart. But if this line of conversation upset or confused him he didn't show it.

"No," he said. Right away, like he knew exactly what I was talking about. "I guess not. Not like the movies. But nothing ever is."

At what may well have been the first of the sleepovers that would see everything from Lindsey's education in how to use a tampon to the first instant message any of us ever sent, and, yes, the birth of the prank war, we were all keeping Nina company for what may well have been the very first time. I know it was early, because we were only just old enough to understand the concept of death. Not fully. But just enough to understand that sometimes things were here and then gone in some permanent way. We were old enough to have some sense of its finality, but not old enough to lock up any talk of it far away from idle conversation, as if any breezy, casual mention might be taken as invitation. We were still curious enough to want to exchange notes on what it entailed, because we didn't know yet that, like everyone else, we would go through our entire lives without ever landing on a firm answer.

Nina told us that the woman who did her mother's nails had had to cancel her mother's appointment that afternoon so she could go home for her father's funeral, a piece of news that had made us all fall silent, though we weren't sure why. Nina asked us what we thought happened when you died. Not testing us, the way she would have been if she had asked us five years later, but really wanting to know. I don't remember, but I'm sure Lindsey said something about heaven, always convinced that her mother was somewhere better than she would've been if she had lived. And I imagine I said I didn't know, because even then I was not imaginative or eager enough to lie to make myself sound smarter than I am. But I remember almost word for word what Nina said, because it was just the kind of thing she was capable of when she wanted to be—unexpected, but just right; the kind of thing that stuck with you and drifted back up in the middle of other, unrelated thoughts and conversations long after you heard it, sometimes for no reason that you could think of when you tried. She said she thought that when you died you got to watch your life from the beginning. Not fast, in one big flash, but like it was a movie. And you would know, watching your movie, what you didn't when you were living it. That the last Starburst you ate before you threw up Starbursts at the outset of the five-day bout of flu that assaulted all five of your senses when you were seven was going to be the last Starburst you were ever going to savor, and that while for the rest of your life the smell of Starbursts on someone else's breath would make you homesick for being young, the taste of them would make you nauseous. And that after the last meal you would ever sit at with both of your parents before they told you that one of them was moving to Orlando or Tallahassee or the moon, you would miss the taste of the very pot roast you complained about the very last time you ate it. It was your father's mother's recipe, so your mother would never make it again after that dinner. And at the very end of the movie you could take the time to process and acknowledge the things you had taken for granted at the time—the last time you would ever walk into an air-conditioned room after even a minute out in hundred-degree heat, or hear a small child laughing by the side of the ocean. The last present you would ever open truly believing it came from Santa Claus. The last bowl of macaroni and cheese, the last episode of your favorite sitcom. The last new dress. The last orgasm. And you could maybe even enjoy the drama of your own death, the way you do at the end of *Love Story* and *Titanic*. I remember she said that's probably something people bragged about in heaven—the crazy or glamorous or tragic way they died—the way people on Earth brag about how long their people have lived in this country or the exotic places from which they came. They would deliver these details, when describing their movie to potential viewers, because that was how you became friends with someone in heaven: You got them to watch your movie, and you watched theirs. They would master their delivery, pausing in just the right places, for maximum effect. Capturing perfectly the texture of the piece of steak that just wouldn't slide down their throat, or the ad on the side of the bus that shattered their skeletal system. What the breath of the man trying to save them with CPR tasted like.

Maybe because, as on most topics, I took Nina's word and made her opinions my facts, that's always how I've thought about death, which I became grateful for after Sam Decker died. Maybe only selfishly, since it meant we got leading roles in his movie, getting as much screen time as we did in that march to the big finish. Or maybe only because it means we got to give him a little of what he gave to us, which I suppose means that, for all the things we couldn't give him that night, we were friends. I have always thought of reciprocity as a central tenet of friendship, probably because of something else Nina said or did. Everyone knows that the end of any story has a huge effect on the whole thing. Maybe we gave him an ending that made the movie he was left with okay. It took only one night to learn how hard he was on his own movies.

He didn't let the favor sit unreturned. I don't know why I attribute my leaving with the night we met Sam Decker, even outside their proximity in time, but I do. Maybe it is because we always attached luck to celebrities, even just their images on buses and on movie posters in the lobby of the one theater in town. It was understood that the first person to spot the poster for the new Sam Decker movie would find favor with the universe, at least temporarily, and we could not begin to fathom how much luck there was in spending an entire night with him. Surely enough to get me somewhere else. Maybe it was because I thought his death left a vacancy in the population of people who lived lives with sweeping scopes that didn't end where they began. Maybe it was because if I couldn't convince him not to get stuck in the empty noise of Florida, I could take the advice he was wasting.

Maybe it was because until that night I had never seen

firsthand that people sometimes leave even when there is still good reason to stay, or maybe it was just because his name was on the note that accompanied the funds I would need in order to leave.

That morning, as the bus pulled out of town, it didn't quite pass Lila's house, but it came close, stopping at an intersection only a few blocks away from where Golden Creek started, and the house her father bought right around the time Nina was released to us, and where Lila stayed when she was home. I hoped it was not too far for the silent dispatch I sent her to make it, the kind you send only to people you know you won't see again, at least not often. Something not unlike a blessing. I wished her a life filled with more Ninas than Carines, knowing that for girls like her, there will always be both. I wished her well.

Decker is the only one I gave a proper, face-to-face good-bye to. I passed a billboard for his latest movie on the way out of town, the one that would remain there for months after it flopped, and was finally taken down not because it finally occurred to the men who rented the space that it was insensitive to leave him exposed up there like that, but because other, better, newer movies were coming out and needed to be advertised. I mouthed *Thank you* at him as we passed but didn't turn around for one last wave after, not wanting to make it any harder on him, knowing how he probably hated to see me go.

Acknowledgments

I owe many thank-yous to many people for their help in shaping this manuscript, but special thanks are due to my agent, Monika Woods, and my editor, Sarah Stein, under whose guidance I added and expanded scenes that now seem like some of the most central elements of the story I set out to tell here. That both women are wonderful, dynamic company in addition to being supernaturally wise and patient has been my good fortune.

I am a firm believer that the key to writing a book is reading as many of them as humanly possible, and I am grateful that reading contemporary fiction has been part of my job for the last nine years. Thank you to my work wives of yore, who became some of my closest friends, and who continue to surprise and inspire me with their intelligence and generosity: Katie Freeman, Josie Kals, and Lena Khidritskaya. And to my current work wives, who make the hours pass, and for whom even the most panic-inducing work crisis is no match: Leslie Brandon and Sarah Bowlin. Thank you to David McCormick for the internship that started it all. And to Ann Close, Deb

Garrison, and Gillian Blake, the three gracious and talented editors I've worked for. My wish for womankind is that every recent grad who moves to a new city and hits the pavement with an overly formal, shoulder-padded business suit and a stack of still-warm résumés finds someone like you.

Thank you to Michele Nix, the only high school friend I ever needed, my Lila, Nina, and Lindsey in one. And to my Kenyon cohorts, especially Meghan Elster, Joy Bullen, and Lindsay Junkin, who kept the party going with me for all those years after graduation, and to Haley Dorsey, for being our glue. How fun it was to be young with you, how lucky I am to know you still. And in memory of Amanda Block, who continues to influence who we are both as individuals and as a group.

Thank you to my teachers at Bennington, David Gates, Sheila Kohler, Bret Anthony Johnston, and Jill McCorkle. And to my friends and fellow writers, Louise Munson, Sarah Fuss, Shevaun Brannigan, Katy Simpson Smith, Meghan Gilliss, and Liz Solms. Let's meet for cake and champagne at the end of the world every year.

Thank you to the community of people who have kept me in New York, a city I love, but which I never would have lasted in as long as I have without friends to soften the blows the city can deal, and raise a glass or two in both the best and worst of times: Feldman and Aria and Kerry and their Chrisses, Sam and Sasha, Ben and Julia, Ira and Katie, Tara and Andrew, Rachel and James, Will and Georgia, Danny and Tim, Seth and Andrew and Amos, Josie and Katie (again). Please don't ever move.

Thank you to Carmen Johnson at Day One, my first editor, and another person I have been lucky enough to count as both colleague and friend. And to Mel, for making me feel pretty in my author photo.

I have never suffered writer's block so badly as I did when trying to come up with the words to adequately thank my family, both for shaping the person I am, and for being such good company. There is no group of people whom I enjoy drinking red wine and laughing with more, and I have always cherished the extent to which we are more than the sum of our parts. Thank you to my siblings, for sharing their childhood with me and letting me hang out with them even though I was not nearly as cool, and to my parents, for standing by that old parental adage that you can be whatever you want to be at every turn. And to Emma, whose imagination and wonder spark my own—I hope you not only continue to march to the beat of your own drum, but invent new instruments.

And to my husband, Ben Mathis-Lilley, burrito maker extraordinaire, trivia whiz kid, intramural king, who doesn't think that much less of me for getting lost every time I get off at the West 4th stop even though I've lived here almost a decade, who turns a walk to the corner bodega into an adventure, and with whom all things are possible. Thank you for your endless help and counsel on this book, but also for all you do, every day. Let's go on vacation.